"It seems we're destined to share more than pleasantries tonight."

"What—"

A huge boom sounded, and the floor under her feet reverberated. Before she had a chance to react, strong hands yanked her from her seat and she found herself facedown on the floor, James on top of her. Protecting her.

She gulped for air, unable to utter a sound as she heard screeches of panic from all corners of Ricco's.

Another boom was followed immediately by its force shaking the building. Her head turned to the side, she saw ceiling tiles hit the floor amidst other patrons doing exactly the same: taking cover from a deadly blast.

"Get ready to move as soon as we can." James's voice was steady in her ear, her only anchor as panic threatened to set in. The image of Iris's eyes, her gurgling laughter, melded into a single thought.

I can't die.

Dear Reader,

Welcome to book four of the Coltons of Colorado! Blue Larkspur is the perfect setting for the danger Rachel and James must survive so that their love, and their family with precious baby Iris, can thrive. Surrounded by Colorado's stunning spring beauty, Rachel learns to trust a man she thought was too much like her father, who'd stained the family with his crimes. James proves otherwise, but before they can be together there are not one but two villains out to sabotage them. I had great fun writing Rachel, James and Iris. What's more exciting than a new family—chased by bad guys?

I am so grateful to my editor, Carly Silver, for giving me yet another opportunity to "play" with the Coltons, and to keep them alive to love another day.

I love to hear from you! Please email me via my website form at www.gerikrotow.com. You can also find me at Facebook.com/gerikrotow and Instagram.com/geri_krotow.

Happy reading!

Peace,

Geri

STALKING COLTON'S FAMILY

Geri Krotow

HARLEQUIN

ROMANTIC SUSPENSE

Special thanks and acknowledgment are given to Geri Krotow for her contribution to The Coltons of Colorado miniseries.

Recycling programs
for this product may
not exist in your area.

ISBN-13: 978-1-335-75969-6

Stalking Colton's Family

Copyright © 2022 by Harlequin Enterprises ULC

For questions and comments about the quality of this book, please contact us at CustomerService@Harlequin.com.

Harlequin Enterprises ULC
22 Adelaide St. West, 41st Floor
Toronto, Ontario M5H 4E3, Canada
www.Harlequin.com

Printed in U.S.A.

Former naval intelligence officer and US Naval Academy graduate **Geri Krotow** draws inspiration from the global situations she's experienced. Geri loves to hear from her readers. You can email her via her website and blog, gerikrotow.com.

Books by Geri Krotow

Harlequin Romantic Suspense

The Coltons of Colorado

Stalking Colton's Family

Silver Valley P.D.

Her Christmas Protector
Wedding Takedown
Her Secret Christmas Agent
Secret Agent Under Fire
The Fugitive's Secret Child
Reunion Under Fire
Snowbound with the Secret Agent
Incognito Ex
Stalked in Silver Valley

The Coltons of Grave Gulch

Colton Bullseye

Visit the Author Profile page at Harlequin.com for more titles.

Dedication

To Steve, Alex and Ellen; thank you for always being here. I love you with all my heart.

Acknowledgments

Many thanks to USNA 86 sister Diana Selberg Pointon for having my six on the white water rafting—I owe you a coffee.

Chapter 1

Rachel Colton stared at her infant daughter Iris's innocent face, soaking all the cuteness up from her bright red wisps of hair to her adorable chin. "I love you, darling daughter, but you're making me late for work. Again."

With an expertise she hadn't had before Iris's birth six months ago, Rachel cleaned up the dirty diaper—or more accurately, the contents of said item that had messed up her only clean going-to-court suit—as she spoke to the most important person in her life.

Iris Colton, the wonder baby who'd surprised everyone with her appearance—Rachel included. Those first few moments of realizing she was pregnant last year had been some of the most trying of her life. And yet, here she stood, getting through another morning with Iris, facing another day as Blue Larkspur's brand-new district attorney after several years as assistant DA. There wasn't one minute that went by that Rachel didn't feel the weight of both her job and motherhood on her shoulders. But being Iris's mom was, hands down, the best job she'd ever had.

"Ba ba." Iris's chubby, six-month-old cheeks puffed out as she babbled and melted all of Rachel's irritation away. She'd come to think of Iris as her "joy baby" because her precious daughter brought her a heaping heartful of happiness each day. Being a new mother was like that—one minute Rachel had no idea how she'd get through the next hour; the next, she wanted to stop time and revel in her joy baby forever.

"We both need to clean up, Iris girl." She held Iris out at arm's length and carried her to the changing table, where she made quick work of getting the infant back into a clean outfit. The sound of the back kitchen door closing alerted her that Iris's nanny had arrived.

"We're back here, Emily!" She smiled at Iris and made silly sounds to keep the baby from squirming until Emily's smiling face appeared at the door of the nursery. Not for the first time, an immense wave of gratitude pulsed through her heart. Emily was the perfect nanny for her baby and had come at the highest recommendation of her mother, Isadora Colton, and her older sister, Morgan. Isa's best friend's granddaughter had Emily as her nanny for her first three years, and Morgan's friend had also employed Emily for a few months before eventually taking a break from her career to stay home. Emily's skills and gifted ability to handle young children put her in high demand in Blue Larkspur. She came with the highest levels of recommendation. Rachel wouldn't have it any other way.

"Good morning, ladies. Oh my." Emily's gaze took in Iris's and Rachel's appearances, from the ruined suit to the soiled onesie on top of the hamper.

"She had a major blowout. I'll put the dirty clothes in the laundry, then I have to do a quick change myself."

"Here, let me take her." Emily reached for Iris at the same moment Iris lifted her arms to greet her nanny. Rachel's heart swelled with relief alongside bittersweet longing. It was a gift to have such a loving, kind nanny for Iris, someone she trusted her daughter with for her often twelve-hour days. But the reassurance of wonderful childcare did nothing to ease the sense of her heart being torn from her chest each time she left her precious girl, knowing she'd invariably miss out on some milestones. It also bothered her that Iris was lacking in the father department, but at least her brother Gideon was a superb uncle and around a lot, most often with Sophia, the love of his life. They'd recently reunited, and the entire Colton family was thrilled for them. Sophia was a pediatrician and both she and Gideon were hoping for a family of their own soon, which would give Iris her first cousin. Rachel had five other brothers in her total of eleven other Colton siblings, but between their jobs and own lives, Gideon remained the one she relied upon most.

It had been a cruel blow to find out that her one-night stand at a legal conference in Helena, Montana, was unavailable to be a responsible father. Rachel had learned the cold, hard truth when she'd tried to call Iris's father, and instead of him answering or being put through to voice mail, another woman who'd identified herself as his fiancée had answered. Which meant he'd most likely been in that committed relationship during their Montana fling.

Rachel had decided on the spot that it was better for all involved that he went on with his own life, and she with hers. The last thing she was willing to do was risk her baby's emotional stability and sense of security with a part-time parent. She'd tucked him away as a bad memory, a mistake, except for the gift of her joy baby. No way would she ever reveal the name of her child's father to her family. Her brothers were protective and wouldn't hesitate to find the man and make his life miserable. Not that she thought of her brothers as criminal stalkers or anything; they were simply very typical brothers who didn't take kindly to anyone messing with their family.

Besides, James Kiriakis had shown more of his true colors the morning after their night of passion; all he'd talked about was the high-profile firm he worked for and how he prided himself on winning his corporate litigations. She remembered the regret that had pierced through the incredible chemistry they'd shared only hours earlier. James's ego-driven boasting had reminded her too much of the worst parts of her father, the long-deceased Ben Colton. As a judge, her father had taken the Blue Larkspur, Colorado, community for every nickel he could, supplementing his legal income with kickbacks from sending offenders of all ages to detention centers. It still stung, twenty years later, that her father had been dirty.

Which validated why Iris didn't need James for a father.

You've got to stop assuming every man is like Dad.
True, but the discovery of her father's nefarious un-

dertakings when he was a judge was a long shadow to not only outrun but a deep wound in the community that she was determined to help heal. Her eleven siblings and she had formed the Truth Foundation for this very reason. Now that she was DA, she'd had to recuse herself from the foundation's work, but there was plenty she could do for Blue Larkspur at the most basic levels. Getting the real criminals locked up while ensuring the innocent got the rehabilitation they needed was a good start.

"I'm going to make you proud to be a Colton, Iris." She spoke to the quiet as she stripped out of the pale gray sheath dress she particularly liked for the way it complemented her figure. As she changed her attire, she tried to ignore the now-familiar struggle to leave her precious infant for another full day at the office.

Iris is safe. I have a good job to support both of us. Our family has our backs. We have Emily.

And that was the crux of it. Emily Chase was the nanny Rachel only would have dared dreamed of, not actually believed existed when she'd been pregnant and the realities of becoming a single parent were sinking in. The last fifteen months had been the most trying yet happiest time of her life. Becoming a single parent had never been on her list of life goals when she'd decided to pursue the law but neither had learning about true love and commitment—in the form of wide-eyed Iris—been the remotest possibility for her.

A text lit up her phone.

Where are you?

Her assistant, Clara, had gotten into the habit of checking on her if she was more than a minute past her self-appointed show-up time for court. Before Iris, arriving thirty minutes early had been an easy parameter to meet. Since becoming a mother, however, she'd scraped the time down with only a handful of minutes to spare.

This morning was going to push that to the limit. She wrestled with a sleeveless shell and skirt, her skin slick with stress sweat. Her ob-gyn assured her that the excess perspiration from hormonal changes while she was breastfeeding Iris was temporary. But being overheated and feeling as though she was always disheveled never left. As if she was just shy of the professionalism she'd taken for granted before Iris.

A soft groan escaped her throat as she threw together the outfit on the fly, grabbing a bracelet while shoving her feet into too-high heels that were the only match for the navy blue.

She forced herself to get her mind focused on work. Emily had Iris; it was okay. Did all new mothers have to reassure themselves like this, all day long?

No wonder Mom stayed home with us in the beginning.

Her mother was an accomplished graphic designer these days but had devoted many years to full-time homemaking. Before her husband's crimes had been exposed and their family driven to near bankruptcy.

As assistant DA, she'd relished putting away the crooks her father had wheeled-and-dealed with years before. Now, as DA, she spent most days proving the culpability of local losers. Her commitment to Blue Larkspur ran as deep as the Colton blood that coursed through her veins.

She was able to serve on her current case only because she'd taken the necessary steps to legally detach herself from the family's Truth Foundation, formed to right the wrongs of Ben Colton. It was imperative that she resign from the nonprofit a few years back, so that she could avoid a conflict of interest to be able to serve as a public prosecutor. But a disgruntled judge or pushy defense attorney could derail her goal to get a crook who'd worked with her father behind bars. That was the thing about the law that Rachel both loved and detested. Justice had to serve all.

Which meant she needed to keep it as professional as possible and show up on time. Today's defendant had made hundreds of thousands of dollars in kickbacks before Ben Colton had died. She'd refrained from investigating him when she was part of the Truth Foundation, of course, but his time was up, now that she was DA. The crook, Brian Parson, had earned enough from the rig he and Ben had set up to support his family with the dirty money for the last twenty years, not to mention all he'd earned as the area drug boss. The Truth Foundation had been supportive of the DA's relentless pursuit of Parson, sitting on its hands so as to not jeopardize the DA's prosecution. It wasn't the first case the Truth Foundation had needed to scale back on, in support of the legal system. Because Rachel had been meticulous about remaining legally unattached to the Parson case, it allowed her to prosecute now, as DA. She relished bringing Parson down. It was time he paid the price.

But he wouldn't if Rachel was late—today's judge was a stickler for promptness and wouldn't hesitate to delay, or worse, throw the case out if she appeared at all unprepared. And what was more evident of piss-poor prep than tardiness?

She hit the speed dial to her assistant.

"Yes, ma'am? Are you here?" Clara's voice was smooth, but she detected a lilt of anxiety.

"No, but I will be. Give me fifteen minutes."

"That takes it to—"

"One minute before showtime. I know. I'll be there." She disconnected and prayed she'd make it.

"You've got to be kidding me."

James Kiriakis let out a sigh as he stared in aggravation at the large mechanical arm lowering in front of the hood of his black BMW, preventing him from crossing the railroad track before what appeared to be an endless line of shipping containers began to click by. Blue Larkspur, Colorado, was nothing like Denver. He'd mistakenly thought the traffic would be a breeze after the constant congestion in the state capital. Wrong assumption, on all fronts. Blue Larkspur was tiny compared to the state capital but mighty in its desire to get to work on time.

He sent a quick hands-free, voice-activated text to the paralegal he was meeting at the courthouse, his fingers in a death clench on the steering wheel. He frantically used his rearview and side-view mirrors, the action automatic at this point as his heart pounded in time to his spike in stress. James was certain he was awash in cortisol as his body poised for yet another nasty confrontation.

There were no signs that he'd been followed by the one person he was running from. The main reason he'd left Denver, truth be told. It didn't stop the hairs on his nape from rising, though. Since he'd departed the city, the nasty sense that he was being watched, followed, *stalked* hadn't lifted. No matter how much he reassured himself that no way could Bethany Austin know he'd moved, had cleared out his high-rise condo and sold it for a tidy profit.

Could she?

"Relax. You've left it all behind." He did the box breathing he'd read about, the method used by navy SEALs. It eased some of the tension in his shoulders, which only seemed to allow the flow of nagging thoughts back into his mind.

It had to be his tardiness that was making him so much on edge. He'd taken all the steps to excise himself from the hellish predicament he'd lived through these past months. Yet as he continued to watch his rearview mirror, he noticed as a vehicle six cars back pulled out of the waiting traffic, made a quick U-Turn and sped off. His gut tightened at the familiar action and he gripped the wheel to pull himself closer to the rearview mirror, tried to make out the license plate on the unfamiliar car that didn't even resemble Bethany's. It was a blur. Probably for the best. What would he do with it if he was able to discern the plate's letters and numbers? Tell the police he thought an unknown vehicle was occupied by his stalker when he hadn't been able to see the driver?

He sucked in another breath, held it, let it go. Disappointment thumped against his chest, under his sternum. How foolish was he to think he'd rid himself of the awfulness of being stalked with one move?

You're just stressed because you're going to be late.

It wasn't like him to be late to anything, ever. But since he'd hit an emotional bottom in his personal life—thanks to stalker Bethany—he found himself questioning everything from his ability to discern fact from fiction, to real emotion from passing illusion. It all boiled down to the fact that he'd lived the life of a victim—had *been* a victim—something that, as a six-foot-one former college athlete, he wasn't accustomed to. But Bethany, the woman he'd briefly and most casually dated—they hadn't gone to bed, hadn't gone past two dinner dates—had turned out to be a stalker extraordinaire.

He'd ended it with her, made it clear they were going to be a friends-only deal, right after he got back from a legal conference in Montana. After he'd spent one incredible night with a woman who made him rethink his personal creed to remain single for at least a while longer. Bethany and he had had zero commitment. He'd only agreed to go out on that second and last date because she'd surprised him at his apartment, telling him how much she'd missed him while he was gone. Her nearly frantic behavior raised red flags that night. So he'd called it off. But Bethany never heard anything she didn't want to. He'd been forced to get a restraining order only a month later, but her chilling antics had continued for the next eight months. He'd put up with a stalker for almost a year.

A stalker. He still struggled with it, that he had his own personal harasser.

He'd dealt with ugly scenes before, when he'd stopped dating someone. But he soon found Bethany Austin wasn't any run-of-the-mill, bitter-that-the-relationship-is-over pursuer. Her methods to get his attention had accelerated into Mach speed without lingering in any manageable area within two days of him telling her that they were no longer even friends. From showing up unannounced at his office to breaking into his condo with a key and digital codes she'd bribed from the doorman—now fired—she'd shattered James's sense of well-being.

His repeated pleas that she seek medical attention for her obvious issues hadn't worked. But even after he'd been forced to get a restraining order, Bethany had still found ways to tail him. Showing up at restaurants, retail stores, recreational parks, always unannounced. She was careful to always maintain the exact distance needed from him so that he couldn't report her presence as a violation of the restraining order but made certain he saw her.

If he hadn't found this new job in Blue Larkspur, he'd have gone back to court to tighten the order's restrictions against her. Bethany wanted more than any man could give her, in his opinion. She'd wanted to be in a committed relationship with James after one date, so he'd immediately backed off, insisted they be friends. No matter how much she assured him that she "got it" and only wanted his friendship, no strings attached, it became clear within days that Bethany saw James as the sole object of her affections.

Affection that had turned creepy in a Denver minute.

Getting Bethany physically out of his life didn't keep her from occupying his mental and emotional space, though.

He blamed himself for her continued harassment; he should have pressed charges each time she broke the restraining order or did any one of myriad definite stalking actions. His empathy for her distress, his guilt that maybe, somehow, he'd encouraged her, had always won out.

James was counting on a new setting, miles and

hours from Bethany, to allow him to finally let go of the constant fight-or-flight drain on his adrenals. That's what his personal trainer had said was wearing him out and flooding his nervous system with cortisol.

He shifted in his seat, stretched his back. James didn't discount that theory, but the observation had struck a chord. Bethany had wormed her way into the most dangerous parts of his mind, the neighborhoods no one should ever wander in alone. Her stalking ignited his most primal defensive behaviors. It didn't matter that she hadn't bothered him for months. Some crimes leave deeper scars than others, and invisible marks can be worse.

Which is why he'd taken so many precautions as he left Denver to prevent Bethany from being able to track him, follow him to Blue Larkspur. She'd always found him in the past, though, was always able to worm her way around any security he'd put in place. It was easy to tell himself that being haunted by Bethany would never end.

Enough.

He was in the midst of his new start, free from Bethany and all the baggage her actions brought with them. He raised the volume on his stereo, allowed his favorite band to drown out any unwanted thoughts.

Today was the first day of week two at a premier Blue Larkspur litigation firm, where he'd accepted a not-unimpressive position that practically guaranteed he'd make partner in short order. Otherwise, would he have ever before considered moving out of Denver, quitting the high-pressure, highly successful job he'd worked, representing major corporations for the past decade, where partnership had been offered only three months ago?

He knew he wouldn't have. He'd fought a deep internal battle and decided to turn down the partnership. Bethany's continued and escalating exploits continued to haunt him, even months after she appeared to have given up on him. A change in address was a good solution. He had his family's support, and that was the deciding factor for James.

His mom, Helen Kiriakis, and his siblings were all close, as his father had died when James was six years old. The Kiriakis clan took care of its own. That said, they all agreed that short of them becoming vigilantes against Bethany, James's move was a smart response.

He'd been eager to transition here anyway. The hustle and bustle of Denver was getting to him, and while he still opted to live in a contemporary luxury condo in Blue Larkspur, he was trading big-city life for more of a quiet-city vibe.

And there's a certain district attorney in Blue Larkspur who caught your vibes fifteen months ago.

He ignored his heart's musings. Rachel Colton had refused all of his calls after they'd shared an incredible night together at a Helena, Montana, legal conference. It'd been all over the state news last month that she'd been recently appointed to Lark's County DA, remarkable for her young but solid career. The Colorado bar association's professional periodical had done an impressive profile on her, and when he saw her stunning features beaming out from the page-sized glossy photo his heart had raced. As if they'd shared more than an evening.

He'd been disappointed to read through and see that it included zero personal information. Why he was still thinking about this woman, though, when she hadn't taken his calls was beyond him. He had to blame this one on the stress of being stalked. Why else, when she'd patently ghosted him, would he allow his mind to flash back to their incendiary night? He couldn't deny that she'd cut him off. Or blame her, for that matter. They didn't even know each other, and it had been the classic one-night stand, on paper. What gnawed at him was how harsh her rejection felt. How hard is it to answer, or at least text, with a "sorry, not interested"?

Besides, for all he knew, Rachel could have turned out to be a stalker, too.

No.

He wasn't going to allow the situation with Bethany to mar his entire future, shadow every thought he ever had about another woman. He'd finished dating Bethany before he'd connected with Rachel. In all his past one-nighters, he'd thought of them as hookups, and as much as he respected great sex, he never expected more. James wanted nothing to do with a permanent relationship until he'd made his mark in the world and he knew his career was solid. He'd been feeling a sense of missing out on what was important as he saw his siblings and close friends get hitched, have kids. That was why he'd tried to get in touch with Rachel after their too-brief connection in Montana. Rachel had struck him as more than a one-nighter. Maybe, daresay, the kind of woman he'd be willing to be committed to.

"All in the past, buddy." But it wasn't. Not in his mind, anyway.

He shifted in his leather bucket seat at the mere memory of *that* night. James was great at putting unwanted thoughts and distractions aside from whatever the task at hand, but his body had never forgotten the pleasure the beautiful Rachel Colton had gifted it with.

He'd been unable to shake the sense that Rachel had been different from every woman he'd met before. James snorted, then all-out laughed at himself, banging his palms on the steering wheel.

Why did he think he was an exception to human behavior? He'd still been emotionally vulnerable after evading Bethany and wanted some companionship. That's why the time with Rachel was still imprinted on his mind. Nothing more.

She lives in Blue Larkspur. Had nothing to do with why he'd picked here for his relocation. It'd been more about the first job offer that would allow him to escape Denver. Okay, mostly. All right, there was some hope that if he let Rachel know he'd moved here, she might bite.

It still bothered the heck out of him that he'd basically been chased from his own life. And yet, he'd also grown tired of his job as he'd done it for so long. It was time for a change.

The train cleared and he tried to clear all thoughts of women out of his mind as he made the last half mile to the courthouse. Not willing to chance there'd be an open spot available in the main, smaller courthouse parking lot, he parked in a garage a block away and sprinted, laptop bag slung over his shoulder, to the front steps. He zigzagged between people also heading to the same single entrance.

Exhilaration pumped through his veins as he hit the top level, skidded to a—

Bam!

"What the—" A female voice continued into a rather

succinct, albeit quiet, stream of profanity that would have made James laugh if he wasn't doing all he could to remain upright, to keep from landing on his ass or worse, atop this stranger. His efforts were futile, and it was with horror that he realized he couldn't stop his fall.

Fortunately his hands landed on either side of the person he'd slammed into, and as his knees hit the unforgiving stone ground, he didn't know what was more surprising: the searing pain of marble-on-kneecap or the sexiest blue eyes he'd ever known staring up at him in complete shock.

"Rachel." Her name came out on the *whoosh* of air that expelled from his lungs.

"James?" Her intense gaze jolted him back to their time in Helena, to when she'd begged him to be this close. To when he'd wondered where she'd been all his life. Sure, he'd expected their paths might cross ever since he'd searched for her on the Internet, when he'd wondered why she was completely icing him out. And he'd all but decided to look her up. But literally running into her wasn't part of his plan.

She never returned your calls or texts.

Not. One.

Even the harsh reminder couldn't make him move, stand up, walk away from Rachel Colton and get to work.

Work. His new job.

"Aw, crap."

Chapter 2

The last time James had been on top of her they'd been in a swanky, minimalist executive suite, and his breath had carried the distinct scent of single malt mingled with her own essence. As she caught her breath, no doubt sucking in his exhales, she smelled peppermint and something…green.

"Let me guess, smoothie for breakfast?" She shoved at his chest, wanting him up and off her *now*. She needed to be in court three minutes ago.

His eyes widened the tiniest bit, which she took as surprise. "What?" Recognition lit up his irises which only annoyed her further. He gave her a slow grin. "Do I have kale in my teeth?"

"Get off!" She pushed harder, struggling to get back on her feet. Anywhere but this close to the man she'd worked every waking hour to free from her mind, ever since that last, lingering kiss well over a year ago.

He adroitly got to his feet and grabbed her elbow, helping her up. Too flustered to fight the unwanted assistance, she figured the quickest way to get away was to keep it simple. She leaned against him, fought to regain balance on the blasted stilettos, to get her breath back. This wasn't any kind of pleasant surprise; it was a scary-as-all-get-out shock. What the heck was James doing in Blue Larkspur?

Fear stabbed through her racing thoughts. Did he know about Iris?

James was a powerful attorney, wasn't he?

No. No way could he come in here now and change the life she'd built. One where Iris was protected from any upset. Like meeting a father she'd never known.

Rachel wasn't worried that she'd have to share her baby with James, was she?

Are you?

"Thank you." Once on her feet she turned away and made a straight shot toward security, James on her heels. Which made her angry at herself for picking the too-high shoes that she hadn't worn since before Iris was born. If she'd stuck with her black flats, no matter that they didn't match the suit, she'd never have been knocked down. She would have made it through security moments before this buffoon—James—had barreled into her. But today was an important court day, as was every day for the DA. She wanted to look her best. To feel her best. So she'd picked the sexier fashion choice.

A scream welled in her throat and she bit her cheek, threw her laptop bag on the X-ray machine's belt and walked through the metal scanner under the keen gaze of the security guard.

"Wait!" The urgent note in his deep voice reached out, grabbed her focus away from getting into court.

She spun back to him so quickly that she teetered for a brief moment before stilling. He leaned in, as if ready to catch her.

"Folks, keep it out of the surveillance area." The guard was not impressed.

Rachel waited for James to clear security.

When she faced him this time, she made no disguise of her contempt as she batted away his smile, his attempt at a friendly greeting.

"James. It's been, what, fifteen months? And while I appreciate that you remember me—"

"You remembered me, too." Issued like a challenge, as if he was out to prove a case. "Otherwise, how would you know the exact amount of time that's passed?"

"Right." She looked at her smartwatch, which dinged with a frantic text from her assistant. "I'm due in court, and I'm late."

"Meet me for dinner."

"I've got to—"

"Please." His hand was on her forearm, his intensity undeniable. She glanced at his left hand, which rested on the laptop case slung across his shoulders. No ring. Sure had to be some long engagement. Or maybe...

No.

"I'm sorry, James. I'm unavailable." She tugged free of his light grasp, and this time, he didn't try to stop her from going through security. The twinge of emotion that tore at her heart was her annoyance at being late for court.

It had nothing to do with disappointment.

* * *

"You're going to have to work harder to get this loser behind bars." Her assistant looked at her across Rachel's massive desk, a tablet balanced on her lap.

"I know that, Clara. Don't you think I do?" Rachel sighed, unable to forgive herself for being late, for not giving her best impression in court this morning. Her mistake had made the judge raise his brows at her. His Honor had seemed more congenial than usual to yet another one of the men who had profited by her deceased father's criminal doings. Ben Colton had been a judge who willingly took bribes to incarcerate innocent people. As a juvenile detention center administrator and board member, Brian Parson had facilitated kickbacks to Judge Colton for providing prisoners who were given harsher sentences than called for and become a very successful, menacing drug kingpin. "We're dealing with not only the slimiest of scum but the richest, too. Brian Parson won't go down without a fight, but we've got him by the…throat." She tried to keep it classy as DA, but sometimes her words got away from her. "I'm just lucky the judge hasn't recused me from the case yet."

"He can't, not since you've resigned your position with the Truth Foundation. Plus, you've never worked on his case before, even when you had my job."

"No, I didn't." She'd made it clear to the then-DA that unless Parson was up for trial she didn't want to be privy to any information about him. She'd never expected to become the DA this soon, though.

Being able to work this side of the cases that the Truth Foundation helped bring to light was important to Rachel. It had cost her years that she could have been working closely alongside her siblings to right her father's wrongs, but she was doing her part to keep Blue Larkspur safe. Parson was a notorious drug kingpin in the area and could go to jail none too soon, as far as she was concerned.

Rachel let out a long breath, wondering what Iris was doing. She missed her baby. A quick glance at her watch told her the baby was taking her afternoon nap. "I know that, but I absolutely can't be late ever again. I'm going to undo all my brothers and sisters have accomplished in twenty years in two months if I'm not careful."

"Stop it. I may be overstepping, but none of this is your fault." Clara was ten years younger and a newly minted lawyer, just as Rachel had been in the same position. Rachel knew her assistant aspired to someday have Rachel's position. Rachel sincerely hoped Clara achieved it. Being DA wasn't all that she'd thought it'd be, and it wasn't just because her father, as well as his widow and kids, had become Blue Larkspur's pariahs after his death. The pressure and quickly evolving cases kept her on her mental toes, which she loved. But combined with the stress of raising an infant, being a new mom, it felt like a bit much at times. Rachel suspected she'd want a quieter position when Iris got older.

"Now you're smiling."

"I've got to call Iris before we go back in session."

Clara nodded, never slow to get a hint. "I'll meet you back in court in fifteen minutes." As Clara opened the door and walked out, the receptionist arrived, holding a huge bouquet of creamy white tulips in a vase that didn't look like a typical florist's inexpensive type.

"These just came for you, ma'am."

"Thank you." She nodded at the corner of her desk, doing all she could to appear unaffected by the gorgeous spring bouquet. Mother Nature had dumped ten inches of snow just last week, not atypical for a Colorado spring, so the reminder of warmer weather wasn't unwelcome. Though she suspected the sentiments might be.

As soon as her office door shut, leaving her alone, she sprang from her chair and whipped off the note card from its stake above the blooms. Her fingers shook as she removed the classy white stationery. "Have dinner with me. James."

He'd left his cell number below his signature. His handwriting was definite, the slant distinct. And her libido responded as if their time together had been only last weekend, not over a year ago. It had to be because he was Iris's father, a purely biological reaction.

She pulled up his contact information in her phone, noting that this was a new number. Her hands shook as she updated his profile. Before she could allow herself to think, Rachel did a most uncharacteristic thing and texted him one word.

Yes.

"I don't want to be the one to tell you you're letting your past run your life, bro, but have you considered your Spidey senses are tingling because you're in a new place?" Jake, James's older brother, had a point. James spoke to him via his wireless earphones as he stacked books on his office shelves. The shipment from Denver had arrived this morning.

"I haven't had any thoughts of Bethany since…"

"When she crashed your farewell party?"

James groaned. "Yes." The reminder of how she'd

shown up at the upscale restaurant, in front of the senior partners and staff, still gave him heartburn. Bethany had worn a dress more suited for a private lover's night out than a business function. He experienced the embarrassment all over again as he remembered his shock at her behavior. In front of all of his colleagues, no less. She'd sidled up next to him, squeezed his butt and tried to kiss him. Since his former firm knew about the restraining order, the office receptionist made a quick 9-1-1 call and Bethany had been removed from the premises in cuffs. But not before the jovial celebration had been doused. "I should have pressed charges then." She'd been let out on minimal bail and an agreement to do community service.

"Stop blaming yourself for her behavior, James."

"I know you're right."

"I always am." They both shared a laugh. Jake was older by five years and also a lawyer. He'd set up his own family practice in the same Denver suburb they'd grown up in. "Seriously, try to let go of what you've been through here. The cops told you that Bethany has a history of stalking boyfriends, right? You're just another bozo on the bus, James. She'll forget about you and latch on to someone else when she finds it impossible to find you. The odds of Bethany following you to Blue Larkspur have to be equal to the odds of you switching to family law."

"Nil." James liked the thrill of the chase for justice in a commercial setting.

"You're such a softie."

"I am." James knew his limits. Jake was well suited for family law as he'd been the one to help his mother and younger siblings when their dad, Stefanos Kiriakis, died. James had never been able to shake the trauma of losing a parent when he was only six. As he grew, he more fully comprehended the legal mess his father had left for his mother. He didn't have a will, which in itself was no problem, as the law provided that his mother and Stefanos's children would inherit the meager coffers left behind by his father. Still, his mother had had to fight off several unscrupulous, distant relatives who battled to gain family heirlooms that in the end provided James's family with the minimal security they needed to eat and keep a roof over their heads. His mother had sold the jewelry and artworks, all to keep her family going.

Back then he'd been too young to understand anything but the intense sadness that permeated the family for several years, at least until he was an adolescent. He was very conscious of the fact that he avoided involved relationships with women for this reason. He never wanted to leave any child in the lurch the way his father had, no matter that Stefanos's mistake was unintentional. "Give me a cold, calculating business suit over a family dispute any day."

"Speaking of which, how's the new job?"

"So far, so good. I thought it'd be slower in a smaller city, but the partners aren't afraid to stack my caseload."

"Have you been to court yet?"

"Only to observe. I begin trying a case next month."

"That's a good amount of time to get your feet wet, to allow you to get settled."

"Definitely."

They spoke for several more minutes about the family, their mother and, of course, the Rockies. Both brothers were baseball fanatics.

When they disconnected, James's mind immediately went back to this morning and how he'd literally run into Rachel Colton, the one woman in town he'd been hoping to see. If it wasn't the definition of serendipity, he didn't know what was—although they were both lawyers in the same small city, there'd been no guarantee they'd see each other again anytime soon, not unless he reached out. Which, he had to admit, he might have procrastinated about. And best news of the day, the week, the past two years? She'd agreed to meet him for dinner tonight. He'd shared neither fact with Jake. Which meant only one thing.

He was hoping for the best of outcomes tonight. First, that Rachel wouldn't think he'd moved here just because she lived here. It was especially important to him that she didn't believe he was any kind of stalker. He knew too well how that felt. Second, he'd be thrilled if Rachel would realize what they'd shared in Montana was more than a mountain fling. That maybe it was worth their while to spend some time together.

It was a great feeling, hope. A lot better than the gnawing fear of being followed.

"I can't thank you enough for helping me out here, Mom." Rachel undressed in her bedroom closet while Iris lay in the middle of her queen-size bed, gurgling with what sounded like glee as her grandmother gave her raspberries on her belly. Isadora Colton was chronologically seventy-two but cut the figure and had the activity level of a woman twenty years younger. Her shoulder-length blond hair with barely a whisper of silver threads was still soft, and a favorite of Iris's. The infant tugged on the long strands with her pudgy hands.

"I would have been offended if you didn't call me. I don't get to see this rosebud enough, do I, Iris?" Iris responded by grabbing another baby fistful of hair and yanking, prompting a deep belly laugh from Isa. Rachel didn't have any memories of her loving mother being so playful with her or any of her siblings. The sixth of twelve Colton kids, she'd been enlisted to help with the younger ones as she become old enough. By the time Rachel was in middle school, Isa seemed exhausted from child-rearing and was often distracted. Rachel remembered a parent who was caring but had little patience for youthful antics. In hindsight she realized worry over her husband and family had consumed Isa's every waking moment.

Ben Colton had enjoyed the esteem and privilege that came with being the local judge for years. His noted career had kept their family in the spotlight, always the ready example of Blue Larkspur's thriving community. They'd remained in the public eye, though, as it turned hostile. An investigation revealed Ben had accepted bribes. He'd been on the take from local private prisons and juvenile detention centers to ensure they remained filled. All Judge Colton had to do was assign the harshest penalty possible to a convict.

A tenacious reporter had uncovered the scandal just before Ben's untimely death in an auto accident twenty years ago, right as Rachel turned fourteen. Her prior idolization of her father and desire to follow in his footsteps had been shattered, but when she emerged from the grief and shame, Rachel knew that there was no path for her other than the law. She vowed to never become corrupt like her father, and in fact, along with her siblings, had been instrumental in helping establish the

Truth Foundation. The organization's goal was to exonerate wrongfully convicted people, including those
their unethical father had sent to jail.

It was to her dismay that as district attorney she
couldn't continue to work on making certain all victims of Ben Colton's crimes received the justice they
deserved. Rachel had recused herself from all of the
Truth Foundation's legal dealings, with assurances from
her siblings that she need not worry, they'd handle it.
Plus she was the new Lark's County District Attorney—
she'd be serving justice across the entire community,
not just Ben Colton's victims.

"What am I doing?" Her gaze froze on the two
dresses she held from hangers, knowing that she
couldn't go on this date—no, not a *date* date, it was
only to find out more about Iris's father—with James.
No matter that her heart had flipped along with her
stomach the second she'd locked gazes with him. She
had to stay the course, though, and not get sidetracked
by James's too sexy looks. First she had to figure out
why he was in Blue Larkspur, and then see how much
he'd heard from the locals about her…and Iris.

"You're getting back to the life you deserve." Isa
stood next to her, expertly balancing Iris on her slim
but strong hip. Isa Colton never missed a yoga or spin
class and could out-lift her daughters nine times out
of ten.

"Mom, you are the last to talk. You've never even
dated since Dad died." It used to be hard to mention her
father's demise, but after two decades, it was a natural
part of their family history. Grief, however, was a different story. Despite his wrongdoings and faults, she

still loved her father, the man he'd been before corruption sunk its sharp teeth into his soul.

"And that might not be the best example for you to follow."

Whoa! Was Isadora Colton—family matriarch and the last word for most Colton disputes—showing a crack in her stoic veneer?

"Mom?" She searched her mother's expression, which was resolutely set in a joyful smile reserved for her grandchildren.

"Oh, don't act so surprised, Rachel. You're a woman who knows what's important in life. You've shown remarkable grace in the midst of a surprise pregnancy and now an unexpected promotion and election to DA. More importantly, you're much younger than I was when Dad died. There's no reason for you to be alone for all of Iris's childhood. If I had to do it over again, maybe I would have been going out with my girlfriends while you babysat your brothers and sisters. Right, Iris baby?"

"Is there someone you wished you'd dated, Mom?"

"Back then? No, not really. A man or two caught my eye, but, well, I was so ashamed by what had happened and we were so busy keeping it together after your dad died that dating wasn't anything I seriously considered. And when my parents died only a year later, I was swamped with grief, again." Her mother turned away and bent down to retrieve a soft elephant rattle Iris had tossed onto the floor earlier.

Rachel knew that while losing her grandparents had been a gut-punch loss to all of them, it had affected her mother the most. Isa had thankfully inherited enough money from her parents to support the Colton clan until all of the kids reached adulthood. It had taken savvy reinvestment and a much tighter budget than they'd ever been accustomed to, but Rachel remembered all the years of struggle as the best family time ever, save for the fact they were grieving Ben Colton and Isa's parents.

"What about now, Mom? Is there someone special?"

Isa's eyes flashed, and for a second, Rachel thought her mother was about to confide in her. But then her walls went back up. "Look, enough talk about me. This is your night. Who again are you meeting?"

"Just a new lawyer in town. It's not a date."

"Uh-huh. Well, I'm perfectly prepared to sleep over if you decide to have your own kind of pajama party on your 'not a date.'"

"Mom!"

"Stop it with the false modesty." Isa nodded at the navy dress with the plunging neckline. "Wear that one. It's the least like your stuffy court suits. Add the diamond earrings I gave you last Christmas and the necklace from Grammy. Put some color on your cheeks and rev up the lipstick while you're at it. That bright pink brings out your blue eyes best. Iris and I are going to go rustle up some dinner while you finish primping."

"The breast milk is in the kitchen freezer." She kept all the milk she pumped at work available for times like these, when she had to be away. Sadness tugged at her peace of mind. Maybe she should cancel the date. She'd only be able to nurse Iris for so long—

"You can nurse her when you get back in, before she goes down for the last time." It was as if her mother read her mind. "I've got it, Rachel. Relax. Twelve kids, remember?" Isa's delicate brow raised in amusement as she sauntered off, singing a medley of sixties soul to her granddaughter.

"I do, Mom." She looked at her phone. "We've got to go." Her car was in the shop due to an unexpected issue and Isa was going to drop her off and pick her up. "Let's get Iris in the car seat. I feel like a teen again, needing my mom to drive me to a date."

Isa laughed. As they left the house and then strapped in Iris, Rachel was glad that the baby wouldn't be visible from outside of the car. In case James arrived at the restaurant entrance at the same time she did.

A nibble of doubt sprinkled with guilt gnawed at her insides. She'd deliberately lied. James was not "just another" lawyer. He was the father of her child.

Had the time come to tell him?

Chapter 3

"Hi, James. I'm so sorry I'm late. It seems to be a theme today." Rachel stood next to the table he hoped might be the location for the start of the relationship they'd never begun. She slid into the seat across from him. So smooth was her appearance that he barely had time to register the dark blue dress that clung to her curves, her impossibly long legs, her slim feet tucked into heels even higher than this morning's. Besides, he was too preoccupied with her face. Rachel's classically high cheekbones accented her sapphire eyes. Eyes that he'd never forgotten. Especially the way they'd flashed indigo when she…

Stop. Keep it out of the gutter, dude.

"No problem. Does work always keep you late?" He figured it was a definite "yes," since she was DA.

She opened the menu, gave the waiter her drink order when he silently appeared. "No, not all the time. The office works well enough most days. This afternoon I had car trouble of all things. My car wouldn't start, so I switched with my mother's. She's, ah, um, she lives nearby." Odd. Rachel wasn't the type to get flustered. At least, not the Rachel he'd met in Helena. There was something she'd stopped herself from saying.

"So your car's in the shop?"

She grinned, and the sight of her dimples hit him in his solar plexus. Rather, the memories of how many times he'd made her smile like that during their time together in Helena was what sucker punched him.

"I've got six brothers, and a couple of my sisters are great with cars, too. My car should be fixed by the time I get in tonight. One of my brothers, Gideon, promised me he'd take care of it. He's always looking for an excuse—" She grabbed her water glass and took a large gulp.

"An excuse to what?"

A soft flush rose up her throat, her cheeks, and he had the distinct impression she'd kept herself from saying something she'd regret. Which was ridiculous since they barely knew one another. How did he know what her actions revealed, or hid?

Except for how she'd reacted to his touch, his kisses...

"You know what I mean. Be around me. Check out my house—I bought it pretty recently—and see what changes I've made. Stuff siblings do." She stared intently at the menu. He reached across the small table and gently tugged on the middle of it.

"May I?"

"May you what?" Her quizzical gaze struck a chord of compassion in him. She really was out of sorts. He could only imagine the private and public pressures of her job.

"Fix this so that you can read it. Unless you like an extra challenge?" He turned the menu right side up, and at first, he wasn't sure if Rachel was going to bolt from the dining room or break down in tears. So many emotions played across her usually confident, serene face.

What he didn't expect was her laughter. It came out in a surprised gasp, not unlike when he'd undressed her—

Whoa. His desire for her kept making his thoughts jump the gun. This was a first date, what would have happened if she'd answered his calls last year. Not an invitation to pick up where they'd left off.

Slow and easy, that's what he'd promised himself when he moved here and again after running into her earlier. He'd decided that if Rachel were amenable, he'd like to pursue their relationship on more than a physical plane. To see if they might cultivate a friendship. Or, well, something in parallel with the sexual chemistry they obviously shared.

"I'm not good at hiding my feelings, am I?" She put the menu on the table. "There's a lot I need to talk to you about, James, and well, can I be frank here? I don't know where to start." The votive candle flame in the table's center reflected in her eyes and he felt a tug in his gut. Why hadn't he driven to Blue Larkspur sooner, figured out why she hadn't answered him?

Because you didn't want to come off like a stalker. No, that was the last thing he'd ever want.

"Why don't we start with where we left off?"

Her raised brow reflected desire and surprise. Too late, he realized how the words must have sounded.

"No, no, I'm not trying to get you in the sack again. Not that I don't want to, I mean." He reached for his water, took a gulp. Where was his composure? "I'd never put that kind of pressure on you until we're both on better footing with a friendship. I think we deserve a shot to get to know one another more than a weekend at a legal conference affords. I've thought of you a lot since we met, Rachel. For whatever reason, you didn't return my calls back then, but this is now. We're both in the same city. I'm asking you to give me a chance." His voice cracked on the last word. Sweat trickled down his back, and nothing had ever seemed more important to him. Who was he? This had to be from the stress of the last several months with Bethany, changing jobs, the move.

"That's fair." Were those tears glistening in her eyes? Or was it the crystal votive reflecting in their blue depths? Before he could discern which of the two, a movement in his peripheral vision drew his gaze. When he focused on the distraction, recognition froze him to the spot. Dread like no other twisted with the bile in his stomach.

A woman whose profile exactly matched Bethany's walked past the dining area, toward the direction of the piano bar at the far end of the spacious restaurant. Was this the fallout from being stalked for months on end? That he'd imagine seeing Bethany at every turn?

Or was it worse? Was Bethany really here, in Blue Larkspur, at the very restaurant he'd invited Rachel to? Was he unconsciously sabotaging his chance with Rachel?

"James, is something the matter?"

"I'm not sure, but if there is, I'm going to take care of it. Stay here."

He'd explain later. After he told Bethany to stay out of his life.

Well, that was odd. Rachel knew she'd behaved like a flighty squirrel since she'd arrived, but had her behavior put James off so much that he'd needed to flee the table? She'd been almost fifteen minutes late, which had totally stressed her out before she even arrived at Ricco's. Punctuality was the key to her peace of mind, something that Iris tested on a daily basis.

She regretted starting the evening off on a rude note, when James was being so accommodating, so…attractive. She hadn't stopped thinking about him since Montana, either, but blamed it on him being Iris's father. Since finding out he was engaged, there had been no way she'd considered him in any other manner.

She lifted her phone so that she could see the screen saver. Iris's face filled the display, her irresistible smile lighting up her big green eyes, which were focused on her Uncle Gideon as he took the photo.

Her stomach grumbled and she put the phone back down on the table. She hadn't eaten since she'd chowed down on the salad in her bento box, six hours ago. The best way to deal with any new situation was to focus on what she knew, so she studied the menu. Right side up this time. Her choice was made easy since her favorite, lobster ravioli, was tonight's special.

The waiter reappeared with her wineglass and what looked like a scotch for James. She'd been so flustered when she arrived that she hadn't heard his drink order. All she'd been concerned with was keeping her eyes from devouring him. Vulnerability wasn't her favorite emotion and James stirred it up in her big-time. And she hadn't told him the truth yet.

He was Iris's father.

Seeing him this morning had been such a surprise. She still hadn't processed it—Iris's father was here, in Blue Larkspur. A ball of nervous energy had consumed her by the time she arrived at the restaurant.

"Have you made your decision?" Their waiter looked at her with polite expectation. Before she replied, James returned and sat down, his expression unreadable.

"I know what I want, but do you need more time?" His courtesy was like a warm hug after her chaotic thoughts. With a little bit of a sexy squeeze.

"Actually, no. I'm ready." Rachel knew she lived up to her family's description of "control freak" with zero question. Normally she arrived at a restaurant with her choice made, having already perused the menu online. There hadn't been time today, though. Not a spare second between Iris, work and her car. This had to be what was making her so aware of James, of the way his athletic build filled out his white dress shirt and black slacks.

But then he flashed her the same smile that had gone a long way to convince her to step out of character and spend a wild, passionate night with a stranger almost fifteen months ago. He nodded for her to order first, unaware of her thoughts, much more significant than any food order. It hit her that while they'd only spent that one night together, James felt like someone she'd always known. An important part of her life.

Well, duh. He's your daughter's father.

"Ma'am?" The server's prompt brought her back, and first she, then James placed their requests.

With them alone again until their meals arrived, she couldn't keep what she knew was anticipatory awareness from flitting across her mind, triggering the warm curl of attraction in her belly, between her legs. It was a constant reminder of how excellently they were matched.

Physically. You don't really know him.

Not yet.

"Before we go further, I need to understand why you didn't take my calls." James fired the first verbal shot. "I saw that you'd reached out to me a few weeks after we met, but when I called you back you never picked up."

"Are you certain you're not a prosecutor?" She tried to make light of their situation. For now. It was going to get superheavy right about the time she revealed that he was a parent. Guilt sucker punched her yet again. No matter that James was engaged, possibly married by now. He needed to know he had a child. "And what exactly brings you to Blue Larkspur?"

"Nice sidestep, Rachel. Fine, I'll go first. I needed a change and received a compelling offer from a large corporate firm in this county. It's number three in all of Colorado."

"Oh, Schmidt, Thungston and Turner?" She rattled off the firm that employed many of her law school classmates.

He nodded. "That's the one. And while I recall that you're not a fan of corporate law, the practice has taken on many cases that are unusual for a firm with its success and reputation."

She knew this to be true. James's new employer

wasn't afraid to help out smaller ventures as needed and often filled in the gap between small-business law and full-on corporate litigation. But it wasn't enough for her to get her hopes up that James wasn't as power hungry as she'd ascertained when they first met.

And it didn't matter. She was going to do the right thing and tell him about Iris. But as for more between them—

"James, are you married?"

His head reared back ever so slightly but just enough for her legal scrutiny to catch the movement. "Absolutely not. Why do you ask?"

This wasn't a time for tiptoeing. Not when she was going to reveal that the most precious thing in the world to her, her daughter, was also his.

You don't have to tell him.

She did, though. He deserved to know.

"You're correct—I did call you a few weeks after we'd met. And frankly, wondered why you hadn't called sooner."

"I wanted to, believe me. But I was out of the country." Her expression had to be doubtful because he leaned over the table, nose to nose, his eyes reflecting honesty. "My sister got married in Edinburgh."

"Oh."

"The entire time I was in Scotland, I couldn't stop imagining you there with me. We'd only had that one night—hours, really—and yet I couldn't shake you. You were different."

Stunned, she sought for reprieve from the possibility she'd made a mistake and found none. If he was being truthful, if he'd been gone when she'd called, then—

"Wait a minute. I called you no more than three and a

half weeks after we met." This date she knew by heart, as it had been the earliest her doctor had assured her that the pregnancy test result was valid. Positive.

"You didn't leave a voice mail." He tilted his head. "I always check."

"I would have left a message, but a woman answered before it switched to voice mail. James, she told me she was your fiancée. I didn't leave my name or try to call you after that. I...couldn't."

It was her turn to observe James's discomfort as his eyes sparked with rage and he leaned forward, his gaze sincere. "I've never been engaged or married." He took a swig of his drink, collapsed back in his chair. "It seems we're destined to share more than pleasantries tonight."

"What—"

A huge boom sounded, and the floor under her feet reverberated. Before she had a chance to react, strong hands yanked her from her seat and she found herself facedown on the floor, James on top of her. Protecting her.

She gulped for air, unable to utter a sound as she heard screeches of panic from all corners of Ricco's.

Another *boom* was followed immediately by its force shaking the building. Her head turned to the side, she saw ceiling tiles hit the floor amid other patrons doing exactly the same—taking cover from a deadly blast.

"Get ready to move as soon as we can." James's voice was steady in her ear, her only anchor as panic threatened to set in. The image of Iris's laughing eyes, her gurgling laughter, melded into a single thought.

I can't die.

Chapter 4

Screams rent the air. As he observed from his location under their table, James saw patrons react on instinct, hitting the ground on their bellies, covering their heads with their hands. Others raced for the main exit. All the while he was aware of the precious charge under him— Rachel. If anything happened to her, he'd never forgive himself. Especially if the cause of these explosions were from what he thought. *Who* he thought.

The blasts suddenly ceased and his stomach sank at the large group near the closest exit. It'd take too long to get out through that door. He stood up and looked around the dining room, spied another neon EXIT sign in the far corner of the room. Already, several people were running through the more distant door.

"Let's go!"

James reached for Rachel's hand at the same time

she got to her feet. With zero fuss she took his lead as he ran around several tables and out the back door. The fading daylight was bright but welcome as they sprinted from the building across the paved lot. Cold wind hit his cheeks. Rachel's dress was thin, offering no protection. But he couldn't worry about keeping Rachel warm, not yet. He had to get her far from the restaurant as quickly as he could.

Only when they reached the edge of the asphalt did they stop, leaning into one another as they caught their breath. James folded Rachel into his arms and she clung to his biceps, her fingers digging in as if she was drowning. He willed warmth and reassurance through his hands, holding her to him.

He put his forehead against hers. "Are you okay, Rachel?"

She blinked, her eyes still glazed over in shock. "Yes, yes, I'm fine. And you? Are you hurt?"

He shook his head, sucking in air like her. "No, no injuries. I'm good." They were both good. Relief began to douse the flames of fear, the rush of adrenaline.

"What on earth was that?" Her voice shook and he knew the reality of what had happened was hitting her, digging past the shock. "Oh my gosh, James. I've got to get home, back to…" She pulled back and her frantic gaze searched the lot, presumably for her car.

"I'll get you home." He quickly dialed emergency services and reported what had happened. He didn't think he'd be the first to call it in, since the loudness of the blasts must have reached for at least a mile or so. But the weight of responsibility that cloaked him made his shoulders ache. And not from an old college injury, aka his torn rotator cuff. If he'd seen Bethany, she was behind this.

The dispatcher took his information and confirmed that they already had units en route. "One more thing, I saw a possible perpetrator." He described Bethany in detail, hoping against all odds he was wrong. That the woman he'd spotted was no more than a doppelgänger.

Rachel's gaze never wavered from his face as he gave a definitive description of the entire event, including providing a description of a bar patron she'd never noticed. Hyperaware of her scrutiny, he felt his gut tighten. Sure enough, once he disconnected, she wanted answers.

"James, what just happened? And who is the woman you were talking about? Is that why you got up from the table so quickly?"

He placed a hand on her shoulder, hoping to dispel her concern. "Don't worry. You're not stuck here. The police and bomb squad are on the way."

"Stop it. Answer my questions." She shrugged out from under his touch, the stubborn streak he was more familiar with emerging. Gratitude hit him sideways. *She was okay.* Rachel was uninjured. If the explosion was Bethany's doing—

He pinched the bridge of his nose, forced himself to calm down enough to answer Rachel's valid questions. But his hands shook as his anger soared. He was furious with himself for dragging her into this nightmare, if indeed his stalker was behind this.

"Let me answer your questions one by one. The explosives first. My guess is it was something like an M-80, possibly homemade due to its strength. But it wasn't a legit bomb, or we wouldn't be here to talk about it, not in as small a space as that building. A strong fire-cracker, nothing more."

"How can you be so sure it was a firecracker? And what woman were you telling the dispatcher about?" Blue eyes emanated determination, control. Like a shark assessing its victim. Her scrutiny was the antithesis of *pleasant*. James needed no further reminder that Rachel was a gifted prosecutor. She had to be tops at her job or she wouldn't have been elected to it so early in her career.

"I can't be certain it was an M-80 or cherry bomb, but my past experience matches what just happened." He ran his hand over his face. "I'm so sorry, Rachel. I put you, the entire restaurant, in danger."

"That's ridiculous." She moved closer, put her hand on his arm. "How can you blame yourself for some random explosion? Unless you're some secret agent posing as a lawyer?" A ghost of a grin flitted across her face.

Tell her.

Confronted with Rachel's generosity of spirit, he had no choice but to level with her.

"I moved to Blue Larkspur to take a fantastic new job. And yes, I'd hoped that maybe you and I would re-connect. But another big reason I moved was to get out of Denver. I needed to go anywhere else a good distance away. I thought heading to the other side of the state would be the end of it."

"It?" She looked like she was pulling teeth and he cursed his lack of directness.

"I've been stalked by a woman I briefly dated before I met you. I thought I'd taken every precaution to keep my transfer confidential, but somehow she's apparently found out."

"How do you know for certain she's followed you here? Because you think you saw her in the restaurant?"

Sirens sounded and snippets of panicked conversation from several small groups of patrons floated around them. Rachel reached for his waist and leaned against him, her body telling him that she wasn't a threat. She supported whatever he was going through.

He tightened his arm around her waist. Her gesture gave him hope that this horrible scourge that Bethany had been in his life could, and would, pass. Eventually.

"I've been stalked for the better part of two years by a woman who has told anyone she can that she's my fiancée or even my wife on several occasions. I believe she answered my phone the day you called. She's the woman who said I was engaged. I should have realized that there had to be a valid reason you wouldn't take my calls. The good news is that I haven't seen a whiff of her for at least three months. But now I think she was biding her time."

"Has she harmed you before? Set off other explosives?" Rachel kept close contact with him but exuded intense energy. He swore he saw the cogs whirring behind her beautiful eyes.

"No, not a bomb per se. This wasn't a bomb, either, but I'm not an explosives expert. Blue Larkspur PD will be able to identify the cause soon enough. It's probably nothing more than a powerful homemade firecracker, meant to scare, to instill terror. She knows how to make them. If it's Bethany, it's because she wants to throw me off balance again. She set one off in the hallway outside my condo door back in Denver. I have a restraining order against her and I thought she'd finally backed off, moved on to her next target. I was wrong."

How many times had he told this story? *Too many.*

"Wow. That's a lot. I'm so sorry, James." Her gaze remained steady on his, her compassion licking the deep wounds.

"Thanks. All of this being said, you've probably figured out that you can't see me again. To be fair, I don't want you to see me again, not until I know Bethany isn't a threat."

His chest and throat tightened with the crushing disappointment of his decision. The woman he'd put hopes on for being the best thing about Blue Larkspur was out of his reach.

He'd thought dealing with Bethany for so many months, constantly looking over his shoulder for her, had been the worst days of his life. Nope. Not even close.

Saying no to any hope of a future with Rachel was his rock bottom.

"Rachel!"

The familiar voice reached her but still in the midst of trying to corral her emotions, she didn't trust her ears. What would her mother be doing here?

"Rachel!" At the second yell she turned from James and faced Isa, holding Iris.

"Mom! What are you doing here?" She ran to her mother's side, leaving James. "Baby girl!" Iris had her arms up, her face an expression of pure happiness at seeing her mother again. "Come here." She enfolded Iris in her arms.

"We hadn't gone home yet."

"Let me guess, the toy store?" She smiled at her baby.

"Toy aisle at the supermarket. I needed a few items.

But then…I got a phone call, I mean, I found out that the explosion happened, and I had to get here, to make sure you're okay. I wouldn't have gotten out of the car if it didn't look safe." Isa pointed at her vehicle, only a few yards away.

"You sure have your ear to the ground, Mom."

"I had to see for myself that you're okay. Is that your date?"

James.

"Um, yes." James must have heard them as he walked up and stood alongside Rachel. "Mom, this is James Kiriakis. James, my mom, Isa Colton."

They exchanged the briefest greetings, and she noted that both her mother and James had the same strained smile. Did she look just as frazzled?

"Is this a granddaughter?" James's gaze flitted over Isa, bundled up in a pink snowsuit, the hood snapped to only reveal her cherubic face.

"Yes, this is my mom's first grandchild." Rachel shot her mother a stern look. Isa was no dummy and she remained quiet. Rachel prayed James's curiosity was cursory. Her prayer was quickly answered as sirens permeated the air.

"Nice." James's reply was distracted as he searched the street for the response team.

"Mom, why don't you and Iris get back in the car and stay warm until I'm ready to leave?"

Not one to miss a hint, Isa smiled. "Sure thing." She took Iris back and retreated to the car. Rachel let out a breath and stood next to James, wondering how on earth she'd just survived not only an explosion but an explosive situation.

James had family he didn't know about yet.

* * *

As they waited for the police, Rachel realized James was blaming himself for everything.

James wouldn't meet her gaze; the combination of despair, resolution and determination etched on his face aged him well beyond thirty-six. She remembered he was two years older than her along with many other details she shouldn't have hung on to. Facts she didn't need to know about a man she thought she'd never see again. Definitely not if she was going to remain detached, perhaps just co-parenting with.

Nothing more, certainly nothing romantic. Because being with him again for such brief, albeit intense, interactions was enough to inform her that she wasn't ready for a relationship with any man, especially James.

But James's palpable frustration blew away her resolve as effectively as the explosion had ruined their quiet dinner conversation. And she had lots to offer him as far as dealing with stalkers went. Memories of always looking over her shoulder for the boyfriend-turned-stalker through her entire senior year of college tried to resurface, but she'd experienced enough life since then to know it was behind her. James was still going through his hell, though.

In for a penny...

"James, listen to me. You are not going to go through this alone. You're living in Blue Larkspur now, part of our community. It's a small city, yes, but we pride ourselves on being a city with a small-town feel and an urban flair. We look out for each other around here. I know what you're going through better than you realize. I had a stalker in college, and it took months to convince him that he was wasting his time. I was fortunate in that he never got violent, but it honestly didn't make the ordeal less scary. He finally stopped after I moved back here, and he moved east. Plus, he got the help he needed."

He swung his gaze from the arriving cruisers to her. She recognized the pain in his eyes, the wariness.

"That sucks, Rachel. I'm sorry you've been through this, too."

"I know more now and have a different perspective, thanks to working in the DA's office. Crimes like stalking require tireless reporting and persistence in not only getting the culprit to back off but getting them the help they need so that no one else becomes a victim. If I hadn't had my family around me, my friends, the support of the university, I don't know what I would have done."

He gave a curt nod. "Yeah, it's a multifaceted issue." His tone was pure attorney, but his stance was 100 percent defeated victim.

She reached out and gave his shoulder a quick squeeze. "You'll get through this, James. And no way are we going to allow Bethany, if it was indeed her, to interfere with our friendship."

His face turned, and when their gazes met, a sudden shock of bonding, laced with awareness, coursed through her. They stood for what seemed like hours but couldn't have been more than a few heartbeats, lost in each other.

Red flag, girlfriend. The chemistry here is bigger than you.

Sirens screeched as the cruisers neared, and she forced her gaze away. What was wrong with her, getting all hot in a parking lot after she'd just been through a potentially life-threatening event?

Two words. *James Kiriakis*.

Blue Larkspur FD's main engine pulled into the lot and she used all of her energy to refocus. To look at anything besides James. "They're not messing around with the response."

James put his hands on his hips and shook his head. "Nor should they. Whether it was a firecracker or bomb, both have the potential to become a whole lot more than a one-building event. Someone could have been hurt in the rush out of the restaurant. Thank goodness it's been a rainy spring so far. It takes less than a firecracker to start a forest fire when it's drier."

"Did Bethany get charged for the illegal use of fireworks in Denver?" Short of looking up the case file for herself, she had to rely on James's account.

"Yes, but her attorney got her off with a fine. But that doesn't seem to affect her behavior. She broke the restraining order several times, always let off with community service and a fine. It's my fault—I should have insisted that she have the full charges pressed against her. But I felt sorry for her and always petitioned the court for leniency. My mistake. If this really was her, she's broken the state fireworks law. Again."

"Maybe they'll catch her, and the charges will hold this time. If she has any extra explosive ingredients in her possession, she's in violation of terrorist laws, too." Colorado did not take its fireworks laws lightly.

He sighed. "I'm not holding my breath. Bethany's as intelligent as she is determined. It's how she's wriggled out of all previous violations related to stalking me. That, and a good lawyer."

"You mean a slimy lawyer." She hated disparaging her own vocation, but there were good and bad players in all professions. A good defense counsel for Bethany would, at minimum, suggest the woman get medical help for her ailment, if she had one.

"Yup." Her fingers itched to soothe the furrows on his tanned brow. She drew in a breath, held it and resisted the over-the-top gesture.

"Fill me in, James. You saw her right before you ran out of the room, didn't you?" She knew the answer but needed to know what he was thinking.

His attention on her had splintered when they were at their table. He'd been distracted, not hearing her as she'd tried to engage in small talk. She'd thought maybe it was because she'd been late, made him think she was going to stand him up. Now she saw it'd been his internal struggle after seeing Bethany. Or at the least, a woman who looked an awful lot like her.

"Yes." He rubbed his nape.

"And you second-guessed yourself."

"Yes. I can't be certain, but I thought I saw a woman who looked just like Bethany walk through the dining area to the bar. She had the same build and facial profile but very different hair, so I wasn't sure. I knew I wouldn't enjoy our time together until I proved I was wrong. I went and looked, but before I got there, she was gone." James spoke with regret. "If only I'd reacted sooner—"

"If it was her, from what you've told me, she's very resourceful. It sounds like she wanted you to know she was there, to know she set the minibomb off. If it wasn't her, you had no way of knowing something so nefarious was going to happen."

James's gaze met hers and she thought she recognized appreciation in its green depths. Rachel understood. When her father's misdeeds had been fully revealed, she and her siblings had sought reassurance from their friends that no one blamed them, only Judge Ben Colton. Not everyone had been supportive, which was why she wanted James to understand she was on his side.

Especially if this Bethany character was all that had kept them from reuniting, from James finding out that he was a father.

Iris.

"Hey, Rachel." Chief of Police Theodore Lawson, an attractive older man with a full mane of silver hair, stood next to them. Theo was an imposing figure no matter where he went, but especially when in his element as police chief. "I'm going to need you to tell me what you witnessed."

"Hi, Chief." The chief was a permanent fixture in Blue Larkspur. Rachel couldn't remember a time when he hadn't been a friend of her family's. Even in the dark days of first finding out about her father's criminal activity and then Ben's tragic death, Theodore had never exuded an air of judgment or blame. He'd shown nothing but the utmost compassion and support to all of her siblings. Most importantly, to their mother, Isa.

A flicker of a memory flashed across her mind, momentarily distracting her. When Isa told her about having second thoughts over remaining alone for the rest of her life. Another memory triggered, from when Rachel ran into her mother with Theo at the local coffee shop. They'd been chatting away, oblivious to her presence until she announced herself. She'd thought it was coincidence that the two were there at the same time, that they'd simply run into one another. But had it been more?

"I'm the one who called it in, Chief. James Kiriakis." James offered Theo his hand, and Rachel shoved her musings on her mother's romantic life to the side.

"Did you, now?" Theodore nodded and accepted James's handshake. "Well, then, come along. This shouldn't take much time."

James nodded at the chief, then looked at Rachel. "I'm sorry about our first date... I'll make this up to you."

"Please." She waved him off, as if it were customary for a date to end on such an explosive note. A date. He'd said it was a date.

"First date, eh? I wondered where Iris was." Chief Lawson grunted but she saw amusement in his gaze. "You don't have to end it now. Just give us fifteen minutes."

Rachel nodded, alarm bells clanging in her mind. Was he going to ask who Iris was? But as she searched James's expression, there was no indication he was paying the chief's words much attention. He was focused on how to stop his stalker, she surmised. How to survive the present was more than enough for James. She got it. Hadn't she been unable to take her siblings' advice all those years ago when they'd told her to stop obsessing about her stalker? To let the cops handle it? It had been impossible for her and it was clearly the same for James. He wanted all of this behind him.

At least the current traumatic incident had kept James from paying too much attention to Iris.

Self-loathing reared and she had to work to not gag at how she was behaving. Grateful that James had something else to worry about that kept him from asking the question she dreaded most. Where was her integrity? She couldn't second-guess her original decision to forget about James, and to keep Isa from him, no matter how difficult it may have proven, with his having a fiancée.

And yet she knew the time was closer than ever for her to tell James about Iris's paternity. No matter the consequences.

Chapter 5

James found Chief Lawson to be incredibly professional while maintaining an aura of relaxed expectation. But James wasn't fooled by the man's obvious years—he put him in his late seventies or early eighties, impressive to still be on active duty—as his astute gaze and pointed questions indicated he missed absolutely nothing.

"That's enough for now, James, but I want you to stop by the station first thing in the morning and give us all the information, legal and otherwise, that you have on Bethany Austin. If this proves to be her, the more details we have, the better. In the meantime, I'll have my department cross-reference your statement with Bethany's record, and contact your former local PD."

"Thank you, Chief." They shook hands and James searched the parking lot for Rachel.

"She's over there, under those aspens." Lawson nodded at Isa's car, and paused. "I've known her family for a long time, James. A lifetime, you could say. Rachel Colton is as good as they come. She deserves the best."

"Good to know." James heard the subtle warning in the chief's statement. Rachel hadn't been kidding when she'd said Blue Larkspur looked out for its own. He headed toward Rachel, wondering what she was thinking. She leaped off the large, sturdy picnic table where people probably enjoyed eating takeout outside when the weather cooperated. Before he could get anywhere near the car, she reached him.

"That didn't take long. Here." A smile lit her face and she handed him his coat. "The coat checker brought out the rack so no one would freeze."

"Why didn't you wait in the car?" He nodded at Isa, still in the driver's seat.

"I'm fine." Concern had replaced panic in her wide blue eyes. "Did Theo agree that it's probably Bethany?"

"Thanks for this." He shrugged into his long, charcoal-wool coat. "Actually, Theo didn't comment much. He said they had half a dozen firecrackers go off in different businesses over the last few days. They've caught three juveniles, thanks to cameras, and he's going to look over Ricco's security report. We'll have to wait and see."

"Blue Larkspur High is out for its spring break." Rachel slid over from the center of the picnic table and patted a spot next to her. "Have a seat."

He complied, not wanting the evening to end. "It might not have been Bethany. It'd be a relief if it wasn't."

"But the woman you saw walk into the restaurant?" The wind grew stronger and caught at her golden hair, whipping strands across her face. He longed to cradle her head in his hands again, press his lips to her full, luscious, strawberry ones.

"It could have been my overactive mind. It's a common malady amongst attorneys, wouldn't you say?"

She grinned. "Absolutely. I hope, for your sake, that's all it was. You said she hasn't bothered you in months. It would be a long shot to expect she'd follow you out of Denver, wouldn't it?"

"Let's hope so." He checked his phone and saw that it was about the time their meal would have wrapped up with coffee and aperitifs. Instead they stood on cold asphalt while a leftover winter wind blew. "I am sorry about tonight, Rachel. How can I make it up to you?"

"Tell you what. Why don't you let me make us dinner? Nothing fancy, just a quiet night in. Away from mischief makers with fireworks." Did he detect a tremble in her voice? Why would she be afraid or nervous about having him over?

"I'd love that, and I promise I'll make certain no one's following me." He said it teasingly but knew he'd continue to put himself through all the checklists that he'd learned about since becoming a stalker's target. Which he obviously hadn't done well enough when driving to Blue Larkspur in the first place, no matter that he knew he'd been religious about all of the safety precautions. The only people who knew he'd moved here were his family, the Denver police, a few colleagues he trusted and the real estate agent who'd sold him the condo. He'd spent any free time getting settled and working out.

"You don't have to come over this week if it's too much, with being new to town and now this. But I'd like to have you to dinner." She arched her brow and motioned her hand in a circle. The last thing he wanted was for her to think his scowl was directed at her or in reaction to the thought of dining at her house.

"I'd love to see you again. But like I said, I can't risk that Bethany might be on my tail."

"Nonsense. If it is her, we'll deal. But she's going to figure out who I am, and that may be enough to keep her at bay. No one wants to tangle with a district attorney. My new job does have a few perks." White teeth flashed, and her chuckle gave him respite from his constant worrying.

"Since you put it that way, what about tomorrow?" The words flew out of his mouth, proving his mind had zero control over his actions. He held his breath, hoping he didn't scare her off by being too eager. Where was his usual savoir faire, which he'd cultivated after years of defending big corporations against heady lawsuits?

Her wide smile was its own reward. "That's great. See you tomorrow night, my place. I'll text you the address." She looked over her shoulder at Isa's car. "I've got to get home."

He watched her get into the car before he turned away and headed toward his own. No matter what Chief Lawson thought about the probable culprits, James couldn't shake the ugly sense that it had been Bethany he'd seen, that she was at the root of this. Somehow she'd found out he'd moved from Denver to Blue Larkspur.

Which meant someone had betrayed his trust, or Bethany had found a weak link in his chain of what he'd thought was an impenetrable security wall. Neither option was palatable.

* * *

Bethany sat on a battered aluminum picnic bench next to a combo gas station/convenience store. She was across a wide boulevard from Ricco's and watched the result of her brilliant actions. The fancy clothes and blond wig she'd worn to gain inconspicuous entry were bunched in a bag in her car, which she'd left parked in a big-box store's lot on the other side of the restaurant. Right now, Bethany knew she looked like a teenager in a huge baggy sweatshirt under a down vest. Skinny jeans and lace-up lumberjack boots completed her anonymous alias. She'd picked the clothing up at a local Goodwill, eager to blend in with the locals.

Bethany was pleased with what she'd accomplished since James's first working morning in Blue Larkspur. Was that only yesterday? She'd been keeping tabs on him since she'd found out he was moving here a week ago. Once she'd figured out where his new place was, that spiffy contemporary condo downtown, she'd promised her boss she'd be at work tomorrow. She'd planned to get back to Denver and keep her job, with frequent weekend trips back here to Blue Larkspur. To win James back.

Except her employer had gotten sick of her frequent bouts with the "flu" or "food poisoning." She'd been fired over the phone today. Which was perfect, because this gave her several weeks of unemployment. By her estimation, she wouldn't need that long to convince James that he'd made a mistake. A mistake she was willing to forgive.

Following James was easy, too easy. The security team he'd consulted at the same time he'd filed the restraining order against her was long behind him in Denver. It helped that she'd borrowed her stepsister's beater. It kept James from identifying her via her usual, more familiar vehicle. Not that he'd know it was her—she had eight different wigs and twice as many outfits equally distributed in the back seat of each. Bethany chuckled. She'd become an expert at quick costume changes. The battered car with tinted windows helped—she didn't draw attention as she undressed.

She'd like to undress in front of James. He'd never allowed their dating to get past flirting, but she knew he wanted more, wanted all of her. She hoped he would know the special cherry bomb she'd created was from her, especially for him. Hadn't he told her she lit up a room? He had. The night they first met at the fancy bar near his firm. Bethany had found many men in that bar before, but it had never lasted past a date or two. And trailing them was too much effort. Besides, whenever she hung on to a guy for too long, she got in trouble and it wasn't worth it.

Except when it came to James. He was special.

James, James. He was smart but not necessarily discerning when it came to where he lived. Of all the places he could have left Denver for, he picked this crap-kicking place? The highway sign read "Welcome to the City of Blue Larkspur" but in her mind, Denver was the only city in Colorado. She smirked as she sipped the super-sugared concoction she'd bought in the stop-and-shop place. A Blue Larkspur Latte Bomb, according to the sign. Fitting for today and what she'd just made happen.

A thrill whistled through her midsection as she watched the restaurant patrons pour out of the building. It wasn't what she'd expected. She'd meant to let James know she'd never left him by using the same explosive she'd made for his Denver condo. When she'd needed to get his attention same as today. But she couldn't drop it in the dining area without being caught, so she'd settled for the women's restroom off the bar.

It hadn't occurred to her that James would be able to recognize her, but she'd watched through the cracked restroom door as he stomped around the bar, acting like he'd seen a ghost.

A giggle escaped her before another memory stifled it.

That unexpected interloper. Rachel Colton.

She hadn't planned for another woman in James's life so soon. Hadn't he learned from Denver? That he shouldn't waste his time with anyone but Bethany herself?

District Attorney Rachel Colton was nothing more than another one of James's passing interests. It was Bethany's job to know everything about James, so she'd followed Rachel home after she'd seen how James had interacted with her on the court steps when the conniving woman had slammed into him, definitely seeking his attention. Bethany had been sitting on a nearby bench—disguised, of course—and witnessed the whole event. Dressed as a street sweeper, she'd gotten close enough to overhear their conversation while Rachel clung to James's jacket collar the way a praying mantis grabs its partner.

James knew Rachel. Rachel had acted all huffy, as if their fall was his fault. The drink turned sour in her gut and she shoved a scream down deep into her chest.

Keep your cool. Patience.

James turned heads, male and female alike, as he

was a fine specimen of a human being. But those people didn't know him like she did. Didn't know that he was a very sweet man under the lawyerly veneer. Bethany knew James Kiriakis better than anyone. Once they had more time together, she was certain he'd see what she knew in her bones.

She was the only woman for him.

This date must be very important to Rachel, because she'd had to figure out how to get not only to work this morning but to the restaurant without her car. Bethany thanked the video she'd found online about how to dilute the fuel in Rachel's tank for at least making her rival's life more difficult. Next time Bethany would make it impossible for Rachel to be with James at all.

Her butt was sore from sitting on the metal bench, her drink near its end. The fire engines were gone, and she counted only one police cruiser left in the parking lot.

And then she saw them. Her skin tightened across her face and her belly, and she gripped the plastic cup until it collapsed, crushed under her fist. James was walking Rachel across the lot. She acted like the kind of rich bitch Bethany wasn't. Bethany knew what mattered in life. True love. Like she had with James.

Without further thought she sprang up and bolted to her car, got in and started the engine.

It was time to follow Rachel again.

Rachel had never been so relieved to pull into her driveway. Isa had left her to her thoughts during the drive from Ricco's, and Iris was asleep in the back seat. Rachel's white Jeep was back in its usual spot, parked next to the trees that separated her property from her neighbor's. Gideon and one of his buddies had dropped it off for her. She sent Gideon a quick text to thank him for taking care of her, again. Rachel relied on her brother more than was probably reasonable, but it was the Colton way. They all depended on each other.

"Mom, I can get Iris out so that you can leave right away."

"Nonsense. I left some things in the house, anyway."

"All right."

The car was still running as shivers continued to race down her spine, despite her seat warmer and heater being on full blast. Rachel had always considered herself intrepid, willing to dive into any case, take on any bad guys. Before she became a mother, that is. Iris had changed everything.

When Isa stopped the engine, shivers ran down Rachel's spine. The leather car seats were still warm, but the reality of what she'd just been through sank in further as she peered through the windshield into the dark night.

What if James's stalker was watching him all the time, as he feared, and had seen her with him? What if she'd taken note of Iris or Isa?

She opened the door to exit and heard a soft rustling to her left. The noise was immediately followed by a definitive *snap*. Her nape prickled with dread and she peered into the shrubs that surrounded her home, up close to the house walls but not touching, as she didn't want to invite any critters to make nests under her siding or on her roof. More sounds drew her attention to the tall aspens that lined the short drive. She let her shoulders sag down in relief. Many nights found deer or fox traipsing through the neighborhood, and with the wet spring, she'd not seen any yet as she'd been mostly inside with Iris.

"What is it, Rachel?" Isa, still in the driver's seat, spoke.

"It's just an animal." She slammed the door shut to warn off the wildlife as much as banish her jumpy nerves. Nothing like taking charge to put fear on the back burner. Before she reached the back driver's side door, Iris's cry rang out. Just great. She'd woken her innocent baby with her own fear.

No. She was not going to let anyone or any threat infringe upon Iris's life. Rachel gathered the infant into her arms, where she quickly lay her head on her mother's shoulder and snuggled in.

Walking into her brightly lit home was the medicine she needed. She kicked off her heels and padded barefoot into the living room.

"I'll be right back, Mom. Let me put her down first."

"Take your time." Isa was distracted with her phone. Her mother sure spent a lot of time texting these days, more than Rachel ever could recall.

Iris went down with zero fuss after Rachel nursed her. She walked back into the living room to find a steaming mug of tea waiting for her on the coffee table.

"Ah, thank you, Mom."

"Not such a great date after all?" Isa always intuited Rachel's mood.

"No. I'm sorry I didn't text you right away. I had no idea you were so close, at the store. I didn't want you to worry, and I figured Theo might mention it. If you talked to him." Could she be any more obvious? *Mom's love life, if she has one, is none of your beeswax.*

"Well, I appreciate that you thought of me." Isa regarded her, compassion lighting her eyes. "Care to fill me in, now that we're home?"

Rachel kept her description of escaping what she'd thought was a bomb explosion to the barest facts, not wanting Isa to freak. Fortunately her mother got distracted when Rachel mentioned Theo.

"Theo does not know the meaning of slowing down, I'll tell you. He should be retired by now."

"He is the chief of police, Mom."

"I know, but he needs to learn to take better care of himself. I told him that this morning."

"Did you?" It was great to be able to turn the tables a bit and put her mother in the hot seat.

Isa drained her mug, stood up and gathered up her things. "I did. To continue on in the vein we spoke about earlier, I was hoping this date would lead to more. Maybe not with the same man, but don't you want to have a full family life? For Iris?"

"Mom, Iris and you are my family. I also have eleven siblings, remember?"

"Oh come on, you know what I mean." Isa paused. "Have you given any further thought to reaching out to Iris's father again?" Suspicion tugged at Rachel's nerves. All she'd told Isa was that circumstances had made Iris's father unavailable. Did Isa have an inkling that James was Iris's father?

She knew her family might have suspected she'd been involved with a married or otherwise-committed man, since she'd made it clear she was not going to contact him for "personal reasons." To their credit, they never questioned her, never made her feel judged. They'd done what Coltons do best—bonded together to make sure she, and now Iris, knew how loved they were.

"I have, actually. And…I just may." She couldn't tell her mother about James. Not yet. Not until she saw how he handled finding out about his daughter. "But I do have another date tomorrow with this same guy. It was the least I could do, after the explosion."

"The things you have to put up with these days to find love." Isa let out a long sigh. "When your dad and I met, it was easy. At a work party, where we found out we had a lot in common. And the chemistry!"

"Mom."

"I know. You don't want to know, but doesn't twelve children tell you something? After I met your father, that was it. All I cared about was the next time I'd see him. He was focused on his career and wanted a partner to share it with. I loved being a paralegal but always wanted to be a mother. It happened a lot faster than we'd planned, but that was okay. It seemed perfect timing, for both of us."

"Life was less complicated forty years ago, Mom."

"Yes and no. People are still people. Human beings with both assets and flaws. We all know your dad's."

"I'm sorry, Mom." She knew this was hard for Isa, to talk about Ben's steep climb and exponentially precipitous fall.

"There's nothing for you, or any of you kids, to be sorry for. Maybe if I'd been further along in my life when we'd met, like you are, I'd have paid more attention to the warning signs. I was already almost thirty but very coddled by my parents and immature, now that I look back. You're head and shoulders ahead of where I was at your age."

"You were having your third and fourth child by

my age, Mom. What did you mean by 'signs'? Did you mean red flags?"

Isa nodded. "Yes. Ben was the type to just skirt the edges of the rules. Do you know what I mean?"

"I think so, but I'd appreciate examples." No matter how much they hurt, no matter that Isa's admission stunned Rachel. It wasn't a secret what Ben had done to the community and his family. And Isa had never shied from admitting the truth about Ben once she knew it. But Isa had never mentioned any indications of Ben's dark side existing before their marriage. Rachel and her siblings were close and kept one another informed about Isa's life as needed. She knew that her sense of obligation to protect her mother from life's unpleasantness wasn't unique. Her sisters and brothers all wished Isa could have somehow been spared the havoc Ben's criminal actions had caused.

Her father had been a bad man, no question. But it didn't change that she'd loved her father—he'd always be her dad—but her job, her vocation, her passion was to set things right.

Isa was poised to leave but stood stock-still. "I don't know, Rachel. There's no good rehashing the past."

"I'm not asking for your lovers' secrets that you shared with Dad." *Ew.* "It's just that with going on this date tonight, it's got me thinking. I need to know what you wish you'd picked up on before you got married."

"Ben preferred to work jobs that were under the table." Isa referred to income that wouldn't be reported to the IRS. Illegally tax-free. "You're a DA, honey, and I know you'd never dream of breaking the law like that. But back then, it wasn't an unusual circumstance. We didn't have two nickels to rub together in those early years. So I let it go, overlooked it. But then he got his first big job, making a salary he'd never dreamed of. Yet he still looked for ways to cheat the system. Always." Isa balanced on the sofa arm, her expression distant and gaze unfocused.

"At the time I believed him when he said it was 'just what affluent folks do, Isa. It's not illegal, just protecting what's ours.' He was very showy, you know. Loved the spotlight at all costs. And he insisted on only the best when it came to material things—from our home to the cars, our clothes. Nothing but top-shelf."

"I remember having nicer things right before he died." She and her siblings had riding lessons and fancy summer camps on the West Coast at an exclusive California beachfront property.

"Yes, we sure did. He was furious when he found out I'd been buying baby clothes at the consignment shops and Goodwill. I'll never forget it. I did the family household budgeting and showed him the figures. Do you know the very next week that man had a raise, doubling our income? Of course, now I realize it was the first time he took a bribe."

"Mom, stop." She'd seen Isa's face stamped with regret too many times. "None of it was your fault. You were doing the best you could, and why wouldn't you believe him? He was your husband. You can't blame yourself for his crimes."

"I'm not blaming myself for your father's transgressions, trust me. But I know that in a twisted way, I was complicit. It was easier to shove my head in the sand and focus on raising our beautiful children than facing such an awful reality. At this point in my life I realize it wasn't right to look the other way. I'm so relieved and grateful that you and your brothers and sisters are working toward restitution for all of his victims and others wrongfully convicted. The Truth Foundation is helping me make amends, you know."

"I do, Mom." And she did. Rachel still had survivor guilt that she and her siblings had lived such a nice life at the expense of juveniles or adults who received longer sentences or ones they didn't deserve. All to fill private and youth detention centers that in turn lined Ben Colton's, and his family's, pockets.

"Take one bit of advice from your old lady. Always trust your gut and follow through on any doubts with the man you love. Always."

"Thanks, Mom." They hugged, then Isa slung her tote over her shoulder and left. Rachel watched her get in her car and drive off before she closed and locked the door.

Just as she was ready to jump into a hot shower, Rachel remembered that it was trash day tomorrow. She turned off the water and shoved her feet into slippers, threw a coat over her robe. She pushed the button for the garage door and waited for it to open before she wheeled the trash and recycle bins down the drive.

Rachel froze on the spot when she saw the muddy footprints at the front of the drive, behind where her brother had parked her repaired car. Icy tremors shot through her gut. They weren't prints from deer, fox or a bear.

They were boot prints.

Chapter 6

"She's a woman I'd love to get to know better. I think we might have reunited sooner if Bethany hadn't intercepted her call over a year ago." James looked out the window of his corporate law office as he spoke to his older brother. Birds flitted between aspen branches and the April rain made everything slick. The view was a far cry from the Denver office tower he'd worked in for over a decade.

"Wow, bro, that's a lot to deal with in the first week you move to a new city." His senior by five years, Jake wasn't one to hold back. "Are you certain it was Bethany you saw in the restaurant?"

He swallowed the hot coffee he'd grabbed moments earlier. "I'm positive. And then the explosion, just like when she shot off the homemade M-80 in my condo building last year."

"That woman doesn't understand the constraints of a

restraining order. I thought maybe she was running on anger, at the humiliation of being dumped by you. But now I wonder if she needs help, bro. I'm sorry you're dealing with this."

"Yeah, me, too." He looked at his watch. Five more minutes and he had to get back to his caseload. "I thought a geographical move would be the end of her stalking, but somehow she's found out I'm here."

"Maybe she hasn't. Maybe it wasn't her. Give it a bit before you assume. Although the explosion is too close to home—I get it." He heard his brother's chair squeak, meaning he was leaning back from his computer desk. "Tell me more about this DA you took to dinner."

James confided a lot in Jake. But his sibling didn't need to know that part of the reason he'd moved here was to maybe—well, okay, *definitely*—run into Rachel again. He'd looked her up and knew before he moved that she was the new DA, and hoped that she was single. At least, there was no mention of her relationship status in the media or on social accounts.

"The local DA happens to be an acquaintance I met at a conference over a year ago, is all."

"Uh-huh. 'Met?'" Jake knew James was holding back—why else be evasive? But James couldn't waste energy on Jake's opinion. Not now, not when he had the pressure of making a good impression in his new job and figuring out if Bethany was really here. If she'd found him again. Just the possibility made the coffee burn like acid in his esophagus.

"Look, if more comes of it, I'll let you know."

"So you're seeing her again? Soon?"

"Yeah. Tonight, actually."

Jake's laugh rolled across the connection and tugged

a grin out of James. "This is the first I've heard of you doing a second, no, make it third date in, like, forever. Since Bethany."

"Yeah, well, Rachel's not Bethany. And the first time I met her wasn't really a date."

"Good thing she's nothing like Bethany." Jake's voice had sobered, reminding James that he wasn't dealing with a jealous high school crush. Bethany had put him through his paces back in Denver, between showing up uninvited at work events, slashing his car tires and those of any women he was seen in public with, and leaving threatening notes in his mailbox. The restraining order had sent her into her hole for a while, but now he wasn't so certain he was rid of her.

"Yeah."

"Talk to you later, bro."

"Bye." He disconnected and stared out the window, but all he saw were mental images of Rachel last night—how beautiful her smile was, how it warmed him inside out, even as they'd stood in freezing weather while waiting for the building to be cleared.

His phone rang and he glanced at the caller ID, which displayed a number he did not recognize. He'd usually leave it but, being new, didn't want to miss any number of possible callers, from the cable/internet provider to the new health insurance he was setting up.

"James Kiriakis."

Silence greeted him. He listened. "Hello?"

The sound of breathing was soft but detectable. Someone was listening to him. And in the background the definite strains of the cloying '70s tune Bethany had insisted was "their song."

His stomach clenched with anger, but he kept his

cool long enough to hang up, write down the number, then block it.

He'd need a new phone number. *Again.*

Worse, James had changed his number along with his address. If it had been Bethany on the line, she had his new number. Which meant she knew he'd moved.

And the area code of the caller had been that of Blue Larkspur, the same as James's new number. Definitely not out of Denver. She'd found him.

Icy dread worked up his spine as James realized his biggest fear. He didn't need Chief of Police Theo Lawson to validate his hunch.

Bethany was back.

"Ouch!" Rachel dropped the baking pan back on the oven rack and quickly shoved her fingers under cold running water. She'd forgotten to use a potholder.

With Iris's sudden teething and working an hour later than usual, she'd backed herself into a corner with getting dinner ready in time for James. Iris had fallen asleep in her baby swing, which Rachel had set up next to the dining table and had a clear view of from the kitchen island. Iris was at the end of being able to use the swing, as she was outgrowing it. The baby's nap was a reprieve of unknown duration. There was no telling when she'd wake up, so Rachel was trying to get the chicken baked, rice steamed and veggies stir-fried all at once.

Why hadn't she ordered out? James would never remember what he'd had for dinner the night he found out he was a father, she was certain. All he'd recall was that his daughter looked exactly like him, minus the green irises, and Rachel had kept her from him.

Not one to ever balk at a challenge—it just wasn't in the Colton gene pool—she'd never considered postponing this second meetup. Having James over sooner rather than later was the absolute right thing to do.

She mentally replayed their conversation as she shoved silicon-coated oven mitts on. Rachel still couldn't believe what he'd revealed last night. He'd been stalked, and it sounded like it was the stalker, Bethany, who'd answered his phone when Rachel found out she was pregnant. Self-recrimination loomed, threatening to batter her normally positive esteem into smithereens. So many doubts and questions about her motives railed at her. Why had she so easily accepted that James was engaged? Worse, what difference should that have made? He was her baby's father, period. He had a right to know.

Her phone rang with the distinct tone she had for her mother, but the noise still made her jump. She was letting James's stalking issue get to her.

"Hey, Mom."

"How's Iris doing? Poor thing. Growing new teeth tuckers a little soul out."

"I'm not so sure about tuckering her out, Mom. She's sleeping now, but she's also in her swing and the house has been pretty quiet. She was hell on wheels when I got home from work, though."

"I can come over and help you through the night with her. The Lark's County DA needs her rest, even on the weekend."

"Uh, I'm fine. I appreciate the offer, though." She pierced one of the chicken breasts with an instant-read thermometer. "And thanks again for driving me to

Ricco's. I don't know what I would do without your support these last months."

"You'd do what you have to. That's what mothers do, dear."

"Well, the shop Gideon took it to thought maybe a squirrel or other rodent got in there and chewed a bunch of random wires. That would have taken a long time to fix. As it is, they flushed the fuel tank and it's up and running. The mechanic said she's checking something out about the fuel, but I know I didn't put the wrong type in." Of course, her mind had been all over the place, between work and Iris.

"That's odd for this time of year. The rodents, I mean. It's been rainy, sure, and still below freezing some nights, but not so cold that critters curl up on engines."

A hint of doubt edged into Rachel's thoughts. She'd thought it unusual, too, as "critters" finding shelter in vehicle engines, gas grills or garages wasn't unheard of—in the winter. Spring was making its mark these past weeks, warming up the Colorado Rockies enough to ensure most their precipitation was of the liquid variety. As for the fuel tank, she hadn't given it a lot of thought as her heavy caseload required all of her mental faculties today.

"You still there, honey?"

"I am, Mom. Look, I've got to get dinner finished and on the table."

"Ah. This isn't anything about your date last night, is it?"

"What are you thinking, Mom? Let me guess. Theo said something about when he interviewed James? What did he tell you? Spill it, Mom."

"Nothing. Well, okay. Theo thinks James is a very nice young man."

Rachel laughed. "Neither James nor I are particularly 'young,' Mom."

"Wait until you are seventy-two and then tell me thirty-four isn't young."

"Hmm."

"I'll let you go. Listen, if that sweet little grandbaby of mine looks like she's not going to give you any sleep, call me. Have a nice dinner!"

"Bye, Mom. Love you."

"Love you, too, sweetheart."

Rachel disconnected and stared at the phone for a second. She could have been honest with Isa. Her mother was the least judgmental person she knew, and she'd be thrilled to know Rachel was planning to tell Iris's father about his daughter, no matter who he was. But she needed the mental and emotional space to first let James know and then see where it was going to go. His attitude about wanting to get to know her better might cool as quickly as the sautéed veggies.

The chicken was done, so she set its pan on two cork trivets to cool and made haste with the zucchini and summer squash, already sizzling in the drizzle of olive oil she'd given the heated pan. The rice wasn't a problem as it cooked automatically in her favorite kitchen appliance—her electronic pressure cooker. Finally she let her shoulders relax, took a sip of the herbal iced tea the nanny had made a huge pitcher of.

The doorbell rang, followed a split second later by Iris's piercing scream. So much for letting James in, allowing him to adjust to his surroundings before introducing his daughter to him.

"Come here, sweetness." She unstrapped Iris from the swing, hugging her. "Time to meet someone for real this time. No quick intros." Iris settled into her, gumming Rachel's shoulder. The bell rang again, followed by a soft knock. Rachel hurried to the front door.

Butterflies attacked her insides and her stomach swooped, just as it did going down a class-A roller coaster. Life was going to change for her, but more importantly for Iris, in the next few moments. Without her hood, Iris's red hair was a dead ringer for James's locks. Rachel's hand shook as she reached for the handle and opened the door.

"Good evening." James's smile lit up his face, dispelling the sterner expression she'd noticed last night. He held out a potted orchid and box of fine chocolates. "Thanks for having me." His gaze was on her, her face, until Iris let out another shriek.

"It's okay, my baby." She looked at James, whose puzzled expression went from surprise to disbelief to thunderous rage in two seconds flat.

Maybe she didn't know James Kiriakis so well.

Chapter 7

James knew people claimed to have "out of body" experiences. But he'd never fully comprehended until he stood in front of a woman he'd come to with hopes of a deeper relationship, to find out she already had a family. And a *kid*.

"Are you babysitting? Or is this your child?" He looked past her into the house. "I never thought to ask you if you were in a relationship, or married, did I?" His fists balled and he fought to not turn and stalk to his car. Finishing this off here and now was best for all of them.

"I'm not going to talk to you while you're like this." Rachel's attorney countenance showed in the steel glints sparking from her eyes, the way she held the kid as if prepared to make a run for it. "Calm down."

"Oh, I'm calm." His jaw ached from clenching, and the knot between his shoulders intensified into a throbbing mass of pain. He looked past her, tried to see into the house. "Where's the father?" Did he know Rachel had been out with him last night?

He was done being anyone's fool.

"Come in before you come to any conclusions, James."

Rachel hated how James's initial pleasure at seeing her had turned to betrayal, and now anger, in the space of a heartbeat. Before she said anything she'd regret, she turned away from him, hoping her refusal to take on any of his anger would dispel the ugly tension between them.

"Aaaagh!" Cranky Iris was back, her cheeks red and eyes watering.

"It's okay, baby." Gently bouncing Iris on her hip, she grabbed a frozen washcloth from the freezer. Cool relief shot through her veins. At least he'd come inside. He could have easily taken off, ghosted her for good. Instead he stood on the other side of the island and observed the überdomestic scene with an air of ticked-off detachment. His gaze never wavered as he set the plant and the sweets down.

"What's wrong with it?"

"Her. Not 'it.' Her name is Iris, and nothing's wrong. She's teething." At his continued stare she added, "Her baby teeth are coming in. It makes her gums swollen, her jaw and ears ache, and her nose has been super-runny."

"Are you married or with someone? Were you with someone when we met in Helena? What about last night, when we met for dinner? Does your family know you were there?" His questions weren't a surprise, but she couldn't help a small smile.

"What's so amusing, Rachel? That I misread you or

that I'm standing here, thinking that I've been made a fool?"

"It's not any of the above. You sound so much like a lawyer. Let's sit down for a minute." She sat on the sofa and he took the loveseat opposite, his movements stilted.

"Naaa!" Iris didn't want anything to do with the washcloth. Rachel ignored her and continued to rub the frozen fabric over the bright pink gums until she relaxed and began to chomp down on the pain-relieving remedy.

"There we go." She smiled at Iris and then looked across at James. "I freeze wet washcloths. They work better than any kind of fancy teething ring."

"Huh." He gave Iris the briefest of glances, as if he thought looking at the infant would burn his eyeballs, before refocusing on Rachel. "Is she your only kid?"

Her only kid? Anger blazed deep in her heart, where her mother love lived. It set off mental warning alarms.

Whoa, girlfriend, rein it in.

James didn't know who Iris was, or if he'd figured it out, he was in shock about it. She had to play fair and give him the benefit of the doubt. It was on her that he didn't know.

"Yes, Iris is my one and only. For the record, I've never been married nor with anyone long-term. I was happily single the night we met in Helena. I still am."

"So you decided to have a baby on your own? I'm not judging, just asking. I have several friends who've decided to go ahead and have a kid with or without a partner. It just would have been nice if you'd have been up front with me about your family from the start." His dismissive tone tossed invisible barbs that dug into her conscience.

Rachel bit her lip, knowing she couldn't keep her

calm demeanor in place much longer, but breaking James's obvious denial too soon wouldn't be productive, either. Maybe she was relying too much on her prosecutor skills, but it would be best for him to figure out as much as possible on his own, at his own pace. Since he was an intelligent man, it wouldn't take very long.

"Iris wasn't planned, James. She was a complete surprise. I didn't know you were averse to children."

"I'm not opposed to dating you because you have a child. I wish you would have trusted me enough to tell me, is all."

"Rachel is six months old, James." She watched him, waited for him to digest not only the age but the fact that she was speaking slowly, deliberately. "I found out I was pregnant about fourteen months ago."

He nodded. "January last year."

"Yes. A month after the legal conference."

He stilled; his facial muscles froze in place. Except for a single pulse visibly pounding at his temple. His gaze muddied. "A month after, you said?"

She nodded.

"Wait a minute, Rachel. You're not—"

"James, this baby girl—" she held Iris facing him, so that he could see his daughter's features "—is yours."

Reality hit James like an ice bath after a college football game. As his university's quarterback he'd sustained countless injuries that healed exponentially faster with the aid of freezing temperatures. The knowledge had never dulled the excruciating pain of putting his game-heated body into the tubs, though. At least he had the edge of the stainless steel to hang on to. As he stared at Iris, there was no thought his mind could grasp at to put him on solid ground.

He had a *daughter*. If what Rachel said was true.

Unless… *Oh no.* Dismay dropped his stomach fifty stories in three seconds. He'd been so wrong about Bethany; was Rachel a different kind of stalker? A single mother who'd do anything to gain a father for her kid?

"She's really mine? That's a strong declaration, Rachel." He meant for the words to come out strong and not a little accusing. Instead, he sounded like a limp version of himself.

"It's the truth." She held the baby up, allowing Iris to pump her legs against Rachel's thighs. "Look at her eyes, James. I've never met anyone besides you with that shape to them. And her cheekbones. Exactly yours."

He'd never given his eyes or facial structure much thought, only knew that he resembled his father, and his siblings. His father's genes came from a long line of Greek Americans, the first of whom had emigrated from Greece in third-class steerage. No one was tougher than his Mykonos-born great-grandfather, what little he remembered of the man. If what Rachel said was true, Iris was the image of her paternal ancestor.

"I'll need a paternity test. For both our peace of mind. Unless you've already done several?"

To her credit, Rachel didn't play the indignant game. Her eyes narrowed and she gave a curt nod. She was a lawyer, though. It was her darn job to stay unruffled, even when caught in a lie. "Of course. Maybe you want to wait to get to know her until you have scientific proof?"

"That's probably for the best." She'd given him an

excellent exit opportunity. All he had to do was get up, walk back out that door and drive away. Back to Denver if he wanted. Or maybe to the East Coast. Some of his siblings lived in Philly. He could just go, keep driving, away from Bethany and her reemergence, away from Blue Larkspur, away from Rachel and the baby doing some kind of Irish jig on her lap.

But he couldn't move. It was as if he was stuck to the loveseat with NASA-grade epoxy. Worse, he couldn't stop looking at Iris.

His Iris?

Iris. It was a word for "rainbow" in ancient Greek. Had Rachel named the baby in a nod to her father— him?

He was an attorney, darn it. Of all people, he knew the power of suggestion. It was one of his many trial tools, used to convince a jury his client was right, on the side of justice. So it should be easy to dismiss what now looked like his grandmother's hair color—Kiriakis flaming red—and his facial features as anecdotal. Yet something about the baby was so familiar...as if they'd always known one another. The same feeling that drove him to keep calling Rachel, despite her rejection of him. The urge to take the job in Blue Larkspur, on the off chance Rachel was still available and had changed her mind.

A breath in, a breath out. As his respiration returned to normal, it was easier to take stock of the situation. Rachel sat quietly, playing with the infant. Most likely his child. He couldn't ignore that Iris looked almost exactly like his sister's twin girls. Yeah, the Kiriakis genes were strong. He and his cousins had all looked alike as kids.

"You never told me—" He held up his hands in sur-render. "No, wait—that's why you called me, when you said a woman answered."

"Yes."

Anger welled. Deep and lasting. Not at Rachel or this beautiful little girl—that was *his* child—but at the woman whose determination to make him hers cost him more than a year with Rachel and the first precious months of his daughter's life. It was one thing when Bethany had come after him, another when he'd been concerned that she was targeting Rachel. But Bethany had kept him from his own child.

His. Own. Child.

"James?" Concern laced her tone.

He tore his gaze off Iris and met Rachel's unflinch-ing yet compassionate gaze. It was as if she thought he was...fragile.

His gut twisted. What the hell had happened in the last year and a half? He'd been on top of his legal game, looking forward to a Denver corporate law career. Then he'd met Bethany, and things started falling apart. His liaison with Rachel had been a bright, happy spot. Until she'd ghosted him. *No, not true.* She'd reacted naturally to the lie she'd been fed.

"Sorry. I'm okay, really. I know I probably look off-kilter. It's a lot to digest."

"I know. But I can only imagine what you're feeling right now. Iris has been with me, a part of me, since I've known you. I've definitely had a lot more time to adjust to my new reality. And for what it's worth, it's been a joyride. Right, Iris, baby?" She kissed her before giv-ing him a rueful smile. "Why don't you stay for dinner at least? I know it's not what you'd imagined it'd be, but since you're new in town, it won't hurt to make a local friend. We can be friends until you get the paternity test results. Then we'll talk about co-parenting, if you're even interested."

"Okay." He agreed without reservation. If Rachel was a conniver, she was over-the-top good at it. And her behavior, her actions last night and now, confirmed that she wasn't going to force the issue. By all appearances, Rachel was confident that things would work out for her and Iris.

So where was he in the equation?

Iris gobbled up the applesauce that Rachel had mixed with a tiny amount of rice cereal, slapping her tiny hands on the plastic high chair tray. She was at the center of the small table, with Rachel at the head and James across from her. If Rachel was one given to worry, it would be wasted on James's reaction to finding out he was a father.

"She's a good eater, I'll give her that." He'd finally tucked into his meal, though she noticed he'd left some of it uneaten. In his shoes she was certain she wouldn't have been able to eat anything.

"I've been so blessed with her, no kidding. She's always been a good eater, from the first time the delivery nurse put her on my breast. She latched on like a champ." Used to telling this story to the women in her life, she halted as she fed Iris, the spoon full of mushy food in midair. Suddenly the word *breast* had a different meaning. As when James had held hers—

"Aaaah!" Iris's squeal happened at the same time her arm swung out and hit Rachel's hand, turning the innocent baby spoon with a bear-shaped handle into a catapult. The sauce splattered across the table, and on James's face.

"Oh man, so sorry about that!" She stood to get him another napkin but he motioned for her to sit.

"If I can't handle a bit of baby food on my face, what kind of court attorney would I make?" He used his napkin to wipe his brow, his shirt. And then, to Rachel's surprise, James stood, not to walk to the kitchen sink and continue the cleanup, but to move his chair close to Iris's high chair.

"May I?" He held out his hand for the spoon. Their eyes met, and she saw the acceptance instead of the resistance that had flashed when she'd first announced Iris's paternity.

"Of course." It was almost too easy to relinquish the feeding duties. Sure, she shared so much of raising Iris with her mother and nanny. But James was a stranger to her baby, even to her. One night of incredible sex did not a relationship make.

It made a baby, though.

Hunger made her stomach gurgle and she realized she hadn't eaten but one or two bites. While she had the opportunity, she shoveled the dinner down. James's rich laughter warmed her, drew her focus from her plate.

"What?"

He was smiling at Iris as he answered, successfully scooping the remaining food into the baby's mouth. "You ate that as if it's your first meal in days."

A grin tugged at her lips. "Maybe not my first meal, but it's my first full dinner. Even with all the help I have from my family, I like for Iris and I to have the evenings to ourselves. We have a dinner-and-bath routine, but since she's started on solid foods, it's been a challenge to eat my meal before she's in bed." Often she skipped it, waking up famished the next day, when having a full breakfast was out of the question. "Smoothies are my go-to, and then I do get a decent meal at lunch, most days."

"Really? Because the last I checked, there's no busier lawyer than a district attorney."

"Long hours include a lunchtime, trust me." His focus on her self-care made her toes curl and she bit her lower lip. From James's perspective they'd gone from one-night-stand acquaintances to survivors of an unexpected blast to co-parents. All in less than forty-eight hours.

"Have you been able to find out if it was Bethany last night?"

He shook his head. "No. Chief Lawson said that unless they can find her on the restaurant's security footage, all they have to go by is my sighting. Which to be fair, was of a woman with very different hair and makeup than I've ever seen her in." He sighed. "Sometimes I think I'm losing my mind. Seeing her where she isn't. You know, like when someone you love dies?"

"I do know." Those first months after her father's fatal accident, she swore she saw him in crowds or heard his voice in the other room instead of the television. "But your stalker's not dead, and if there's any chance she knows you moved here, it's not unreasonable to be on guard."

"There's one other thing you need to know. And I need to call the chief and report it. I had a hang-up call on the way here. It's classic Bethany."

"I get hang-ups all the time. And solicitors. Maybe someone was about to sell you a new source for electricity."

"Ah, I wish I had your optimism. But I'm certain it was her—she played the same song she always does on her crank calls."

"I'm afraid to ask what the song is."

He told her, and she sucked in a deep gulp of air. "I remember that from when my mother played it after my father died. It's kind of a creepy song, saying they'll love you until you're both dead and six feet under."

"Exactly. And perfectly Bethany."

"Look, you'll report it, and the chief will put his best officers on it. There are many ways to catch a stalker these days and tracking her phone will help."

"I'm sure she's using burners."

"You're probably right. But come on, no going negative. Let's enjoy the rest of the meal." She knew she was probably off-putting with her extreme-bubbly affectation, but she'd do anything to get the hopeless look off his face. Surprise sideswiped her, making goosebumps dance across her forearms. How could she care about his feelings when honestly, she hardly knew him?

Because she knew the truth, and a paternity test would prove it to James. It wasn't personal that he was resisting it. Although, seeing how he was feeding Iris, making soft encouraging noises as the baby chowed down, she knew that somewhere inside his walled-off heart he knew the truth. At least, his DNA did.

"What do we do now?" He showed her the empty bowl. Iris was as content as she'd been in days, staring at her daddy. Whether or not James believed it yet, Rachel knew the truth and suspected that with some kind of baby intuition, Iris did, too.

"We sit and finish our meals, then she gets her bath. James, you don't have to do—"

"Rachel, the lawyer in me knows that I need to wait on a paternity test. And I'll use the lab you've recommended." She'd given him a card for a facility downtown. "But for some reason I can't explain, I believe you. If we find out I'm not the father, we'll deal with it then. I don't think it'd change the fact that I want to get to know you better."

This struck a chord of fear into Rachel deeper than any stalker could. It meant that James wanted to be with her for her, not just because he thought she was his child's mother.

"I'll go get her bath going." She stood and all but ran to the nursery. Before James saw the utter panic on her face.

Bethany didn't like having to park a block over from the woman's house and was thankful she'd worn all black. Still, the light didn't disappear until after six as spring had reached Colorado. Only the shadow of the Rockies allowed her to slip up next to the darkened side of the house, which turned out to be her lucky choice tonight. It gave Bethany views into the living room and kitchen area, and a back bedroom with a crib.

Maybe she'd misread Rachel Colton's body language and she was some kind of relative of James's? A sister she didn't know about, with his niece or nephew? It made her feel a bit bad about spiking the woman's fuel so that her car wouldn't start. But James needed to understand that everything about his life was Bethany's business. No one was going to get close to James without her approval.

Aggravation made her itch all over as she peered into the window and watched James talk to the baby girl as if she was someone he knew. Bethany had been infuriated when James arrived here. She hadn't expected that. It was a Saturday night. James liked to watch or attend baseball games. She'd been certain he'd drive back to Denver and go see the Rockies take on the Phillies in a doubleheader tomorrow. She'd arrived at his Blue Larkspur condo too late this afternoon, after she knew he'd be out of work—he'd already left, and that's what she'd assumed he'd done. She couldn't risk tailing him from work, as the city was too busy that time of day. But he hadn't gone to the game, not if he was back in this hick excuse for a city in time to have dinner with Rachel and her brat.

Watching James play with the baby made her womb contract, she was certain. It wasn't her IBS; it was a sign that James was meant to be the father of her babies. Judging from how he was such a natural with the infant, she knew she'd found the right father for her future children.

All she had to do was get him alone, get all distractions away from him.

Which meant she had to find out why James was spending so much time with Rachel Colton. If she was James's sister, or a friend from his past, she'd come up with a strong but safe message. But if this was James's idea of a new girlfriend, all bets were off.

Bethany was going to annihilate anyone in her way.

Chapter 8

"Rachel, your brother is here to see you." Clara spoke from the door to the DA's office, a full twenty feet from Rachel's monstrous red-oak desk. She still wasn't used to the perks of being the top prosecuting attorney in Lark's County. A tickle of concern broke her concentration from the case she had to present at the end of the week.

"Which brother?"

"Gideon." The tickle turned to full-fledged alarm bells. Gideon was the sibling she was closest to, and despite being single-birth Coltons, just a few years apart, she and her younger brother got on as if they were twins.

"Send him right in, thank you."

Gideon entered no more than thirty seconds later, an expression of concern on his classically handsome face. His blue eyes, an exact match to hers, flickered with the energy he put into his work as a social worker.

It was perhaps the single reason they were so close—they shared a unique passion to serve their community. Of course, her new paycheck was the most she'd ever dreamed of making, and Gideon was doing well in his position, too.

"Hey, what's going on?" She rose and rounded the desk to hug him, then motioned for him to take a seat as she sat next to him in the matching chair.

"Sorry to bust in on you like this, but I had to see for myself that you're okay."

"Wha— Oh, let me guess. You spoke to Mom."

"I did, and one of my coworkers was at the same restaurant that night. I heard firsthand how awful it was."

"It was scary at first, sure, but I'm pretty certain it ended up being nothing more than an oversize firecracker." For her the scarier part was that Bethany might be the cause, and had her sights on Rachel, too.

"I'm glad you're okay." His eyes narrowed. "But I know you, Rachel. You're not telling Mom everything. Who is this James dude that you met for dinner? Are you going to see him again?"

"Dang." She let out a laugh. "I should have known you were picking up on my vibes."

"Spill it."

"You can't tell Mom, or anyone else. I need you to promise."

"I have to be able to tell Sophia." His eyes softened and a small smile graced his square jawline. Gideon had rekindled his relationship with the strong, no-nonsense pediatrician recently while working with her to save a little boy's life. Satisfaction curled in Rachel's belly. There was nothing lovelier than knowing her brother was happy.

"Okay, well, I don't see a problem with that. She's used to keeping confidences just like we are." She paused, knowing her next words would interest Gideon, who until now played the major male figure in Iris's life.

"Tell me, Rachel. Neither of us have that much time." She realized he was here on his lunch hour, and she needed to have hers soon, too.

"Okay. The 'James dude?' He's Iris's father and he's in the city. Actually, he's moved here."

"What? And you didn't tell me, or any of us?"

"Hold on. I didn't know it until a few days ago. He didn't move here to find me. At least I don't think he did."

"But you must have told him that Iris is his?"

"Not right away, I didn't. That's what the dinner at Ricco's was about. I had to feel him out, see what his deal is. The explosion cut that date short, so I had him over on Saturday night. I told him then."

"He believed you?"

"Yeah. I mean, he resisted at first, as anyone would with such big news. But I know it's his child, and he will too, after he gets the paternity test. Although I daresay he's already convinced Iris is his. It's hard to overlook the hair color and stubbornness." She grinned but Gideon wasn't picking up on her sense of humor.

"Wow. This is a huge turn of events. I'm proud of you, sis, even though you should have told me as soon as you knew this jerk was around."

"He's not a jerk and what's there to be proud of?"

"You're stepping out of your comfort zone. No offense, but you like things neat and tidy. Controlling, some might say." He grinned. "I know you said you tried to tell him about Iris already, but did you, really?"

She hadn't given anyone in her family one iota of information about James or the circumstances of their meeting, for good reason. Her brothers were too protective for her liking. Which could translate to a black eye for James. A snort escaped her at the thought of her brothers acting like some kind of gang. They were all softies at heart, with their family's security being the one exception.

"No, no, you've got me there. I didn't try hard enough to tell him, when I should have. When I was pregnant." She explained what had happened, how a woman she now believed to be Bethany Austin had answered and said she was James's fiancée. Gideon listened in his unique attention-to-detail manner as she dumped the entire story, leaving no stone unturned.

"Let's distill this down, sis. You've got your kid's dad in your life, and I hope for his sake he'll become involved in Iris's life the way a father should." At her movement to fight him on his dramatic concern, he held his hand up. "Hang on. Let me finish. Besides finally getting the truth out in the open with this man—James—you find out he has a stalker? And you've entered her sights?"

"Yes." There was nothing to deny, even though she wanted to. Anything to avoid the fear that circled around her consciousness all day since the explosion.

"You've got to go to the police, Rachel. Talk to the chief directly. I don't give a rat's butt if this James dude wants you to or not. A stalker is nothing to mess with."

"He's not what's kept me from reporting any of this. He has a restraining order out on her, for heaven's sake."

"Then, I don't understand why you're here in your

office and not down at BLPD headquarters. You and Iris need round-the-clock protection."

When Rachel had called James and asked him to meet her within the next hour, alarm bells had gone off. Was she going to end their brief relationship already? Refuse him access to Iris? He'd agreed to meet her ASAP and told himself to stop jumping to conclusions.

"Thanks for meeting me here." Rachel's eyes were unreadable behind her oversize sunglasses, but her posture, hunched over her coffee, bundled in the long raincoat, suggested she was still wary of him, his intentions. "I realize that you probably need time to process everything I told you, but I have to ask you something."

"Okay." He sipped his black brew, full strength, even though it was the middle of the afternoon. They sat at a table outside a popular Blue Larkspur coffee shop, a block up from the riverfront.

"I'm going to go to the police with the additional incidents I believe Bethany Austin might be involved in. Above and beyond the Ricco's explosion."

"The explosion and your car's sabotage?"

"There's another thing. The morning after you were over, I took Iris into the backyard for fresh air. We had a break in the rain and it was sunny... Anyway, there were footprints on my back deck and patio, similar to ones I'd found in my driveway after our night at Ricco's. That night after Ricco's I blamed the prints on my overactive imagination and thought that maybe they were from neighborhood teens playing tag or hide-and-seek at night. They do that every so often. But after seeing the prints on my patio, I'm not so certain. Plus the shrubs and plants near each of my windows had been disturbed. Then there's my gas tank. The mechanic called me today because she'd sent off a fuel sample when she serviced my car. My engine failure had nothing to do with errant rodents but was caused by someone tainting my fuel."

Her mouth was in a grim line and she didn't need to elaborate.

"I wish you'd have called me. Of course you have to go to report this, all of it. I'm so sorry I've involved you in my mess, Rachel. And Iris…" He choked on the little girl's name. His daughter. He had to get the DNA verified for legal purposes but he knew that girl was his, as clear as he knew Rachel wasn't lying.

Slow down.

But no matter what his lawyer instincts said, he knew in his heart what the truth was. The DNA test would only validate his instincts.

"Iris is fine." Two lines appeared between her eyebrows. What had he done that puzzled her?

"I want to get the paternity test over and done with." The words sounded harsher than he'd intended. "For all our sakes."

"Of course you do." The wariness was back in her voice and she leaned back in her chair, putting more space between them.

"I have an appointment later today to take care of it, at the lab you recommended. They told me it'll take up to five days." He said the last part so she'd have the information, but what he didn't mention was that he was paying to have the results expedited. By this time tomorrow he hoped to know if he was a father.

You already know.

Rachel stood, and he followed. "And I've already sent

Iris's in. We're in good shape as far as that's concerned, then. Look, I've got to go—I'm due in court in forty-five minutes. I'll let you know what Chief Lawson says."

"I'd appreciate that."

She gave him a nod, then walked toward the center of the city. He watched her departure, unable to take his gaze off her slim figure, the way her legs looked in what must be her courtroom shoes. Sexy, strong, the most attractive woman he'd ever met.

More importantly, the smartest person he probably knew. And she was most likely the mother of his child. What did his divorced friend call it, raising kids with his ex? The same term Rachel had used on Saturday. *Co-parenting.* He and Rachel were going to co-parent Iris if the paternity test proved his gut instinct and her claim correct.

She turned a corner and disappeared from view and he had to fight the urge to catch up, walk alongside her. Instead, he took their empty cups to the recycle bin, pulled out his phone to see what was waiting for him back at the firm.

Anything to ignore the sensation that the term *co-parenting* elicited. It wasn't pleasant, the idea of only being Iris's daddy and working with Rachel in what would be a more businesslike relationship.

James wanted more.

"Thanks for seeing me." Rachel sat in one of the comfy chairs in front of the chief's desk at BLPD. "I hate to bother you when there's so much on the station's plate these days."

"Please, Rachel. I know you're the DA, and rightfully so, the best Blue Larkspur could ask for. But you'll always be family to me." His eyes twinkled and belied the hard-core crime and hardened crooks he'd dealt with in his decades-long career.

"I'll get right to the point. Somebody put a thinner in my fuel tank last week so that my car wouldn't start. The mechanic says it's a deliberate act, and while it could have been bored teens, she doubted it."

"You use who for your auto repair?"

She named the shop. "I've known her since high school. Laurie used to fix our family beaters when we were all still teens and saved me so much money as I hustled tables through college and law school. She knows her stuff, Chief."

"Go on." He was taking notes on a bright yellow legal pad, using the same brand of all-wood pencil that she preferred. It made her heart warm to see someone else who needed the tactile motion to get his thoughts together.

"This part is harder. I haven't even told my mother yet."

Theo's brows raised, but he didn't say anything. He understood the heft of her statement. Rachel was close to Isa and kept little from her. Their bond had cemented at a time that most mothers and daughters struggle, when Rachel was fourteen. The same year Ben died and the broad-scale damage he'd done to the community had come to light.

"I, um, well." Rachel stopped, took a deep breath. It wasn't usual for her to be timid or without words. "Iris's dad is here, in town. You met him the other night, at the restaurant explosion. James Kiriakis. He moved in from Denver, for a job. He has a restraining order on his former girlfriend, Bethany Austin, that he took out when he resided in Denver. He's certain she's followed him here, that she's in Blue Larkspur. You already know all of this, right?"

"Right."

She spilled the rest of it. The sense of being watched, the odd sounds around the house. "And there's one more thing. When I got home after the explosion, I thought I heard animals in my yard. Until I found footprints on my drive. They were similar to the patio prints."

"Has James mentioned if he's been contacted by Bethany?"

"We only spoke today, briefly. He had a crank call with the song Bethany thinks is theirs. He didn't mention anything else." She'd been tempted to reach out to him sooner but knew he'd need time to process. And she hadn't known if he'd received the results of his paternity test yet.

"Do you have a problem with me talking to him about this, Rachel?"

"Not at all. He knows I'm here speaking to you. I'm sorry for all this extra drama. You don't need an additional action item today, I'm sure."

He chuckled. "At my age, I'm happy to be able to continue to do the work I was cut out for."

"Did you ever consider doing anything else? Or, if I may utter the word, retire?"

"A few times. Especially after a hard case, one with kids getting hurt. Yeah, I looked at contracting—you know, that HGTV kind of stuff—and I thought about teaching at the police academy. But when it comes down to it, I'd miss the community, the people."

"I understand." She'd worked in public law her entire career.

"I know you do. Not many would have the courage or means to rectify the sins of their fathers, Rachel, but you and your siblings have. The Truth Foundation is the pride of Blue Larkspur."

"As much as Ben Colton is its dark stain."

"I knew your father, and while I was always suspicious of many of his dealings, his original motives were from the heart. He wanted to provide for his family. Raising twelve kids isn't easy or inexpensive."

"But it's not an excuse to take bribes and put criminals away for longer than what's fair, or convict innocents." She shook her head. "My only regret with accepting the DA position is that I can't work on the Truth Foundation any longer."

"You're doing a lot of good right where you are, Rachel. Give it time. The case against Clay Houseman is about to get interesting. We've got evidence that substantiates he's been involved in the illegal activities he was arrested for, unrelated to Spence. But he's still claiming to be responsible for crimes that Spence is serving time for." Theo referred to Clay Houseman, who had recently been arrested for a variety of transgressions. But suspiciously after his arrest, Houseman claimed to be responsible for drug crimes that Ronald Spence, a longtime criminal and prisoner, was incarcerated for. It was suspected that Spence had somehow bribed or threatened Houseman into pleading guilty for Spence's offenses. Spence was the last case that Ben Colton presided over, after Judge Colton had admitted to previous wrongs and vowed to uphold the law in all his future endeavors. Rachel was certain her father had done the right thing, that Spence was guilty no matter his continued claims of innocence, all these years later. Caleb led the Truth Foundation in its investigation of Spence, to determine if the man's claims of innocence had merit. The foundation was all about justice and the absolute truth, no matter any family member's personal opinion.

"I can't be involved in it, Chief." While she'd taken steps to be removed from the Parson case, when it came to Spence and Houseman, she couldn't be partial.

"No, but your staff can. If he gets convicted, there's a good chance we'll find out that we need to free Ronald Spence."

Frustration rushed heat into her cheeks. "I don't know how I feel about that, to be honest. Spence may not be guilty of what Dad sent him to prison for, but he's no innocent victim, either." Ronald Spence had gone to jail for drug smuggling, the last case Ben Colton had heard. Drug dealers decimated families and the overall sense of well-being normally enjoyed by Blue Larkspur citizens, but now the Coltons were not positive whether Spence was actually guilty.

"No. This is one time I wish I could still be on the Truth Foundation as well as DA. It'd be like waving a wand and fixing everything all at once. Except I don't have all the information on Houseman, and I doubt anyone does. Just as with Spence—all drug lords are the slimiest of pond scum."

"You've got that right, Rachel." Theo sipped what had to be a cold break-room coffee by now. "As you said, this isn't your concern. I'm sorry I brought it up."

"No apology necessary. It's a family thing." And he was part of their family, wasn't he? A decades-old friend. Except...

"What's up, Rachel? Do you have another question for me?" Theo must have caught the speculation in her expression.

"I was wondering exactly what your intentions are with my mother." As soon as the words were out, she heard how intrusive and rude they were. She held up her hands in a surrender gesture. "No, wait, don't tell me. That was out of line. And definitely none of my business."

Theo's usual noncommittal expression faltered, his cheeks reddening. His eyes cast downward at the legal pad in front of him. Rachel felt like a heel for being so obtuse. Theo was older than her mom, and their generation did things with a lot more subtlety than hers. Could she have been any crasser in her query?

After a long, silent moment Theo cleared his throat and looked back up. He was still blushing, but his gaze was clear and steady. "It's okay, Rachel. I do happen to care a heck of a lot about your mother. But it's got to be on her terms and her time."

Stunned that he'd responded at all, she blinked and gazed down at her phone, suddenly unable to look at him. His sweet, tender heart was on his crisply pressed dress-shirt sleeve, and a rush of affection for the man who'd become a strong, positive figure in her life stole her words. She bit her bottom lip to keep from blubbering as she spoke.

She copied what she'd seen James do when she'd proclaimed he had a daughter and let herself take a couple deep breaths.

"It's okay, Chief. We're all doing our best, aren't we?"

"Yes indeed. Give me a chance to continue to investigate the explosion. We'll find ties to Bethany Austin if they're there. She's now a suspect if all that James told you, and the events you've relayed, prove true."

"It will come out in the wash, I'm certain." She couldn't explain why, but she trusted James's claims. And not only because of the incidents that had happened to her, with her car and the footprints around her home.

Hold on, girlfriend. She knew it wasn't wise to trust a man she'd spent so little time with. But her heart didn't seem to care. She stood and gave Theo a smile. The man really was a dear, though she wouldn't express it right now while he was in his Chief mode.

"I'm afraid you're right." Theo nodded.

"Thanks so much, Chief. I hope this doesn't amount to a hill of beans, but if it does, I wanted you to have everything I've pieced together. There's nothing more important than keeping Iris safe."

He nodded. "Agreed. I'm on it, Rachel. I appreciate that you've trusted me with your personal life, too." He paused, and she thought she saw a mischievous twinkle in his eyes. "But can I say one thing?"

"Shoot."

"Isa is going to be over the moon with all of this. It's her deepest wish that you find someone to love you and Iris. Provided my impression of James as an upstanding man proves true."

"Uh…thank you? And if I can say something? I'd love it if you became a permanent member of our family." She scooted out of the office before he could reply, not wanting to risk embarrassing him again.

Only a few days ago, she'd be on the phone as she walked, texting or calling Gideon to relay the family gossip. But as she headed for the courthouse in the sunny afternoon light, she was struck by another impulse. Her fingers itched to text James.

Nope, not happening. But boy oh boy, she wanted to.

Chapter 9

The week flew by with work responsibilities and Iris's teething antics. By Friday night, all Rachel wanted was to spend some quality time with Iris, get her to bed and veg in front of her favorite Netflix show. There was a new rom-com she was interested in, even though she didn't need or welcome romance into her personal life. Raising Iris and being a DA was enough, thank you very much.

An image of James smiling, sitting at her dining room table, jolted her off the precarious and defensive pedestal she'd constructed. She and James would be friends. Co-parents. It was going to have to be enough, wasn't it?

"Look at you!" She finished drying Iris off after a fun bath time complete with not one or two but eleven mini rubber duckies of various colors, all gifted to Iris by her adoring aunts and uncles. Her tiny hand still clutched a bright blue one, and Rachel had to avoid getting clocked by her daughter.

"Uuuuu ma ma!"

"What? Oh my gosh, did you say—"

The doorbell rang and the chimes seemed particularly jarring, interrupting a very special baby milestone.

"They can wait, sweetie. What did you say?" And who would be dropping in after eight o'clock on a Friday night? All of her siblings worked long days and hard weeks. The Coltons gathered when anyone who wanted or was available showed up at the main house where Isa still lived. Isa made wonderful meals, but help from all the children turned the former delicious-but-humble food into several-course, gourmet events.

Iris giggled but spoke no more. Disappointment stabbed at Rachel's heart, and to her surprise, tears welled. The combination of all of the past week's emotional upheaval all added up. First James came back into her life, along with Bethany Austin. Houseman's testimony confirmed his guilt for Spence's alleged crimes, raising the probability of Spence's release. Spence was a man she wasn't comfortable with being back on the streets. Her powerlessness hit her in the face and her shoulders felt as if she'd spent all day hauling rocks. Bone weariness settled over her and she blinked back more tears.

Iris's big blue eyes gave her an uncannily adult look, as though her daughter knew what she was feeling.

"It's okay, baby girl. Mommy's just got some hormones and emotions zipping around." Rachel's milk production had slowed down since Iris was eating increasing portions of solid food. Her GP, a nurse practitioner, had warned that Rachel shouldn't discount her hormones from wreaking havoc as her body adjusted to Iris's gradually diminishing need for breast milk. She'd nurse for at least twelve months, but there was no hiding from time. Iris wasn't the tiny infant she'd brought home. These past six months had raced by, and—

Ding dong ding.

"Dang it!" She bundled Iris more tightly into the bath towel, tucked the hood sewn into the corner around the baby's head.

"Coming!"

Gathering Iris in her arms, she headed for the front door. She'd meant to get surveillance cameras she'd ordered online for the front and back entrances installed, but it had to wait until Sunday. Gideon had promised to come over and install them for her. Isa had recently had a system installed. As DA, Rachel would be able to write the expense off and, frankly, should have installed the security measures sooner. Evidence that someone had spiked her gas tank, and that maybe the same person had been snooping around her property, combined with Bethany Austin's probable role in it had pushed her to decide to act now.

Still, the boxes of unopened cameras sat in the corner of the foyer, worthless to her in this moment. Looking through the peephole, she let out a shocked squeak and opened the door.

James's profile was stark against the bright white of the front porch light.

"James!"

"Hey, Rachel. Iris, how are you, baby?" He cooed at Iris as if he did it all the time, not as though he'd just met her last week and was seeing her for only the second time.

"Come in. I don't want her to get chilled." She stepped aside and opened the door wide. Only then did her gaze catch on several stacks of items that surrounded him. "What on earth have you brought?"

He flashed a quick grin before getting to work, hauling in his bounty. "I realize I'm months late and you may already have a lot of this stuff, but I've brought Iris a few things." He spoke as he paraded back and forth from the porch and into the house.

"Here okay?" He indicated a spot next to the stairs. Rachel nodded.

"I'd help you, but Iris is still damp from her bath. Let me get her dressed."

"Go ahead. It'll give me time to set up some of this."

Rachel didn't want to even ask him what, exactly, needed to be set up. If the oversize colorful boxes were any indication, James had decided to play new daddy and Santa Claus all in one fell swoop.

James got to work as soon as he had all his bounty inside. He hoped to be rid of the packaging before Rachel returned with Iris. His stomach jumped with giddy nervousness at the thought of Iris's eyes growing wide at her new toys.

His fingers stymied his progress, however, as they behaved like they were all thumbs. When had plastic packaging become so difficult to open?

Scissors.

He needed help opening the heavy-duty seals. Looking around the living room area, he saw no sign of a tool to help him. Finally, he spied a pair of scissors in the kitchen knife block and helped himself.

Fifteen minutes and ten open packages later, he smiled at his creation. Wait until Iris saw this!

"What on earth?" There was no missing the disapproval in Rachel's tone as she spoke next to him, Iris in her arms. His baby girl was in pajamas and looked cute as all get-out.

"Did you buy out the store, James?"

Rachel's surprise was evident but it wasn't the happy kind he'd expected as she gaped at what he'd worked on. The kid-sized kitchen had what he considered the most fun potential. The pink-and-orange appliances were perfect replicas of Rachel's kitchen. His lungs pressed against his rib cage as he watched her gaze move over the play kitchen, the pile of plastic utensils and dishes, and on to the fully equipped play construction bench. Because his girl was going to be completely self-sufficient. By the time she was an adult, he hoped she would be able to cook, bake and put together a wooden deck with minimal effort.

"Check this out." He held up a miniature plastic cordless drill not that far off from the real one he owned. "The drill bit really turns!"

"Okay. But James—" He could hear the concern in her tone and had to fix it. "It's, it's a lot. That's all. Not in a bad way, necessarily. I'm just…surprised."

"It's not finished. There's a toddler-sized table and chairs, and I grabbed some lawn equipment. A lawn mower and snowplow, plus they had this little gas grill that I thought would be perfect as the weather warms up." He tried to see the toys from Rachel's perspective and noticed the large pile of cardboard and plastic.

"I had a hard time getting started. I guess I'm nervous." *Stop talking, bro.* "I can move it wherever you want it. I got both the kitchen and workbench sets because I don't want Iris to ever feel she has to conform to being anything other than who she is."

"How thoughtful." Rachel looked like she'd swallowed a bird.

"What is it?"

A low giggle sounded and at first he thought it was Iris, but the baby had her fist in her mouth, chomping down as she had on the frozen washcloth last week. The only source of glee had to be Rachel. Whose laughter made her shoulders shake like aspen leaves in a breeze.

"James, Iris is barely seven months old. She won't be ready for any of this for another six months to a year, at the least."

"She'll be pulling up on stuff soon, right? As soon as she starts crawling." He'd been doing some reading. If Rachel saw the stack of parenting books he'd pored over after work this week…

"I suppose you're right." Bemusement gave her cheeks the same rosy glow as Iris's. Awe sucker punched him. He didn't think, no, he knew, he'd never seen a more beautiful image than Rachel holding Iris, both of their attention completely focused on him.

"Kiriakis kids walk early, by the way. My nieces and nephews all started by nine months."

"Okay, well, good to know."

Defeat tried to smother his happy buzz, but he shoved it away. He wasn't about to let Rachel's reluctance get in the way of bonding with his daughter. "I figured you already had all the baby things you needed. Since I missed out on that, I wanted to get a jump start on her next development phase."

At Rachel's sharp glance, he decided to elaborate.

She'd find out soon enough. "I've read the latest editions of *What to Expect the First Year* by Heidi Murkoff and *Caring for Your Baby and Young Child* by the American Academy of Pediatrics. And I've been an involved uncle to five nieces and nephews. I'm not a beginner." But he was a new parent, no question.

"You've had a lot to digest since we ran into one another again."

He sighed. "I'm a hot mess, aren't I?"

"No more than any of us are. Right, Iris girl?" Her response was generous. If he were her he didn't think he'd be so accommodating. He looked at how comfortably Rachel held Iris, and when he smiled at the baby, he was rewarded with a lopsided smile.

"She has my mother's smile." The statement came out in a whisper, but he didn't care. This was his daughter and not only was he going to make up for every second he'd missed, he was going to fill them with fun. No way was Iris ever going to have the heartbreak that his childhood had.

"Oh." Rachel stared at him until he caught her gaze, then looked at Iris. "I was wondering about her smile. And her feet. Look at these tootsies." She held a foot in her hand. "No one in my family has that wide of a space between their big and second toes."

Warmth beyond his understanding burst inside his chest and he held out his arms. Iris had his feet! "May I?"

Rachel handed Iris over, and in the second where they both held her, their gazes met again. If anyone had ever told him he'd be comfortable in any kind of family situation that remotely involved him, he'd have howled with laughter. But that was before Rachel. Before he held this precious gift that was his baby daughter in his hands.

"Rachel, I want to make this up to you. To Iris." Rachel turned away, her expression guarded. He allowed Iris's weight to settle against his chest.

"I take it you've gotten the DNA results back by now?" Rachel spoke from the toddler kitchen, where she knelt as she tested out the faux appliances. He smiled at Iris who took a second to register the gesture before she responded with her toothless grin.

"Actually, yes. They are proof of what my heart, and your red hair, already told me." He spoke to Iris as he carried her toward the sofa, laughing when her tiny hand reached up and tweaked his nose. "Honk."

Rachel straightened and turned toward him. He couldn't read her mood, not until she moved closer and picked up a baby blanket from a recliner, clearing the seat cushion.

"Well, then that's settled. Legally and heart-wise. Here, use this chair. She likes to be rocked this time of night. It's her bedtime." He complied, acting as casually as he could, not wanting to upset Iris's routine by carrying on a deep conversation with Rachel. He couldn't help but notice that while her lips remained in a soft line, her brows level, there was a spark in her eyes.

Hope.

Anger tightened Bethany's gut as she stared at her phone, furious at the images of the past half hour. How dare Rachel allow James into her home this late at night! And then, to top it off, she handed over her baby to him. What a lazy mother. Just like hers, who'd foisted her kid off on her younger sister and Bethany's grandma before taking off for the big, wide world. At least Bethany's aunt and grandmother had fed her most nights. Unlike Mom, who barely fed herself. If it didn't have a clever name like Harvey Wallbanger or Sex on the Beach, her mother didn't want it.

Bethany's only mistake in her tracking of James was that she hadn't sprung for an audio feed when she purchased the special cameras from the spy store. She'd left no fewer than five of the tiny lenses on various pieces of Rachel's furniture and fireplace mantel, to give her as full of a picture as possible without a moving camera. No audio meant she had to guess at what they were saying, but she already knew the deal. That Rachel was using all her wiles to snare James in her web.

James was too nice; she'd warned him about that. Unlike the other men she'd tried to hook up with, to make a family life, James hadn't dropped her like a wet cat. He'd insisted they stay friends. That's how she knew he still loved her. He just didn't want to disappoint her with his long work hours, and now that she knew he'd had to change jobs, it was all the clearer to her what had happened. James was struggling at work and didn't want to drag her into it. So typical of him, to be that thoughtful!

Still, it'd be better if she could hear what they were saying. Although not having audio kept her from having to deal with the brat's crying. The kid's mouth sure was open a lot, and Rachel was always holding or feeding her.

Maybe she could go back to the spy store... *No.* There wasn't time. She'd had to drive clear to Colorado Springs and back for the equipment, because thanks to that pesky restraining order, she couldn't risk leaving any kind of digital footprint around James's apartment. Rachel's house was another matter, in Bethany's opinion. She couldn't help it if James was at her place all the time. If the cops caught her, she was going to claim she'd been tracking Rachel, as a concerned citizen. Rachel was a public servant, so Bethany thought her justification made sense. And Rachel was around him a lot—too much. Way too much.

No, she couldn't worry about getting audio equipment. Not yet. Plus, where would she have a package shipped right now? No way was she risking having it sent to her permanent address in Denver, and setting up a P.O. Box in Blue Larkspur required an ID. Nope, not happening. So she'd gotten all she could with her limited cash funds at the brick-and-mortar location.

She grinned to herself as she mentally ran down her equipment. Wireless cameras that Rachel wouldn't be likely to find, check. Nearly invisible sensors at each door to let her know when Rachel or the babysitter, or Isa Colton, was coming and going, check. Getting James to see that Bethany was the only woman for him— almost a check but not quite yet. It looked like she was going to have to get this woman out of the picture first. Some scare tactics were in order, but Bethany had to bide her time.

Time wasn't her friend right now, though. Paying cash was getting to be a pain, as she didn't dare use her ATM card anywhere near Blue Larkspur. She was down to her last few hundred dollars, too. When her cash ran out, she'd have to use credit or debit.

She refocused on the screen in front of her. A thrill shot through her and made her laugh aloud in the small car's confines. It had been too easy to plant the cameras, one in the living room and one in the kitchen, covering the entire front of the house. She had a third for the kid's bedroom but the darn babysitter had prevented her from placing it. Bethany had had to run and hide when the nanny came back into the house unexpectedly. Bethany had put a neighbor's package that she'd stolen on Rachel's porch and rung the bell. The babysitter hadn't taken the package to the correct address as Rachel had hoped. Probably because the kid was sleeping in the crib. Rachel had looked at the brat but didn't have time to linger. She didn't care about a stupid kid.

Unless.

She watched the video feed as James held the baby and made funny faces at it. Maybe he liked babies. Bethany wasn't ever going to have kids—she'd made sure of it and had her tubes tied when she was still in her twenties. She'd convinced the ob-gyn that she carried a horrible genetic disease with DNA results she'd stolen from a work acquaintance who'd confessed her family's plight. But if James was set on having a baby? No problem. If he wanted this kid, she'd make that happen. Women got their tubal ligations reversed all the time. It wasn't cheap, but James would pay for it. Whatever it took for Bethany and James to make their own baby.

It looked like Rachel Colton was the only thing in her way.

Chapter 10

"How do you know she's still sleeping?" James asked the question a little too casually as they sat across from each other in the living room.

"You mean how do I know she's still breathing, right? That monitor over there." Joy lit a fuse in her heart as she pointed at the kitchen counter to the small white device The ice wall she'd worked hard to keep between her and James was melting a little too quickly for her liking. James, like her father, loved the better things in life, the best things money could buy. Exhibit A, the top-of-the-toy-line household playset in her living room. But how could she resist opening up to him, to his obvious desire to be Iris's dad? And it wasn't for her, but for Iris.

Keep telling yourself that.

"Yeah, something like that." His sheepish grimace

proved her suspicion. "I don't know how you don't worry about her 24/7."

"To be honest, it never ends, the worry part. It's normal from what I've heard. My mom says it's part of being a parent and we'll go to the grave with it. But it does get easier, trust me. You'll get more comfortable with taking care of her, get to know her so well that you'll figure out what she needs before she does." She found herself giving him the same speech her mother had given her in the first hours of Iris's life. "That first night in the hospital, I was certain I'd never be able to manage it all. It's overwhelming at first. You're at the beginning of your journey. I get it."

"While we both have to do the maturing becoming a parent requires, you had the physical side of birth to deal with, too. It's impossible for me to imagine how exhausted you must have been, how you might still be. I can't thank you enough for bringing her into the world." James's voice and words caressed her from the inside out. Again, she chalked it up to gratitude that Iris would have a dad. This had nothing to do with her non-relationship with James.

Co-parents. That was the keyword of the day.

"What made you change your mind, James?"

"About being involved in her life?" He smiled. "I hadn't decided not to be, in truth. I was in shock, you know. Finding out about Iris was like having a grenade thrown at me."

"Are you certain you're ready to begin the bonding process, James?" Toys could be returned. Her baby's heart, not so much. Although she knew he was the father, that the DNA proved it, she feared James would get cold feet. Wouldn't anyone when faced with the overwhelming responsibility of raising a soul from infancy until independence?

He shook his head in one decisive movement that she knew was meant to shut down her doubt.

"I'm not waiting one minute longer to get to know my daughter."

It was a huge turn-on that he was 100 percent committed. She envied his ability to have faith it would all work out.

She observed James's quiet manner and couldn't deny his level of commitment. He appeared to have every intention of being present for Iris.

"For what it's worth, I always knew how the DNA results would turn out." She tried to bring some levity to a most serious subject.

"There was nothing to wait for, except for Iris's sake, and her birth record. She needs to know that she wasn't ever anything but loved from the moment I found out about her. I know you've loved her from the start—it's evident."

She shook her head, but not as sharply as he had. "You know, it was odd, scary and very exciting. All at once. A very big surprise, to be sure. Gosh, when I saw the plus sign on that pregnancy test, I about fainted. I've always been careful with birth control, and we were that weekend. I was certain the test was a false positive. But, well, Iris is here." She smiled.

He grinned back. "Yeah, I remember being extra-careful. Maybe it's true—some things are just meant to be."

She blushed. "Yet nothing is one hundred percent. I did panic and of course got checked for STDs."

"I was clean, like I told you. Still am."

"Thanks for the update." She didn't want to go *there* with him, because they had to remain friends, period. Co-parents. "I don't blame you for doubting me, though. You only knew me from one night. And you did try to reach me for so long... I should have figured out that maybe you weren't engaged anymore."

"I was never engaged, as you now know. I never have been. I'm sorry for any pain my apparent lack of interest has caused. I blame myself for allowing Bethany so close in the first place. If I'd listened to my brother, my friends, I would have shut her down from the get-go. Now she's out of control and has stolen time from me and Iris that I can't get back. *We* can't get back." Her toes curled with aching need at the heat in his eyes. A need that she couldn't fulfill if she wanted to be a good DA and the best mother for Iris.

"I'm sorry about all of it, James."

She eyed the stack of unopened security cameras on the floor and silently reminded herself to check in with Gideon for a good time on Sunday to have him install them. The sooner, the better. Although, sitting here with James, no secrets between them any longer, she felt safer than she had since she found out she was pregnant.

"What happened with Bethany in the beginning? When you first met her?" They both knew where it was now.

"We were acquaintances, then friends, and we dated exactly two times. I never took her to bed, if you're asking that. I don't know why, because she was willing, and I've never been one to turn down some fun. But she was too clingy, and her laughter seemed almost desperate, if that makes sense."

"It does." She respected that he didn't even try to pretend that he hadn't been a player. "Did you date anyone since who she's tried to interfere with?"

"Here and there, but no more than a dinner. I'm putting myself on the line here, Rachel, when I tell you that since we met, you and I, I haven't had the usual interest in dating around. It was a combination of meeting you, then you rejecting my calls and, of course, constantly having to look over my shoulder for Bethany's next twisted act. It made even me, the self-avowed forever-single guy, gun-shy."

"That makes sense. Since we're being on the level with each other, I have to admit it's nice to know that you didn't reject me. I believe you, James. That Bethany was the one who answered your phone when I called. It makes total sense in the context you've provided."

He ran his hand over his head, scratched his nape. "I couldn't risk bringing another woman into my mess, and I didn't want any other woman but you. I know I'm coming on too strong here. You don't even know that I'm sincere about Iris. How could you? But I'll prove it to you, Rachel. I will."

She heard declarations of all kinds on a daily basis from defendants and witnesses. Hadn't she become immune to emotional ploys? When James spoke, though, looking at her with his sexy green eyes, she couldn't breathe. And instead of appealing solely to her parenting concerns about Iris having an involved father, James stirred up the intense desire she'd thought she'd left behind in Helena with their unbridled sex.

As the moment stretched into minutes, the tension between them increased. Rachel swore there was a cord attaching them, belly to belly, tightening with each gulp of air her lungs fought for. Unable to handle the heat that was swirling in her most intimate places, she stood, walked toward the kitchen. Away from James. Before she gave in to the question in his eyes.

"I've got an early start in the morning." She lied. Saturday mornings were for sleeping in as long as Iris allowed, then heading out to either her sister and brother's Gemini Ranch or the Colton homestead to enjoy wider spaces and time with Grandma.

"Please don't shut me out. Give me a chance." James was right next to her at the kitchen counter. She hadn't expected him to follow her, to be so close, where she only had to lean a bit, on her tiptoes, and her mouth would be able to catch his—

No. Dad charmed Mom just like this.

She didn't move, and James took a step back. "I'll let you get some rest. Can I come over to see Iris tomorrow?"

"Of course. Text me when you wake up, and we'll work something out." She risked a glance at him, but the heat of the moment had passed. Her gut sank, and the rest of the evening loomed large and boring. Which left her…confused. Shouldn't she be relieved? "I think we need to come up with a joint custody agreement, for both our and Iris's sakes."

He nodded. "I agree."

"Okay. Well, that's settled."

"And for the record? I never needed to see the DNA results, Rachel. I knew Iris was mine almost from the second I laid eyes on her."

Early the next morning, James marveled at how his life had changed on the proverbial dime. It was still all so new to him. Like Christmas, or a special birthday that kept recurring. He couldn't wait to tell his family. He wanted to do it in person if at all possible, but with Bethany's threatening presence he was unwilling to leave Rachel and Iris. So he might need to tell Mom, Jake, and his other siblings over the phone. Maybe he could arrange a video chat session soon. After he was more settled into his role as Iris's daddy.

"Thanks for helping me with the car seat." He sat on the passenger side as Rachel drove the three of them out to the Colton family home, now solely Isa's. After exchanging several texts this morning, he'd figured out she was planning to spend the day here and asked if her family knew about him. Only her brother Gideon did.

"You'll be a pro in no time."

"Let's hope so, for Iris's sake." They laughed together, then settled into a comfortable silence. He used the time to absorb his surroundings, take in the stark natural beauty that was Colorado.

Unlike the rainy days that had characterized April since his arrival in town, today the sun reflected off every new bud.

"I'm glad you're getting to see this all in spring. I happen to think it's one of the most beautiful times of year here." Rachel must have sensed his appreciation.

He took in the mountains, always standing sentinel, visible or not. "I never want to live anywhere but Colorado. It'd be difficult to not have those to view."

"On that we agree, then. Look, James, if you don't want to tell my mother that you're Iris's dad today, you don't have to. We can say you're a colleague who I'm introducing to the area."

"And I just happened to stop by and ask to spend the entire day with you, butting into your family time?"

"Well, when you put it like that..."

"I've been trying to figure out how and when to tell my family, too. I have no problem with telling the Coltons the truth today. But it's your call. Iris is my daughter no matter when we let our families know." On cue, Iris let out a wail. "That's definitely a Colton trait. Kiriakises don't cry."

They both laughed.

"Guilty as charged. I'm from a long line of very loud, expressive people," Rachel said.

"Why is she crying? I thought babies liked car rides."

"She does, but she doesn't like feeling left out of the conversation, do you, baby girl?" He saw that Rachel used a rearview mirror attached to the usual one to look at the infant without having to take her eyes off the road.

"I'm going to have to get a bigger car. My sports coupe days are over." He lazily thought about the kind of four-wheel drive he'd trade his BMW in for.

"If you're expecting any sympathy, none here." She pointed at the large nylon bag on the floor next to his legs. "Can you get her purple unicorn out of there? It looks like a blankie but has a stuffed animal on the end."

He hoisted the diaper bag onto his lap as she rounded a bend that revealed the subdivision that her mother lived in.

"Whoa. I thought you said your mom lived in the suburbs. This seems farther out of the city. You grew up here, even after your dad—" He stopped himself.

Crap.

Why had he let it slip that he'd been checking up on her family? Rachel was nothing like her father as far as he was concerned. Not with her prosecution record while assistant DA and her most recent cases as a newly elected DA.

"Well, it's a story of timing, as most are. My dad's criminal activities had just come to light when he was killed in the car crash. Before he died, and before there was time for him to be disbarred and face the prosecution he definitely would have, he'd tried his last few cases. Immediately after he passed, my mom was strapped for cash and we had several lean times. But then my grandparents died, leaving Mom with enough money to invest so that she was able to take care of us. Her wise financial strategies also enabled her to refresh her graphic design skills and set up her own business. So it all worked out."

"How old were you?"

"Fourteen. Hard to believe it's been twenty years."

"Forgive me if I'm overstepping, but I've read up on the Truth Foundation, too. Impressive."

Rachel's white smile flashed, but she kept her eyes on the road, hands on the wheel. "Thanks. Yeah, I'm really proud of what we've accomplished. It killed me to have to quit it for now, but my siblings supported me in my decision to run for DA. They told me I could do my part by restoring and maintaining justice in Blue Larkspur."

"They're right." He shifted in his seat so that he could check on Iris. Her tiny profile was backlit by the passing scenery as she looked out her window, absently kicking her pudgy legs and clutching the stuffed unicorn. "Is she always this easy to placate?"

Rachel's laugh filled the car. "Absolutely not. You know how she was wailing a few minutes ago? She once did that for two hours straight, when I drove to meet a college classmate in Aspen. She fell into a deep sleep five minutes before I pulled in. My girlfriend and I spent the entire visit in the car with the heater on, eating takeout. Needless to say, Iris woke back up for the ride home."

She shook her head and laughed as she pulled into her mother's parking garage, and she killed the engine. Taking her sunglasses from the center beverage holder and shoving them atop her blond head, Rachel looked at him.

"Sure you're ready for this?"

"No question."

"Then, strap in, buddy. It's always a fun ride at the Coltons'."

Chapter 11

"Give her to me this second. Did you miss Grammy, honey bunny?" Isa enveloped Iris the minute they were in the door, only pausing for the briefest moment to take James in with her shrewd gaze. To her mother's credit, she didn't ask or say anything. Relief calmed her nerves as Rachel kissed her mother on the cheek.

"Hey, Mom."

"Come on in. We're going to have a cookie party!" The scene around the oversize kitchen island was typical for a weekend afternoon. Gideon stood behind Sophia, the woman Rachel was positive was his soon-to-be fiancée, and rubbed her shoulders as Sophia dropped cookie dough onto baking sheets covered with parchment paper. While Rachel's other siblings were nowhere in sight, she knew that several would be popping in throughout the day, which would allow James to meet them on a casual basis. The less fuss made of her bringing a guy home, the better.

"There's my goddaughter!" Gideon dropped his arms from Sophia's shoulders and walked over to plant a kiss on Iris's red head.

"Hi, sweetie pie." Sophia spoke to Iris from the island before giving Rachel a broad grin along with a surreptitious wink. "Hey, Rachel." Gideon had obviously told her about James, which Rachel had expected. She was so happy for her younger brother, reuniting with the love of his life.

Would she ever want to open her soul to anyone more than she did to Gideon?

You already have. Maybe, but this wasn't the time to psychoanalyze herself.

"Hey, Sophia. Everyone, this is James. He's..." The words stuck in her throat. He was more than a friend, but definitely not her boyfriend. To her utter astonishment, she discovered she'd wanted to say he was.

"I'm Iris's father." James picked up where she'd faltered, hands on his hips, confident. "Not the deadbeat dad you probably think I am. I didn't know about Iris until very recently."

"Well. Mystery solved." Isa bounced Iris in her arms, swaying back and forth. The image tugged at memories of when her younger siblings had been little enough for her mother to do the same with them. "The real questions are, where are you from and how much are we going to see of you?"

"Mom!" Rachel never thought of herself as the indignant type until now. Gideon let out a guffaw that he covered with a series of exaggerated coughs, and Sophia bit her lip and bent farther over her task, moving her face out of view.

"It's okay, Rachel." James spoke as if he dealt with intimate domestic conflict instead of corporate law. "It's a fair and needed question. For now, Rachel's agreed to allow me to see Iris. We are going to work out a joint custody agreement, and my intention is to be as much of a father to Iris as I possibly can be."

"No matter your relationship status with my daughter?" Isa didn't so much as blink. The woman had gone through losing her husband twice. First to his lawbreaking ways, then to death. She'd raised twelve kids, all of whom became contributing members of society. Telling her granddaughter's father to pound sand wouldn't be out of her bag of conversational skills. In Isa's worldview, it didn't matter that James hadn't known about Iris sooner. That was on Rachel. But now that he knew, Isa would expect nothing less than total commitment.

"Absolutely. I'm committed to Iris. Rachel is not going to raise her alone," James answered without hesitation. As if he'd turned into the man she'd hoped he was when she'd met him in Helena but had dismissed the possibility in a Denver minute. During that brief night, his descriptions of his fancy car, the tailored cut of his suit that only a top designer label afforded, had conveyed that James was into material things and financial success. Just like Ben Colton. And she knew the ending of that story with painful clarity. But the James she'd come to know since he'd moved to Blue Larkspur didn't fit her initial impression. Not at all.

The skin of her nape prickled with doubt. Was there a chance she'd misread James? Had she misinterpreted the pride in his voice when he'd spoken of his success at supporting his corporate clients? Instead of being the showy big earner, was James perhaps not as much like her father as she'd feared?

"James and I are going to co-parent Iris." She glanced at him for confirmation. Her stomach flipped as she forged through her self-recrimination one more time. "The only reason James wasn't here sooner is because I didn't tell him about Iris."

"Rachel!" Isa's tone was as good as a scolding. "I thought you told him but he wasn't interested in his daughter."

"Mom, I never explicitly gave you reason to think that."

Iris appeared oblivious to the gravity of the conversation, holding out her arms toward James.

"Aaaagh!" she gurgled at her father. Isa carried the baby to him. Isa handed her granddaughter over to the man she barely knew, a silent communication in the gesture. "She knows you, that's for certain."

Rachel knew she'd never forget this moment. The exact time the three of them had become a family. Without the encumbrance of romantic love, that is.

James received Iris with aplomb, as if he'd been carrying her the past six months instead of the past few days. Iris, for her part, snuggled up against his chest and rested her chin on James's broad shoulder.

"You little stinker." Rachel couldn't stop the laugh if she'd wanted to. "She wouldn't rest for the drive up, but now she's ready for a nap."

"Not allowed! Not until she's fed." Isa looked at Rachel. "Do you have some bottles with you?"

"Yes, I'll get them." She walked over to where they'd dropped the diaper bag and small cooler, producing a bottle of the breast milk she'd pumped before driving over. "I knew you'd want to feed her."

"I'll take her back, James, if you don't mind." Isa held her arms out for the baby, but Iris abruptly turned her face away from her grandmother and cried out. "Well, that's a first." Rachel knew Isa didn't take it personally, though, sure her mother was secretly thrilled that the mystery of Iris's father was solved, and said parent appeared to be every part the man she'd want raising her granddaughter.

"She prefers James over me already." Rachel still held the bottle, which she thrust out to James. "Here you go."

He took the bottle and baby to the nearest island stool and perched on it. Without preamble, Iris started eating.

The quiet was fleeting as the front door opened and a rush of voices carried into the kitchen.

"That'll be your brother and sister. At least one pair." Isa left for the foyer and Rachel exchanged glances with Gideon and Sophia, who still appeared ready to burst out into laughter.

"What?"

Gideon grinned and slowly shook his head. "I have to hand it to you, James. If you can make it through an Isa Colton interrogation, you're practically blood. Welcome to the family."

"Your mother's one tough cookie." James slugged back several gulps of water from the large glass he'd carried out to the spacious back patio. Rachel held a stemless wineglass that she'd only partially filled with sparkling water. With Iris taking her nap in the room

Isa had set up just for her—and many more grandchildren to come—it was the perfect time to escape her family's scrutiny.

"She is. But you handled her perfectly. Thank you for being so understanding."

"Hey, she has every right to ask the questions she did. I know you might not agree. You're her daughter. But as an outsider I have to say I'm impressed with her direct manner and steady demeanor. Is she a lawyer, too?"

"No, she's a graphic designer. But she was Dad's sounding board and knows the cases he judged as well as he did. You can't get anything past her. When we were kids, it was something I hated. But now I hope I can be half as good a mother as she was for all of us. None of us were made to suffer any more than absolutely necessary after Dad died. Mom picked up all of the pieces and kept her head held high."

"And your brother, he's Iris's godfather?"

"Yes. He's done a great job of being around a lot. He was determined to be the father figure—" She stopped.

"That I wasn't?" His brow rose.

"Partly, yes. Now that you're here, he doesn't have to be so obsessive about it. But I was going to say he didn't want to be like our dad. Dad was a wonderful father in that he loved and provided for us. But the way he provided turned out to be wrong. What we can do now, is to prevent it from happening to other kids."

"Gideon sounds like my kind of dude." The words escaped his mouth without hesitation.

"Like any Colton, he can be way over-the-top when it comes to sticking up for his own." She cast her gaze over the mountains, grateful for the great weather that gave them a break from the spring rains. It was nice to be out on the patio without needing a winter parka.

"No such thing if you ask me." James leaned forward, forearms on his thighs, their well-sculpted shapes matching the rest of his athletic frame. "Sure is beautiful out here. What made you get a place in your neighborhood?"

"My job. And yeah, I agree it's really pretty here. I've spent my share of teenaged angst moments on this patio, thinking through my life and what I want out of it."

"But you picked the city life?"

"I did. When I bought my house, I was the assistant DA and I thought I'd be doing that job for years yet. I had no idea different members of the council would ask me to consider running for DA."

"Why not?"

"Well, first off, I'm young. As old as thirty-four can feel some days, especially days when I find out I'm being watched by your stalker." She shot him a reassuring grin, hoping to ease his concern about coming into her life and exposing her and Iris to Bethany's threats. "It's early days for a DA, especially in a place like Blue Larkspur. Folks here can definitely be free thinkers, but they're apt to stick with tradition, the familiar. I replaced a septuagenarian male, and before him, the DA served until he was nearly eighty. I'm breaking the mold, per se."

"More like re-creating it from what I've read on your court record to date. Having the Colton name couldn't have always been a help."

"It hasn't been easy, you're right. My father really messed up his life and so many others', and even ours for a bit. But it helps that he worked hard to right his wrongs during the last cases he heard."

"I'm thinking your work ethic and integrity, not to mention legal brilliance, is the real reason you're already a DA. I'm in awe of you, Rachel Colton."

"Flattery will get you everywhere."

"Will it get me a kiss?"

She froze, suddenly wishing she were as small as the spider who worked his way across one of the paver patio tiles. "I'm sorry, James. I can't see there being any point in us being more than co-parents." Yet when he reached out and grasped her hand, his thumb caressing the inside of her wrist in slow, lazy circles, her body's response let her know that she was fighting against her truth.

Rachel still wanted James, in every way possible.

She licked her lips, heard his intake of breath and looked up to see his pupils dilated no matter the bright sunshine. Apparently James still wanted her, too.

But in what ways?

Does it matter? She knew it was risky kissing him out here. Her family could be watching, and if they noticed the display of affection, they'd jump to the wrong conclusions. Think there was more between her and James than Iris.

"Stop thinking, Rachel. What have you got to lose?"

Everything.

Maybe it was the bright sunshine and spring's promise of warmer days. Or the way Isa's garden, bursting with wildflower blooms that included her favorite creamy columbine, was beginning to fill the air with its honeysuckle scent. All of a sudden, kissing James seemed not only right but the *only* thing to do.

Careful. The risk of getting her heart broken would always exist. So why not enjoy life where she could?

"Okay." She waited for James's eyes to widen, his mouth to curve into a smoldering smile. More of a gambler than she'd ever dreamed, Rachel leaned in for his kiss.

James had wanted to feel her lips against his since Helena, since he'd nearly squashed her on the courthouse steps over a week ago. Which made the feel of her soft mouth under his as sweet as the taste of her. It was all he'd remembered from their too-brief liaison and more. He felt her tongue's dance on his lips, then in his mouth, and knew the same thrill she'd given him before. But this was different. No longer singles finding passion on their own timeline, they were parents.

A chuckle eased up his throat. Rachel pulled back. He really adored her wide blue eyes, the way her irises were etched in black. "I can't say a man has ever laughed at my kisses before."

Her hands rested on his chest, the breeze lifting her long hair from her face. "I'm just glad you're not shoving me away like you did on the courthouse steps."

"What else did you expect me to do? I was late for court." They both laughed before she leaned back. He didn't want to see the quick embrace end, but they were in her mother's backyard with the potential of any of her Colton relatives popping outside. "We're lucky no one's staring out the window at us."

"Would it bother you if they had?"

"No. My family isn't always the best at minding their own business but it's all out of love. Usually."

"I thought your brother might be willing to take me on if need be."

"Gideon?" She swung her arms in circles, twisted from her waist. When she realized he was watching her, she stopped, gave him an apologetic smile. "Sorry. Carrying Iris around, lifting her car seat, putting her stroller in the car adds up on my back and shoulders. I only get exercise in when Iris is napping or after she's gone to bed. Sometimes at work over lunch, but not very often."

"I'll be able to help you with that. You'll have more free time to work out if I'm with Iris."

"I don't want free time from Iris." Their gazes held. James wasn't going to push it. This was too new and Rachel deserved however long she needed to see for herself that he was true to his word. He was committed to being Iris's full-time dad.

"I understand."

"But I'm not going to keep you from her, of course."

"I know. I trust you, Rachel." It gave him pause, thinking that he trusted another woman when he was still being stalked by Bethany. But Rachel wasn't Bethany nor was she like any other woman he'd ever met.

"You trust me, eh? Then, tell me what you were laughing about a few minutes ago."

"Huh? Oh, that. I couldn't help compare our kisses in Helena to this one in Blue Larkspur."

"Oh?" Her brow rose and she appeared ready to call for her brother.

"No, no, it wasn't a criticism. Same sexy kissing, trust me. But we're both different. We're parents now. There's more weight to it, if that makes sense."

"Yes, it does. And yes, we are definitely parents of that beautiful little girl. Before I got pregnant, I thought

I didn't want kids ever, or at least not for a very long time. I'd considered freezing my eggs, you know? Now I don't know how I ever lived without her." She hesitated, the shadow of concern evident in how she puckered her lips, the worry lines at her brows. "James, I don't want to give you the wrong impression, or ever lead you on. You and I are two very different people."

"Meaning?" He fought against the sense that he stood on shaky ground. Was she about to tell him that his trust was unwarranted? That she'd changed her mind about how involved he could be with Iris?

"Meaning you're all about your job. About the more tangible things in life."

"Whoa, pot calling the kettle and all that. You didn't make DA at thirty-four because you're anything but career-driven."

"Yes, I'm career-minded, no question. But look at it objectively. I'm giving my all to putting criminals away, people who are a threat to society. You're a corporate lawyer. Your motives are completely different."

Anger flared, and he banked it with the realization that this wasn't about him, not really. He stood on a platform of eggshells, of letting her know he wasn't her father.

"I'd say my purpose is the same as yours. Sure, it's corporate law and often involves very lucrative corporations. But we're after the bad guys, too. The scum of society who are on the take, going after something they didn't earn. Stealing."

"What about the individual civilians you've kept from receiving settlements for wrongs the same corporations have committed?"

"You're talking about the Lucid Scents case." It had

made the national news due to its sensationalist spin. A man had sued James's client for damages related to a particular cosmetic—a cologne that he'd applied to areas of his body that scents were never meant to reach. Misuse of the product had caused a mild rash, but the claimant insisted his subsequent mental distress had caused him to miss days of work and he was now unable to use any similar product at all, for fear of further skin irritation. The whole thing had been ridiculous, and James had been stunned when the judge didn't throw the case out. But then he'd learned that the judge wanted to make an example of cases like Lucid Scents. Sadly, too many fraudulent cases were on the court docket these days. It had looked like James was going to lose the case, as the judge wanted to show that large corporations needed to care about every customer, not just the majority. Who, in this case, didn't react to their product.

James knew he'd been lucky to win. The claimant's lawyer was a known ambulance chaser, and it was obvious he'd found a case and corporation he thought would become his big catch. Except James had been Lucid Scent's attorney and won the case for the corporate giant.

"That's the most obvious one, sure. And the easiest one to find with a web search. But you have to have represented many of a similar vein." She crossed her arms at her chest.

"Actually, no, that was a unique case. I've done mostly corporate litigation for firm versus firm cases. I'm not the soul-crushing guy here, Rachel. I think you're mistaking my drive to succeed for something else." Like her father accepting bribes for cash to give his family life the appearance of financial success.

"You're right, I wouldn't know about a lot of your work. The records aren't as available as my cases."

Ouch. A blow meant to sting. Of course his cases were often under the seal of nondisclosure, something Rachel didn't deal with unless minors were involved or very sensitive state and/or government information was at risk of being made public.

"I'm happy to provide you with any details that I can. How far back do you want me to go?"

"Forget it. This is silly." Rachel's easygoing nature had vanished, and she turned toward the patio door. "I'm going to check on Iris. Why don't you walk around out here, familiarize yourself with the layout of the yard? Over there is the play set, sandbox and swings that have been there since we were all kids. They need to be replaced, but there's no hurry. Iris isn't crawling."

"Yet. She'll be walking before she crawls if she has her way." He spoke to her retreating form, trying to recapture their more easygoing connection over their daughter. But Rachel didn't respond. The door clicked closed and he was left alone. He turned back to the handsomely landscaped property, tried to let the calming view take away the ugly sense of loss. He didn't have anything substantial with Rachel, save for having fathered a child with her.

Why did he care so deeply about her opinion of him?

Don't ask a question if you're not ready for the answer.

Chapter 12

Rachel swiveled her desk chair from the wide window that overlooked the entire city of Blue Larkspur, where on a clear day she was able to pick out hers, and her mother's, subdivisions.

"This is ridiculous." She spoke to her empty office, a rarity, and tried to focus on her laptop screen. Work was what she'd always used to avoid uncomfortable emotions and situations. Like how her father had betrayed the community twenty years ago. As assistant DA she'd thrown herself into case after case, doing whatever it took, working however long hours, all to fix Ben Colton's crimes. And to ease her broken heart a little more.

Her concerns over her father and the Colton legacy had taken a back seat, though. Ever since James showed up in both her life and Iris's. Almost another full week had passed since Rachel had introduced James to her family and he'd stepped into his role as Iris's father with aplomb. She'd been able to stay a little aloof from him emotionally by focusing on each day as it came, sharing parenting duties with him around both of their work schedules. But at night, when the lights went out and she was alone in bed with herself, her thoughts, she had a more difficult time escaping the changes going on in her heart. Which in turn made her fear of committing to a man like her father, no matter how cursory, rear its head and appear in full Technicolor. Not that she was thinking about a relationship with James—nothing further than co-parenting—but it was only natural her thoughts would wander at times, imagining what they'd be like as a couple. Wasn't it?

"Judge Reed wants to give you extra security." Clara stood in front of her, waiting patiently for Rachel to look up from her desk, where she'd been daydreaming.

"Tell her I appreciate it, but Chief Lawson has already put extra patrols in my neighborhood." She hadn't told her assistant or anyone at work about the potential threat from Bethany Austin. Her relationship with James, and whomever he brought with him, was private. And since Gideon had installed the security system, she was feeling much better about being home alone with Iris. Not to mention leaving Iris with Emily each morning for work.

"She's not going to take no for an answer. Brian Parson is still well-connected with Blue Larkspur's criminal syndicate and he's threatened you three times, counting today." Clara referred to when the defendant had looked directly at her and said "I'll see you in hell, Rachel Colton."

It wasn't usual for a suspect to do that, not once they were in trial proceedings. But it happened. All part of her job.

"The first two times don't count. He was still thinking he was above the law. As for today, he's afraid. We have a solid case against him. This time he's going to be convicted of first-degree murder."

Parson was heavily involved in the area's worst drug trafficking to date. She couldn't prove his ties to Clay Houseman, who was close to getting arrested, according to Theo, but she suspected most crime in Blue Larkspur was related to the syndicate founded by Ronald Spence. Thankfully Spence was still behind bars, but he'd pleaded his case to the Truth Foundation over the years. He proclaimed his innocence, that he'd been framed by Ben Colton. She wasn't sure she believed him, though. Not because she wanted to exonerate her father, but because the evidence pointed to Spence's guilt. And Spence was the bad player she was most concerned about, not some lower player in the drug ring like Parson.

"I'll pass your message to Judge Reed's staff, but expect her to shoot you down on this." Clara didn't budge.

"Fine. But remind them that these criminals don't want to draw the kind of attention to themselves that threatening or harming a government official would bring. They're all a bunch of evil scumbags, but they're business first. No way will they risk their multimillion-dollar revenue in Colorado by targeting a rural county DA."

"Okay, got it. I'm on it."

Rachel tried to get back into her case prep after Clara left the office, but she couldn't let go of the feeling that maybe she shouldn't have been so dismissive of Judge Reed's offer for protection. It wasn't just her, but Iris, too.

And there was the issue that had plagued her since last evening. A bouquet addressed to her, with no return address. The prettiest spring wildflowers, not unlike the ones in her mother's garden. Except for the single long-stemmed rose in the center, which was black. And the note, written with a sloppy but legible hand. "Stick to being a DA and leave James Kiriakis alone."

It had to be from Bethany. If it had been related to her job, James's name wouldn't be on the note. Unless the sender was from one of her cases and had invested in finding out about her most personal details, which she doubted.

She shivered despite the silk cardigan she wore atop her blouse and skirt. While Gideon had been great about setting up the security cameras at both her front and back doors, they hadn't helped when she'd searched the video feed last night in hopes of identifying the flower deliverer. The person had worn dark clothing complete with a hood over their head, a baseball cap brim obscuring their face. It was impossible to tell if the figure was male or female, no doubt what they'd wanted. It especially made sense if it was Bethany, as it still hadn't been determined whether she was actually in Blue Larkspur.

She should at least mention it to the cops, she supposed. It would be their manpower that provided the extra patrols.

As she wondered about whether or not to call Clara back in, her phone lit up with a text from Theo. Serendipity!

Please call me when you can.

Restless with her indecision, she shut her laptop and grabbed her purse.

Ten minutes later she walked into the chief's office, needing the reassurance of his consistency. After her father died, the ability to trust men—and, really, anyone—had perished with him. But Theo's constant presence in their lives, the way BLPD had worked steadfastly to uncover Ben Colton's crimes, had provided the security her life otherwise lacked.

The love of her siblings had been huge, too, and of course Isa's unwavering commitment to her family. Yet the gap left by her father had left Rachel needier than she'd have ever wanted. Academics, the Truth Foundation and the law gave her reassurance, a steady compass point.

Theo had been part of it all along.

She knocked on his door, ajar, revealing the octogenarian at his desk, poring over his computer screen.

He looked up over his glasses. "Rachel, please come in."

She opened the door wide and all intentions of reporting the flower delivery to Theo took a mental back seat as she spied her oldest siblings, Caleb and Morgan, already sitting in the office. As partners in the family legal firm, Colton and Colton, it wasn't unusual to see them working together. But not in here, not since she'd been elected DA. Colton and Colton was the driving force behind the Truth Foundation, and Rachel hadn't seen her oldest siblings in a work situation recently. Caleb was dressed in his usual suit, well tailored and looking like he was about to go into court. But his brighter-than-usual blue tie showed the influence of his fiancée, Nadine. Morgan wore a classic red A-line dress, their grandmother's pearls around her neck. Isa had insisted each daughter pick an item from her own mother's jewelry box.

"Wow, I wasn't expecting this. What's going on?" Alarm bells rang. Caleb was thick into investigating Randall Spence. Was there new information, new evidence that he was dirty, unlike Spence claimed?

"We asked the chief to call you. You didn't have to come in." Morgan smiled. "But I'm glad you did, sis." Her blue eyes matched Rachel's, although Morgan's hair was long and brunette instead of blond.

"Hey, Rachel." Caleb, always the more serious of the twins, offered a quick smile, his brown eyes warmer than they'd been in years. Since falling for his ex-wife's cousin Nadine, he exuded a more relaxed vibe. His expression was stamped with concern, though, which made Rachel's shoulders tense.

"Have a seat." Theo nodded at the usual chair she sat in and she noticed that Caleb sat on a folding chair. It never ceased to give her pause that the folks literally keeping a community secure made do with the least. She never thought of herself in this light, but to be fair, her experience and degree would earn almost three times as much in the private sector. But she'd never pursued the law for financial gain, or even power. "I'm glad you stopped in instead of calling. It'll be easier to figure out our options."

"What options?" She took in all three expressions while her siblings and Theo appeared to be measuring her up, too. Whatever this was about, it wasn't good.

James stared at his phone as dismay scrunched his stomach into a painful ball. Chief Lawson was unavailable, "in a conference" according to the BLPD receptionist. He'd checked in with Denver PD, too, but hadn't been able to find out anything on Bethany's whereabouts. She hadn't been seen in Denver, at least since he'd moved. He wanted to go over his options again, remind the chief how persistent Bethany Austin could be. He had to make sure BLPD knew who he believed they were dealing with.

"You look so sad for our most recent hire." Adam Jones, an attorney hired the month before James, stood in front of his desk.

"I'm good. Wrapping up loose ends in Denver, is all." The last thing James wanted or needed was for his new employer to find out about Bethany. He wasn't ashamed that he was a stalking victim, and he wasn't in denial that she was back at harassing him and now Rachel. But if he could keep her separate from work, it'd help his peace of mind.

"I hear you, man. I moved here from Helena and it's taken me almost a full month to close all my utilities, get my apartment professionally cleaned, you know the deal. All the little stuff nobody thinks about until it has to get done."

James ignored the sensations zinging around his insides at the mention of where he'd met Rachel. Where they'd conceived Iris.

"I do know. I have to say I think I'm going to like Blue Larkspur a lot. I already do. Which makes me antsy to get Denver business settled."

"You won't have to return there, will you?"

"No, no. My family's there, and my brother's been a huge help." He wasn't lying on this; Jake had offered to do whatever he needed to assist James in escaping the hell that Denver had become for him. Even with Bethany's lack of activity the last several months, he'd still looked over his shoulder.

And now he had to check his surroundings in Blue Larkspur. Constantly.

"Why don't we grab a beer sometime this week? There's a great place just outside of town that has an IPA I like."

"I'm not sure about this week yet, but definitely soon. Thanks, Adam."

"Sure. If you need anything, let me know. I've only been here a month longer than you, but I think it's fair to say we've landed at a great firm."

"I agree."

Alone again, James knew that the best thing about Blue Larkspur for him wasn't his new job, its partners or even the city that already felt like home.

It was the woman who'd enchanted him, and the beautiful baby girl they'd made together. Bethany was in over her head this time. He wasn't going to give up until she was stopped.

"Okay, so shoot." Tension screeched across Rachel's nerve endings as she sat next to her siblings. It was the same reason she never read mystery or thriller novels; she couldn't stand not knowing the entire story *yesterday*.

Theo spoke. "I know you're recused from all Truth Foundation cases, but we've had some developments that you need to know about as DA. I wanted to give you a heads-up so that you have time to sort what you can and can't be involved with going forward."

Caleb leaned over, looking past Morgan. "The Truth

Foundation has been involved in investigating Ronald Spence's case, as you know, for the last twenty years."

Morgan nodded. "Since Dad died. But now the chief has arrested Clay Houseman. Spence tipped us off after requesting to speak to the chief."

"We brought him in for—" Theo cleared his throat and used his glasses to read off his computer screen "—drug dealing, racketeering, threatening a minor, and added resisting arrest and attempted murder on a police officer when he pulled his gun and shot at one of our own."

Rachel listened, allowed it to settle. "What does this have to do with Spence?" As far as she was concerned, nothing would ever clear the man for the damage he'd rained down on Blue Larkspur. Nothing. Spence had been a drug kingpin when Blue Larkspur went through its worst time. Hundreds of teenagers were lured into using his products, which were whatever illicit drugs he could peddle. Homelessness, crime, addiction all addled the normally friendly city. Spence went to jail on certain charges but Caleb and Rachel had read his files forwards and backwards. If the charges that put him behind bars hadn't stuck, he had committed plenty of other offenses to be prosecuted for. She found the timing of Houseman's plea suspicious, too. Years after Spence went to jail, and for the exact same crimes. As DA she'd read reports that indicated Spence might still be guilty.

Theo folded his hands on his desk, gave Caleb and Morgan each a glance before focusing on Rachel.

Oh crap. This isn't going to be good.

"Houseman confessed to all of the current charges, and more. He says he was the one who committed each and every crime that Spence was charged for and convicted of."

"That's ridiculous! He can't give a blanket confession like that and expect it to hold up in court. Tell me you see this for what it is." Nothing more than another example of how Spence still somehow held sway over the Blue Larkspur crime network.

Theo shook his head. "It wasn't a general comment, Rachel. His lawyer made sure he confessed to each and every charge that Spence was convicted of. We haven't had time to look into their exact connection, but Houseman might be the fall guy for Spence."

"Spence is claiming that he was framed, as you know, but now he's got weight behind his claims." Morgan watched for Rachel's reaction as she spoke, disappointment etched on her face. "I'd hate to see the Truth Foundation's reputation go up in flames. Because it will if Spence walks. He's always claimed he was the victim of circumstances and faulty witnesses, like a lot of the actually innocent people our dad put away."

Morgan's dismay was justified. Spence had always claimed his blamelessness and had appealed his sentence repeatedly. Rachel strongly suspected Spence had never given up his position of power in the crime organization, but they'd never been able to prove it while she was the assistant DA.

"If Houseman's indictment holds, Spence is going to be freed." Caleb summarized the Colton family's biggest fear. If their hunches were right, one of the bad guys was going to be out on the streets.

Nausea surged and Rachel collapsed back in her chair, wishing she could run off to the restroom and shut herself in the diminutive stall. She didn't want her siblings worrying about her. A sour stomach was the good ol' standby that had plagued her in her teens and throughout adolescence whenever she was faced with what seemed an insurmountable obstacle. Her GP had broken the code on it when she told Rachel it might have been caused by her repressed grief and anxiety.

Morgan placed her hand on Rachel's forearm. "I'm sorry, sis. It was a shock to us, too. From all perspectives it's a certainty that Spence might be guilty of many crimes, but we haven't been able to find enough evidence of his culpability to turn it over to the authorities and possibly outweigh Houseman's confession."

"And I don't need to hear any details about that." Rachel was always eager to put a bad player behind bars but this was directly related to Ben Colton's crimes. She'd never risk her status as DA to prosecute if she didn't have to. "Even though I think that in the instance of Randall Spence, there isn't a judge around who won't recuse me out of hand."

"This is a hard pill to swallow for all of you." Theo's deep baritone reverberated his compassion in the closed office.

"I'm fine, really. It's just— I mean—" What could she say to reassure her siblings she was okay but not lie to them, either?

"I've gone through his case file, the court records at least a dozen times since I was in law school. No matter how much Spence shot his mouth off about being innocent, the case against him was solid, and the DA at the time had done their homework. He shouldn't be up for parole for at least another decade, and now you're telling me he might stroll out of state prison in a matter of months?"

"Weeks, from the court schedule I saw." Caleb's tone held compassion even though he didn't shy from reality.

"*Days* are what I just found out," Theo added.

"Of course. You know more than I do since I'm re-cused from all things Spence and the Truth Foundation." She mumbled as she remained slumped, needing a few moments to let the sick feeling pass. Court schedules were full but high-profile cases were often pushed through more quickly. Clara kept her apprised of those that were most pertinent to the DA's office but had to leave this one off the list today. "I take it you caught him only this morning?"

"Yes." Theo was the largest, most experienced presence in the room and yet he'd gone quiet, allowing the siblings to share their combined grief. Rachel had learned long ago that the sorrow over Ben Colton's demise, both legally and morally, would never go away, but she'd learned to live with it. It didn't take away the difficulty of facing it again and again, however. Events like today's news were bound to reopen the heavily scarred wounds.

"Does Mom know?" Isa's expression that combined sadness with gritty determination flashed across her mind.

"Not yet. I'll go over after work and tell her." Morgan looked at Caleb. "We were both going to do it to-gether but—"

"It's Nadine's birthday." A slow flush crept up Caleb's neck.

"Nice to see you join the rest of humanity, bro." Rachel welcomed the opportunity to tease her brother as it also allowed her to think about something other than her still-iffy stomach. "I'll meet you there, and I'll bring Iris. I can get off work early today."

"You don't have to do that."

"I want to do it." Rachel looked at Theo. "I think it would be good if you could be there, too. Mom draws on you for support."

"I, um, sure. Of course I'll be there." Whatever made Caleb's cheeks red was catching, as Theo's face reddened, too.

"Great. We'll all meet there at five, then? Is that too early, Rachel?" Morgan quickly took charge, which was a relief instead of igniting the usual sibling competition, especially among the three Colton attorneys.

"Works for me." Rachel had no idea how she'd get all her work done before then, but nothing like the threat of a bad guy being let loose on the streets again to motivate.

As she walked out of the police department, a text dinged.

Okay if I come over after work to see Iris?

James. James would be able to help.

Bethany's neck muscles were cramping again. Keeping an eye on Rachel Colton was a pain in all of her body parts. All she had was the tablet she'd stolen from the community college campus from an unsuspecting student who'd left it in her backpack on a picnic bench. The same young woman had unlocked it with a passcode Bethany was able to discern as she'd watched the woman all yesterday morning.

Her personal phone and laptop were off-limits since

she couldn't risk being found by law enforcement. She didn't think James had done anything more about the restraining order, like reporting that he thought she'd been the one to set off the explosion at the restaurant. If he had, wouldn't she have found out when she called her mother, who would have warned her of increased police surveillance around the family, on one of the burner phones?

Finally, finally, she got to watch James without Rachel's ugly puss in the frame. Rachel had left James alone with the baby. And James, because he was the nice guy Bethany knew better than anyone, was being really nice to the kid. But once he saw that Rachel wasn't the woman for him, Bethany was sure he'd let the kid go, too.

Rachel Colton might be a DA, but she sure was a dumb bunny. Bethany thought her flower arrangement would be enough to warn the annoying woman away from James. But no, James was here less than twenty-four hours after Bethany had delivered the bouquet. A grin made her tight facial muscles relax for a millisecond. It had been smart of her to nab the flowers from the highway medians on the outskirts of town. The black rose had been in a pile of garbage she'd found in a dumpster that the local Goodwill shared with a restaurant, along with a crumpled Over the Hill banner. She'd been searching for some more clothes to use as disguises when the rose stem had scratched her wrist. It was a sign, she was certain, that she was supposed to use it to scare Rachel off.

But if the woman had been afraid, she'd not shown it. She'd actually stood on her porch and dumped the flowers into the side bushes and left the vase—also a dumpster find—on the porch. Talk about lack of appreciation!

And now it looked like Rachel Colton was using James as her personal babysitter. How dare Rachel saunter off and leave her brat with James while she went off to do whatever? Her vision blurred and she clenched the tablet, hands shaking.

Calm down. Focus on James.

What she saw was real. Rachel was leaving the house, alone. Which meant Bethany had to follow her, because she'd lost track of the couple and kid last weekend when they'd gone away for the day. She needed to know every place Rachel Colton went.

Weekdays sure were simpler, when both Rachel and James went to their jobs, and Bethany could count on them being in the same places for hours at a time.

Since she had to follow Rachel, she wouldn't be able to check in on James as often, not unless wherever Rachel went had a strong Wi-Fi signal. That was the other thing Bethany relied upon: free internet so that she could log in to the camera system. The surveillance app she'd purchased saved up to six hours of recorded video, but that was it, leaving at least two-hour gaps in the middle of the night. Bethany didn't like gaps when it came to James or the people in his life.

She waited for Rachel to get into her fancy-ass car and back out of the drive, counted to three, then started her engine and followed her out of the subdivision. Bethany's gas gauge had enough left to take her thirty miles or so.

She wasn't a praying person, as she'd learned long ago that she alone was in charge of her fate as well as the fates of those she cared about. But she whispered some words anyway, hoping she had enough gas until she could get back to where she'd hidden her cash and refill the tank.

The drive didn't take as long as she thought it would. In fact, she had plenty of fuel left to return to her favorite stakeout site in Blue Larkspur. But Rachel had pulled into a very, very upscale neighborhood, by Bethany's standards. Who needed this much? And the house she approached was set back from the road, but Bethany had seen enough of the homes on the drive in and knew that this had to be Rachel Colton's family home. Her mother was Isa Colton, a local graphic designer, and her father had been a crooked judge who the family had created a nonprofit around, trying to fix their father's bad deeds.

Bethany laughed. Too bad Ben Colton was dead. He sounded like the kind of man she'd get along well with. One who understood power, what a deal meant. Unlike James, who'd broken the deal of their relationship. Oh sure, he'd claimed they'd never been more than friends, but Bethany had reminded him that he'd made it seem they'd be together forever. And they would.

Just as soon as she got Rachel Colton out of the way.

Chapter 13

Rachel pulled in front of her mother's house, as her siblings had already jam-packed Isa's driveway. She killed the engine and rested her arms on the wheel, needing a few seconds to calm down before walking into what was bound to be an emotional cesspool with her family.

The empty passenger seat and baby car seat in the back underscored that she was on her own, without her family. James wasn't technically related, but as Iris's father, he was a de facto support she was coming to rely on, maybe too much. He'd agreed to meet her at her house early and was eager for more time with his daughter. It was a relief to know Iris was safe with him, that the baby's routine wouldn't be interrupted by a tension-filled scene at her mother's.

Whenever the subject of her father's criminal activities came up, it brought out the worst in her siblings.

Treat Yourself
with 2 Free Books!

GET UP TO 4 FREE BOOKS &
2 FREE GIFTS WORTH OVER $20

See Inside For Details

Claim Them While You Can

Claim up to FOUR NEW BOOKS & TWO MYSTERY GIFTS – absolutely FREE!

Dear Reader,

We both know life can be difficult at times. That's why it's important to treat yourself so you can relax and recharge once in a while.

And I'd like to help you do this by sending you this amazing offer of up to FOUR brand new full length FREE BOOKS that WE pay for.

This is everything I have ready to send to you right now:

Try **Harlequin® Romantic Suspense** books featuring heart-racing page-turners with unexpected plot twists and irresistible chemistry that will keep you guessing to the very end.

Try **Harlequin Intrigue® Larger-Print** books featuring action-packed stories that will keep you on the edge of your seat. Solve the crime and deliver justice at all costs.

Or TRY BOTH!

All we ask in return is that you answer 4 simple questions on the attached Treat Yourself survey. You'll get **Two Free Books** and **Two Mystery Gifts** from each series you try, *altogether worth over $20!* Who could pass up a deal like that?

Sincerely,

Pam Powers

Harlequin Reader Service

Treat Yourself to Free Books and Free Gifts.

Answer 4 fun questions and get rewarded.

**We love to connect with our readers!
Please tell us a little about you...**

	YES	NO
1. I LOVE reading a good book.		
2. I indulge and "treat" myself often.		
3. I love getting FREE things.		
4. Reading is one of my favorite activities.		

TREAT YOURSELF • Pick your 2 Free Books...

Yes! Please send me my Free Books from each series I select and Free Mystery Gifts. I understand that I am under no obligation to buy anything, as explained on the back of this card.

Which do you prefer?

❏ **Harlequin® Romantic Suspense** 240/340 HDL GRCZ
❏ **Harlequin Intrigue® Larger-Print** 199/399 HDL GRCZ
❏ **Try Both** 240/340 & 199/399 HDL GRDD

FIRST NAME _____ LAST NAME _____

ADDRESS _____

APT.# _____ CITY _____

STATE/PROV. _____ ZIP/POSTAL CODE _____

EMAIL ❏ Please check this box if you would like to receive newsletters and promotional emails from Harlequin Enterprises ULC and its affiliates. You can unsubscribe anytime.

HI/HRS-520-TY22

They each wanted to protect their mother but had different approaches. Not to mention that they didn't each have the same daily reminder of what Ben had done. Caleb and Morgan certainly had the most to deal with, as far as the community was concerned. All of the siblings were involved with and supported the Truth Foundation, but most of them had dispersed career-wise and found other ways to give back, whether to Blue Larkspur or the world at large.

Rachel knew the meeting was going to be rough. Otherwise she wouldn't have asked James to be with Iris this quickly on his own. Emily couldn't stay late today, and Rachel had been in a bind. The Colton meeting didn't need the distraction of a possibly cranky baby, and she didn't want Iris exposed to the negative vibes that were bound to come up.

Her stomach still roiled with uncertainty.

Your heart is hurting, too.

For once she wished she could blame her unease on being a new mom, fearing for her baby's safety with a man she'd only known a couple of weeks.

It wasn't that, though. She completely trusted James. He'd bonded with Iris in the best way possible, even though both he and Rachel had heavy work schedules and were still getting used to being around one another on a regular basis. Plus she'd asked Theo to do a background check on James, just to be sure. It was clear. James was as he appeared—an honest, sincere man chock-full of integrity.

Which brought her to what continued to tug at her peace of mind. Everything with James, from their passionate introduction to revealing his paternity, had come more easily than she'd expected. As if it was all meant to be and had been this way for a long time.

Rachel didn't know how or when exactly it had happened, but James had become as important a focal point in her life as Iris. She thought of him as family, whether she wanted to acknowledge it or not.

"Enough." She spoke to the empty car, grabbed her bag and exited. As she walked the gauntlet to her mother's home, she clung to the fact that all her siblings wanted the same thing she did. To keep Isa and their family safe, and to keep the ugly touch of any drug dealers out of Blue Larkspur.

A hard goal to achieve if the ringleader was let out of jail.

"You are your daddy's girl, aren't you?" James tickled Iris's cheek and was rewarded with a dimpled grin. A low laugh erupted from his belly and he wondered how he could have been so afraid to be with his daughter alone. Until now, Rachel had always been with him to help out as needed. He knew it had taken all of her trust and self-discipline to leave their baby with him. Her faith in him touched him as intimately as her kisses had in Helena.

She had some kind of important meeting with her family that she didn't think he'd be interested in, and he got it. Sometimes families needed to be alone.

He took Iris's bib off, since she'd just eaten a hearty dinner, and lifted her from the high chair. The pride warming his chest was silly, but so what? Just two weeks ago he'd had no clue how to work a car seat or high chair or any other infant paraphernalia, and now he felt like an expert.

He carried Iris down the hallway to the baby's bathroom. The table where Rachel left her keys and incoming mail was to his left, just off the nursery, and he made sure to avoid bumping into it. A note sat on the whitewashed surface, his name in bold marker shouting out at him from the crumpled sheet of paper. "Stick to being a DA and leave James Kiriakis alone."

The slant and style of handwriting made him stop in his tracks. He'd seen it before.

Bethany.

He tried to engage his reasoning ability, honed by years in law. But when faced with the possibility that Bethany was not only stalking him again but making trouble for others, logic became unattainable. Now she was warning off Rachel, had become a threat to his daughter.

Blood heated his face, made his ears pound with his frantic heartbeat.

Iris squirmed in his arms, shook him back into the present. He looked into her precious eyes, fixated on his, and let out a long breath. Iris was safe, with him. Rachel was safe at her mother's house. She'd texted when she'd arrived and told him she'd do the same when she left. Bethany was the unknown.

Be prepared.

It didn't matter that he'd taken every precaution to not be followed each time he came to Rachel's. If the message on the table had been delivered here, Bethany knew where Rachel lived. Even if it had been delivered to Rachel's office, the sender knew that he and Rachel were involved somehow. Did Bethany know Iris was his daughter, too?

Anger inched up his spine, his nape and crushed his

head in a steady throb. The need to protect burst from the center of his chest, and he held Iris close, knowing that nothing was more important. It had happened so quickly, this sense of knowing she was his. That they were part of a family of their own making. He, Iris and Rachel. He'd never let anything hurt them.

Nothing.

"Hi, Rachel!" The chorus of voices greeted her when she walked into the house, the front door visible from the dining table in the great room's arrangement.

Five of Rachel's siblings, including the oldest twins, gathered around Isa's large, scratched table. The triplets, Oliver, Ezra and Dominic, were absent, and she longed for their grounding presence. Two years older than Rachel, the three were always involved in international intrigue of one sort or another. Oliver was a venture capitalist, Ezra was in the army and Dominic was an agent with the FBI's International Corruption Unit. It wasn't a surprise that they weren't around, but still, it was never the same without them.

Same for the youngest Colton siblings, her sisters Alexa and Naomi, also twins. Born eight years after Rachel and six years after Gideon, they were the "pleasant surprises" that Isa and Ben had joked about when they were younger. Alexa was a US Marshal and like her triplet brothers, often unavailable. Naomi didn't show up for many of the gatherings, either, but she didn't work for the government—quite the opposite, as she was a reality TV producer. Naomi missed many of their family get-togethers due to being off-site or on location.

Rachel understood the impossibility of having them all under one roof more than once every year or so.

Twelve adults spread across the country—the planet!—with different interests and ages made coming together in person difficult. But it didn't ever take away from the solidarity and love that they shared as Coltons. That unconditional Colton bond wrapped around her, around Isa's dining room table, no matter how many of them were physically present.

"Mom." Rachel gave Isa a quick peck on her cheek before sitting down. It seemed a rather formal place to gather, as they usually opted for the kitchen and its large island. But as she met Morgan's and then Caleb's gazes, the cold truth of their new reality knifed through her center.

"Hi, everyone."

Morgan and Caleb didn't respond, as they'd gone back to discussing whatever was on Morgan's smartphone. Did they have an update?

"Hey, Rach." Her brother Jasper sat next to Aubrey, his fraternal twin. Both were four years younger than Rachel.

"How's life at the ranch?" She referred to the twins' Gemini Ranch.

"The usual." Aubrey grinned. "Usual" in a Colorado spring meant lots of calving and foaling, highlighted by the muddy marks on both Aubrey's and Jasper's jean jackets.

"I take it from your glow that Luke is well?" Rachel teased her about the love of her life, Luke Bishop. A Neapolitan by birth, he'd been on the run for years from the Camorra criminal organization. Rachel silently acknowledged that while her life might seem chaotic, she wasn't alone. Each Colton sibling seemed to have their own personal challenges to deal with. At least Aubrey's had come with a happily-ever-after.

"I'm fine, *grazie*." Luke spoke from his seat next to Aubrey, but his gaze barely met Rachel's as he was mesmerized by her sister. Nothing like true love. She wasn't jealous, or anything like it. Simply happy for her sister.

"Where's my niece?" Aubrey interrupted her thoughts.

Rachel shifted on her seat, at a loss for the best response.

"Does James have her?" Gideon's quiet request was a lifeline, his voice steadying. Rachel hadn't felt on solid ground since James had knocked her off her feet in front of the courthouse.

"Yes." At the raised brows and attempts at surreptitious glances, she relented. "This meeting is not about me, or Iris, but yes, James is getting more and more involved in our lives. I mean, in Iris's life." She looked at the wall for the thermostat that controlled the temperature throughout the sprawling Colton homestead. "Mom, do you still have the heat on?"

"Of course I do. It's April in Colorado, isn't it?" Her siblings laughed and Rachel couldn't help from joining in. Her mother was the quickest with a comeback, always.

"I don't mean to be a jerk, but it seems excessive. Is anyone else in here hot?" She lifted her long locks from her nape, stretched her neck in an effort to somehow cool the heat that made her skin feel like aluminum foil around a baked potato.

Rachel's gaze shifted to her brother Gavin's face, prominently displayed on Isa's iPad. Gavin was six years younger than Rachel and a total loner, happiest when pursuing a hot lead for his next article or podcast. He'd been interested in journalism since he'd been a kid. "Hi, Gavin. Wish you were here."

"Rachel. I am there. Virtually, anyhow. How's being the new DA treating you?" Even through the screen she saw how his eyes glinted with brotherly affection and more. Gratitude took her agitation down a level, the distraction from why they were all here acting like a cool breeze on her hot skin.

"It's good. Looking for a new story? Don't look at me." She shot him a smile.

Rachel went around the table, greeting Nadine and Sophia, too, before the meeting began.

"Good evening." Theo's voice boomed into the room from the front foyer and his purposeful steps echoed across the great room.

"Theo." Isa smiled and indicated he take the seat to her left. Was that a blush on her mother's cheeks? And a smile trying to shift the chief's mouth from its grim line?

"Let's get it going, everyone." Caleb waited for the room to quiet down before he continued, "Mom, I hope you don't mind that we asked Theo to be in on this family meeting. It involves our family, him and BLPD." Caleb sat to the right of Isa, her gaze rapt from her seat at the head of the table. A polished attorney, Caleb couldn't shake his training even with his immediate family. Rachel suppressed an inappropriate grin. This felt a little too much like the county courthouse for her liking. But they weren't here to talk about the Colton Christmas-gift exchange.

Caleb met each of their gazes with a nod before proceeding.

"We've asked you all to join us, and we've sent texts to the others, to let you know some sad news for the family. Spence is going to be released from jail in the near term, possibly as early as the end of this week. As expected, there are significant reports and rumors that Spence has orchestrated all of this. He may still be pulling the syndicate's strings from behind bars."

Gasps and several swear words sounded from all present, but Rachel was used to her siblings and their various reactions over bad news. It was her mother's reaction that she cared most about.

Isa kept her gaze downcast for so long that the room grew silent, and she wondered if her mother was saying a prayer or had been shocked speechless. But when Isa's gaze swung up, all Rachel saw in the blue depths much like her own was steel.

"We always knew this could happen. Prisoners get released when it's determined they weren't guilty."

"But Mom!"

"You've got to be kidding!"

"He's a crook!"

So many spoke at once that Rachel couldn't hear her own response. Which involved the swear words her siblings had previously used. Sure, she'd already heard the bad news earlier, so it wasn't a surprise. But being in the company of her family unlocked the box in her heart where she carefully stored all things related to her father's demise.

Ben Colton's sudden death in a tragic car accident and the aftermath of grief was actually easier for her to remember, because her father had had no power over his passing. But choosing to accept bribes from criminals in the same league as Spence was something she'd never been able to forgive him for. She knew many of her siblings were still working on the forgiveness part, too.

Ben had had his hands full and the pressure on as each of his kids arrived and Isa realized she couldn't balance twelve children and a career all at the same time. His initial salary as a small-city judge hadn't been enough to put decent groceries on the table, much less keep them all clothed and the bills paid. Since she'd had Iris, Rachel had a new understanding of what it meant to be a parent and she was able to muster some compassion for her father. But she drew the line where he'd repeatedly broken the law and continued to accept increasingly higher bribes.

"Hold on, everyone." Isa held up a hand. "I'm not saying it's okay, or the right decision, but this isn't about my opinion. Or any of yours. The law is the law, and it seems Spence is going free, right?"

Heads nodded.

"Well, then, we'll have to keep the Truth Foundation on it, assure he doesn't make the tiniest deviation from what's legal. Meanwhile, can we find out more about Clay Houseman?"

As her mother shifted her focus to Theo, Rachel had to keep her jaw from hitting her sternum. Shouldn't Mom be looking at Morgan or Caleb, or even her, no matter that she was recused from all Truth Foundation activity?

"Theo, your department is going to keep an eye on Spence, aren't you? And you must have info on Houseman that even Caleb and Morgan don't know, right?" Isa's respect for the chief was evident.

"We work closely with your foundation, Isa. But no, we can't tail someone who's being released as a free man. Not unless he breaks the law or reports come in that he has. Unfortunately, Spence may disappear into the crowd unless he does something overt, traceable."

"Which he won't because he's smarter than that. He's always been wily." Isa's use of the old-fashioned word forced a smile from Rachel, which she welcomed in the midst of the distressing news.

"Mom, we're doing everything we can to monitor the situation. You have nothing to worry about." Caleb beat Morgan to the bottom line. Morgan reacted by chewing on her pen cap, an old habit ever since they'd gotten brand-new packages of the blue ink pens at the beginning of each semester. Nostalgia pushed into Rachel's awareness, and she blinked back tears while searching for a distraction from the heavy emotions.

Aubrey and Jasper quietly observed the scene while Gavin pecked away on his tablet. Gavin seemed constitutionally unable to turn off his reporter persona. Sensing her stare, he looked up and shot her a conspiratorial wink. She bit her cheek to keep from grinning. A swell of love for her entire family squeezed tight around Rachel's center.

Isa leaned back in her chair and let out a long sigh. "This is tough, but nothing like what we've been through in the past, right? I can see that you're all worried about me. Stop. Just, stop. This is affecting you more, because you've all been so invested in the mission of our Truth Foundation. The truth of this matter is that if Spence is still dirty, it's going to come out. He'll face justice again. It's all in how you spin it at the Foundation."

"We've already reached out to a PR person who does

contract work. And we're looking into hiring a full-time social media person." Morgan spoke.

"The morning coffee club doesn't go on social media a whole lot." Gavin referred to the older seniors in their seventies and eighties who gathered every morning at Blue Larkspur's most popular diner for breakfast, a cup of joe and local gossip. "They're going to get riled up when they find out, if they haven't heard already."

"That's the breaks of small-city life when it has big-time crime." Rachel let her thoughts out, and quickly looked at Isa to make sure her mother wouldn't take it wrong. "I love Blue Larkspur—it's my home, too. But since becoming DA I appreciate more than ever that we face the same challenges as large cities. It's often worse because we don't have all the law enforcement needed to handle them. Morgan, you're smart to hire PR professionals. We have to spin this for the Foundation's, for Blue Larkspur's benefit. Otherwise we're no more than a social media meme promising justice but delivering zilch."

"My only regret is that we can't say the DA supports us." Caleb reminded her that she was recused from the Truth Foundation's work. "But your personal support is appreciated."

Rachel hid another grin. The Coltons were all very much individuals but shared a common passion for their life's work, whatever it was. Just as Gavin couldn't stop being a reporter for a short time at the family dining room table, Caleb couldn't put his eldest-son and legal hats on the shelf.

"My main concern, besides keeping Blue Larkspur safe, is that all of you, especially Isa, are safe." Theo spoke. "Isa had a security system installed recently, so how about the rest of you? Your other siblings who couldn't make it tonight?"

Theo went around the table and took notes as they each responded. Rachel's stomach churned as he got closer to her. She knew she had to tell her family about the note, which made it more real, scarier.

"Rachel?" Theo prompted.

"Gideon installed cameras at my front and back doors two weekends ago, and they work great. But, well, I've got another problem." She had her family's attention. Even Gavin looked up from his tablet.

"James's ex is a stalker. Not in a joking or casual way. It's gone on for almost two years. She's been arrested several times in Denver since he obtained a permanent restraining order against her. Which she's never followed, frankly. Anyway, when he moved to Blue Larkspur, it was partly for his new job—"

"And to step up to fatherhood," Gideon interrupted. Rachel glared at him.

"For your information James didn't know about Iris." She briefly filled them in on how she'd called James and thought he was engaged. "James is certain it was Bethany who answered his phone. It was when he was still trying to be nice to her, be her friend. Before her threats became dark and twisted."

"We get it, Rach." Aubrey spoke up.

"Right. So, you know about the explosion at Ricco's downtown. I was there, with James. It was our first meeting since he's been back."

"You mean 'date.'" Jasper smirked.

"No, no date. I agreed to meet with him to try to feel him out—"

Gavin guffawed when she said "feel" and the rest

of the siblings cracked into silly laughter. Isa hid her mouth behind an elegantly manicured hand and Theo looked down at his notepad.

Rachel's face heated and she fought to keep her temper as a newly discovered emotion pulsed through her veins. *Protectiveness.* Not only for her child, which she was used to, but toward James.

Like a tigress, the urge to slash out at anyone who threatened her baby's father was primal, unmistakable.

"I get it, everyone. You need some comic relief. Please, allow me to provide it at my expense." She tried to infuse her request with exasperation but found herself giggling, too. No one could make her laugh as quickly or hard as her siblings.

"Sorry, not sorry, sis." Jasper's reply was echoed with nods. "Go on."

"Okay, may I finish now? James thinks he saw Bethany in the restaurant moments before the explosion. Add in that I've had some suspicious things happen. Gideon knows about the fuel thinner that was added to my gas tank. Theo knows about the muddy footprints on both my front and back house entrances." She sucked in a deep breath. "What none of you know is that yesterday I received a threatening note in a package that had a bunch of flowers."

She detailed the note and her suspicions, told them her security video had revealed zilch. "I'll get that note to you ASAP."

"Thanks, as soon as you do, I'll send it to the lab."

"There's one more thing—I keep having the sense I'm being watched. The latter is probably my overactive imagination, but the first rule in self-defense is awareness. I've had the being-watched feeling several times over the past two weeks."

"Since James has come back into your life, you mean." Isa's quiet proclamation made everyone turn to her. "We used to call that something else in our day, didn't we?" Isa winked. At Theo. Who blushed like a middle-school boy caught fantasizing about his current crush.

This time Rachel let the table dissolve into giggles. No sense fighting it. Her only regret was that James wasn't at her side, because he deserved to know what they were up against. If they were going to effectively co-parent Iris, it went without saying that their number one job was to keep their baby girl safe, wasn't it?

The sick sensation was back, stirring up her stomach acid.

Were any of them safe with a stalker around and a dangerous criminal about to be put back on the streets?

Chapter 14

"Hey." The touch of Rachel's hand on his shoulder woke James from his uneasy rest on her sofa later that night.

"Hi." He swung his legs down onto the floor and forced himself awake, wondering how he'd drifted off when he needed to be alert for any intruders. The memory of finding the scary letter jolted him to standing. Rachel blinked, eyes luminous in the lamplight, and took a step back.

"You okay?"

"Yes. And Iris is good—she fell asleep before I could finish *Goodnight Moon*. She ate all of her dinner and loves the new boat." He'd brought a windup bath toy for her, noting that she previously only had rubber duckies and soft squirt toys.

"You did say we need to encourage her engineering

gifts." Rachel's soft smile about undid him. Would she be receptive to another kiss, to more?

Security.

He shook his head. "I did, and we do, but I need to talk to you about something serious, Rachel."

"Shoot." She remained standing, as did he, a foot between them.

"When were you going to tell me about the note from Bethany?"

Her eyes widened before she looked up at the ceiling, and her chest rose on an inhale.

"I thought you were here to spend time with your daughter. To bond. Not to snoop through my stuff."

"You left it on the hall table in full view, Rachel. And really, it's not the point. Is this what you were meeting with your family about?"

"No." A quick shake of her head. "Not at all."

"Do they know? Do your brothers know?"

"You speak as if you're worried more about the Colton men than women. We're all a formidable bunch, James."

He'd gotten her hackles up and he hadn't meant to, not about her family. "I don't blame them for being suspicious of me. If my nephew's father showed up months after the birth, I wouldn't be very welcoming either, trust me. But we're in this together and your safety, Iris's, is what matters most to me. Please answer my question, Rachel. Does your family know about the note? About Bethany?"

"Yes, I told them about the note tonight. I was planning to tell you sooner, but this meeting came up..." She threw her hands up in the air. "Let's go talk in the kitchen. Want some tea?"

He wanted something stronger, but becoming Iris's dad and now the ever-present danger from Bethany negated any desire for the tiniest sip of a single malt.

"Sure." Following her to the kitchen, he gave her a more detailed rundown of his evening with Iris as Rachel made the hot drinks.

"You're kidding? She actually tried to wind the bathtub boat by herself?" The sparkle in Rachel's eyes confirmed that she thought their daughter was advanced for her age, too. "She can hardly hold a spoon steady yet."

He sipped his ginger tea. "I'm telling you, she tried to turn the little lever and chattered at me until I did it for her. She misses absolutely nothing." His chest warmed and it wasn't solely from the drink. Being a father was already his favorite job ever. Although, sitting with Rachel, the scent of her reaching him across the counter—strong, sexy, slightly floral—he had to ask himself if he wanted to be more than Iris's co-parent.

"I'm sorry I didn't come to you first about the note, James. I should have. You've had so much come down on you at once. Finding out you're a father, moving, starting a new job. And lest we forget, the constant reminder that Bethany's trying to destroy your life again. I didn't think it was fair to dump it on you, is all."

"One note?"

"There's more I need to fill you in on." Her eyes reflected her contrition. It was impossible to be angry with Rachel when he knew her motives had been in the right place.

He listened as she rehashed everything that had happened to date, including the footprints, her car trouble. "My family laughed and tried to joke about it when I told them I keep thinking someone's watching me, but that's their way of breaking the tension. They're worried, too. I can't leave my house without looking over both shoulders, I can only imagine how you feel after dealing with this for so much longer. And the cameras Gideon installed aren't enough, not if I can't conclusively identify who left the note with the flowers."

"There's only one solution to this, Rachel."

She shook her head. "I'm not leaving my own house, James. As much as it all points to Bethany, there's a decent chance I'm being warned off by a local crime ring." She told him about her case docket. "There are at least half a dozen culprits but definitely one in particular who'd like to scare me off a strong prosecution."

He wished they were talking about anything but the potential danger surrounding them. His body reacted as if they weren't in the crosshairs of predators. Whether it was Bethany or one of Rachel's suspects didn't matter. A threat to his family was just that. A threat.

She sipped her tea, a lavender concoction that mingled with her scent. His awareness of her every move shot to his crotch. Unlike the previous times Rachel had aroused him, though, this time he wasn't flashing back to how it had been in Helena. Or even that kiss in her mother's backyard.

James wanted to know what Rachel felt like moving against him now. Tonight. It was almost scarier than having a stalker. Accepting she had so much power over him.

"What are you thinking?" She'd picked up on his mood. Always.

"Come on. I have a great poker face."

"You do, except I know you well enough that when

I see those lines at the corners of your eyes, you're either angry or ready to break out laughing."

He grunted. "It's both. I'm beyond mad that anyone would try to threaten you or Iris."

"And the second?"

He stared into her eyes, unable to articulate that what he wanted to do wasn't just a physical need. Come to think of it, neither had it been in Helena. Sure, they'd had a solid dose of insta-lust, no question. But it hadn't been her killer bod or beautiful smile that had attracted him, not at first. Rachel's intelligence, the way she seemed to vibrate with a strength and passion he didn't see in other women. Those had been the draw.

"James?" She licked her lips, leaned in toward him.

James cupped her face. The softness of her cheek under his thumb pad sent zings of sexual awareness down his arms and straight to between his legs.

"Babe." He leaned in and kissed her across the breakfast counter. Unlike the exploratory, almost languid kiss at Isa Colton's house, when their lips touched now, it was the bridge to their all-consuming connection. He needed more; no, not more. He wanted *all* of her.

Rachel's tongue met his at the same moment he plunged his into her mouth, and James let go of all restraint. He crushed her lips with his mouth, his hands around her head.

"I need you, Rachel." His voice hitched, his heart slamming against his ribs.

Rachel stepped around the counter and tugged at him, evidently wanting him off the barstool. "What do you want, James?" Eyes half-lidded, her lips red and swollen.

"This." He stood and turned the stool around so that

the back was against the sturdy nook. He sat back down and grasped her waist to lift her, but she already had a leg over him, wriggling the rest of the way to straddle him. The contact of her softness against his arousal was at once the sweetest and sexiest moment of his life.

"Like this?" She gyrated her pelvis in an ageless move of seduction. Except where Rachel was concerned, no seduction was needed.

"More like this." He strung his fingers through her hair, clasped his hand on the base of her head and pulled her mouth to his. As their kiss deepened, he pushed against the small of her back with his free hand, then trailed it up, up her spine, unsnapping her bra and reaching around her front in a single move. Her breast, heavy as it filled his palm, was hot. On fire, like him. He tweaked her pebbled nipple and she cried out, nipped his neck with frustrated love bites.

"James, please. Please. Never stop this. Never."

"It's a deal." He plundered her mouth again, needing every lick and taste of her. Wanting more, knowing it would never be enough. Not with Rachel.

"I have to taste you, all of you."

"Let's go to my bedroom."

"Wait, what about Iris? What if we wake her?"

She gasped out a giggle. "I have a baby monitor on in my bedroom, too. Look, she's fine." She pointed at the video monitor on the counter where an image of their baby sleeping on her side, the sound of her soft breathing, verified Iris was all right. "I ran the vacuum, made all the usual loud noises when she was tiny. She sleeps like a rock."

"Good to know." He tried to not be rough as he held her ass in his hands and lifted both of them from the stool. Her legs automatically circled his waist, and he thought his knees might buckle from the heady desire that rushed through him. It didn't escape him that the dining table was closest, the sofa nearby.

"Stop thinking, James." She saw his gaze wander and looked over her shoulder at the sofa. "Not this time. Take me to my bed, babe."

James let her down so gently it belied the next moments as he quickly shucked his clothing while she scrambled out of hers. They allowed one another a chance to take in each other's full nudity, but urgency strummed through every single nerve ending as she looked at him and pointed to the side of the bed.

"Condoms are in the nightstand drawer. Not that it helped last time." Her breath hitched and she saw his reflexive breath when his chest rose, displaying his strawberry blond hair, which dusted his magnificent pecs. Not the most stunning part of him, though. She trailed her gaze south, took in the full length of him. Her mouth watered in sync with the dampness between her legs as she trembled with need.

"Are you sure, Rachel?" His slightly raised brows revealed that while he was sincere in needing her consent, he also knew what he was doing to her.

"James I've never been more certain about anything. I have to make love to you. If you don't come here—"

He prowled the two steps to the bed and covered her with his sinewy length before she finished, covered her mouth with his. Had she ever met a better kisser? A better stroker? A better lover?

No.

Her mind wanted to go over how wonderful a father James was, how that had surprised her, how he wasn't the corporate shark she'd judged him to be, but his hands and tongue turned her mind to mush. Well, not mush but a sensuous center that put her entire body, her soul into a pleasure zone she'd never visited before. The time in Helena had been hot and fulfilled not only her fantasies but all of her sexual needs. Now, tonight, she knew James. He knew his child.

James knew Rachel's every need.

"Oh my, that's—that's…" She gasped for air as his fingers plunged into her slick, wet folds while his thumb circled her most sensitive spot.

"Stop thinking, Rachel." His laughter rumbled low in his throat but he needn't have repeated her earlier admonition. Waves of an intense orgasm made her back arch, her insides spasm against his fingers.

Before she came down from the climax, he'd donned a condom. Braced above her, a forearm on either side of her head, his eyes were emerald points of need, his open mouth irresistible. Their lips met at the same moment he entered her.

Nothing about sex or mutual satisfaction was new to Rachel, and James's evident expertise mirrored it was the same for him. But as they moved together, watching each other for what heightened their pleasure the most, she caught glimpses of a place she'd never been before. Paradise. Heaven.

James waited until she began her second climax before she heard his breath hitch again, the deep groan emanating from his chest. They each cried out as the waves hit them, and Rachel knew what was different when she made love to James.

They shared more than a physical, or child, connection. Theirs was a heart pact. When or where it had happened, she didn't know, but what Rachel was certain of was that she'd never have a connection like this with anyone else.

Chapter 15

They lay next to one another, holding hands for long moments after. James was at a loss for words, a rarity for an attorney and definitely for him.

"That was incredible." Rachel spoke first. He dug deep for the strength to rise up on his elbow and look at her. He never wanted to talk to her without seeing her every reaction, the way her eyelashes framed her expressive eyes or how her mouth quirked into a dimple on her left cheek.

"More than incredible, I'd say." He stroked her hair back before allowing his fingers to travel around her face, down her throat, between her breasts. "You're the most beautiful woman in the world, Rachel."

She turned her head to meet his gaze and tugged on his short hair, leaned up for a lingering kiss. "You make me feel that way, for sure."

"I'm not leaving, you know."

She smiled. "I'm glad. I wasn't sure if you'd like Blue Larkspur enough to stay."

An icy splash of reality cut through his sensual reverie. "It has nothing to do with the location." He rolled away, sat on the side of the bed. It wasn't the time to try to express the jumble of emotions tearing his heart wide open. And he wasn't going *there*, to the part of him that knew wherever Rachel and Iris were was where he belonged. Instead he tried to focus on what needed to be done, here and now.

"Hold that thought." She scrambled off the bed, disappeared into the bathroom for a few minutes before returning in a too-sexy, red-and-white-flower-print silk kimono. He liked the way the hem flirted with being just shy of indecent, revealing her robust, creamy thighs. James had zero attraction to superskinny women. Rachel's curves and softness were the ideal of femininity to him.

"So, moving here had nothing to do with Blue Larkspur's geolocation?" A soft smile played across her luscious lips.

"I can't have this conversation with you right now, Rachel. My first priority has to be keeping you both safe. I'm moving in with you and Iris. And not because we just made love." He put his jeans on. "I'll be sleeping on the couch tonight. I have to leave early tomorrow morning, to get to my condo and shower before work. Tomorrow I'll come here straight from the firm, packed for the duration. You and Iris are never going to be alone. Not until your cases are closed and we know for certain if it's Bethany or not. If it is Bethany, then she needs to be caught. Helped."

"Whoa. Hang on a sec."

As she ran her fingers through her hair, his own twitched to feel the silky locks. How could he be hard for her again, so soon?

"You don't have to move in here. Gideon installed the cameras, and I'll upgrade to a better security system."

"Not enough. No matter who's stalking you, they mean business. This isn't kid stuff, Rachel."

"Don't you think I, of all people, know that? Darn it, James! Self-serving criminals, including my own danged father, have wreaked havoc on my life since I was a kid. My father was crooked for years before his death. In fact, you could say I was born into crime."

Regret yanked at his resolve to detach from what they'd just shared so that he could be the protection she and Iris deserved. "Stop it. You're not your father."

"Yeah, look how well being his daughter worked out." The lines above her brow deepened and she blew out a frustrated breath. "Spence is free to be the awful man he is and hurt the innocent citizens of our town again." She crossed her arms in front of her. "No matter how much good the Truth Foundation does, it'll never be enough."

"Rachel." He took a step closer, not missing the irony of having to walk on eggshells after sharing the most cataclysmic orgasm of his life with her minutes earlier. He stood still, steady. "It's not your responsibility to fix the wrongs of your father."

Her eyes blazed. "That's just it, James—it *is* my job. Whether it's with my family's nonprofit or as an elected official on a government salary, I'll never stop making amends for what he did. You can't pay back those who served years of unnecessary time."

"I'm sorry. I'm not trying to do anything here but

support you. My dad died when I was still a tiny kid, so like you, I lost him too soon. But I don't have the crappy legacy your father left you with. And to be honest? I'm not half the person you are. That's what I liked about you from the start, Rachel. You don't back down from what you know to be right."

She shrugged and nodded. "Thanks for that. I know I'm being uptight, but it's hard not—"

The sound of breaking glass, quickly followed by a solid thump, reached them. James held his hand up to Rachel.

"Stay here." He ran out of the room, to the nursery. Iris was safe and sleeping, but he took her from the crib anyway. Rachel was on his heels and he nodded at the master bedroom door. "Back to your room. Fast!"

Once in her room again, he handed the baby to her. "Don't go anywhere until I tell you it's clear. Where's your phone?"

"On the nightstand." She was already there, clutching the still-sleeping Iris in the crook of her arm as she grabbed the phone with her other hand.

"Call 9-1-1. If you hear any kind of trouble, go out the sliding door and run to your neighbor's."

"It's Rachel Colton, DA." Fear coursed through her as she identified herself to the emergency services dispatcher. She hoped that when she'd said "DA," the dispatcher would alert the cruisers in her area more quickly. Theo had already assigned extra patrols on her house, so she was certain the response would be faster than normal.

"Stay on the line, ma'am. I'll have a unit there in two minutes."

"Thanks." She wrapped her arms around Iris, kissed her sweet head. The baby snuggled in closer, knowing her mother's embrace without waking. Rachel thought that if the crashing sound hadn't woken her daughter, then Rachel's pounding heart would.

It was impossible to hear what was going on in the front of the house, and she had to fight to keep herself from escaping through the master bedroom's sliding glass doors. If there was a prowler on her property, she'd be putting them both at risk. But her instinct to run was primal, and her entire body shook with the adrenaline rush.

A dark shadow appeared at the patio door and she gasped, until the motion detector light activated and she made out Theo's form. She unlocked the door with shaking hands.

"You both okay?" In pure cop mode, Theo's gaze assessed her and Iris for injury.

"Yes, yes. James went to see what happened."

He nodded. "I know. He's out front, giving the officers a report. My team's combing your living room."

"I guess you don't need me to keep the line open anymore." She went to disconnect the call to 9-1-1, but Theo stopped her and took her phone.

"Chief Theo Lawson. Who's this?"

Rachel waited as he confirmed the call had been handled and disconnected.

"What happened?"

"Put the baby down and I'll show you."

"I'm not leaving her alone back here. Not yet."

"She's safe, Rachel. You're safe. It's over."

James came in through the bedroom door, took in

the scene of Rachel stubbornly holding on to Iris, nodded at the chief.

"I gave my report, and they're going to take the brick with them."

"A *brick*?" Her voice rose in pitch without effort. "What we heard was a brick through the front window?"

"No, your transom over the front door." James walked to her and took Iris from her arms. "Let me hold her and get her back down while you go with Theo and see what happened."

Rachel didn't want to let go of Iris but realized she completely trusted James. If he thought it was safe, then it was.

She followed Theo into the front room, to the foyer. Shards of glass were scattered randomly across the high-gloss hardwood, and as she looked up she saw the center pane of three that made up the rectangular window was a gaping hole. An officer took photos of the scene, then placed a plain brown brick into an evidence bag.

"Why would someone do this? And why the door instead of the front picture window?" She couldn't keep her voice from shaking.

"They wanted to scare you, to get your attention." Theo's familiar voice soothed her.

Rachel squatted near where the brick had landed. The small scar in the varnish was a reminder that they were lucky no one was injured. "Was there a message with it?"

The officer looked at Theo.

"Show her," Theo said.

The officer turned the rectangle upside down, and she made out the two words painted in bright red.

BACK OFF.

"Wow. No mistaking the meaning." Nausea swirled with anxiety in her belly. No matter what, she had to keep her baby safe. The officers present would file their reports but that took time. Time that her internal warning system told her was running out. "Iris and I are going to have to leave town. Or maybe she should stay with my mother."

Theo looked at her with compassion, and something else. Knowing. "I understand your logic. I'd want to do the same in your position."

"But?"

"But short of leaving the state, whoever this is, one of your defendants or Bethany Austin, they're going to follow you wherever you go. No place is safe for you until they're caught."

"Well gee, Theo, color me reassured." She knew she was being caustic, but her daughter's life was on the line. What if Iris was crawling already and had been on the floor?

James stood beside her. "The baby's back down, and I have the monitor." He held up the device that they usually kept on the kitchen counter. He looked at Theo. "I told Rachel earlier that I think it's a good idea that I stay here until we make sure we know who's behind *all* of the criminal pranks."

"Excellent choice. In fact, the best one, short of having an officer check in on you and Iris hourly." Theo chimed in so quickly that suspicion raised its head in Rachel's thoughts.

"I could go to my mother's…" She trailed off and was grateful James and Theo gave her the space needed to figure it out. Going to Isa's wasn't acceptable. She didn't want any bad guy following her there. Plus, the Colton house was too far from downtown Blue Larkspur. Rachel relished living this close to the courthouse and her office. Not to mention the police.

"I have to say, BLPD was here almost before I'd finished requesting help. I know that you have a team spending more time in my neighborhood, but still, I appreciate the quick response."

Theo nodded. "Yes, that's another solid reason to stay here, in your own home."

"I'll be here." James stood next to her, a steady presence as two more officers appeared and began taking evidence samples with tiny brushes, putting them into small, tightly sealed plastic bags.

Rachel's head pounded, and the heavy weight on her chest made it hard to focus on anything but curling up on the sofa and going to sleep. She had zero fight left.

What harm would it do to have James live with her and Iris? It would give him more time with his daughter, too. Win-win.

"Okay, you two are right. I'll have a professional security team come and install a top-of-the-line system tomorrow. I'll pay for any expenses that exceed the DA private-home budget out of my pocket. James, of course you're more than welcome to stay here. While the sofa in the front room is a queen sleeper, I have a perfectly comfortable guest room. Use that."

Theo cleared his throat. "I'd be more comfortable if James stayed in the front room, close to the window and front door. An intruder would have to pass him first. Combined with our amplified patrols, it'll give you just about the highest level of security possible."

"What's the highest?" She'd thought it would be

what Theo had already proposed, what James had insisted upon.

"When your harasser is either arrested, behind bars or dead." Theo minced no words and didn't wait for either of them to reply. "My team will be out of here within the hour. Go ahead and finish up your usual nighttime routine. We'll make sure the broken window is boarded up. Get it fixed as soon as possible, Rachel. If you can't find anyone, I'm happy to come out tomorrow after work and help."

"That won't be necessary. I'll take care of it." James spoke up. "I'll call in a personal day tomorrow."

Relief flowed through her tense shoulder muscles. "That's not necessary. You've only just started your job! Emily takes great care of Iris and has alerted me to any little change she notices."

"I'm not saying to tell her not to come. I'll need her here to watch Iris. I can work on my cases remotely. I'm not due back in court for two weeks. My job is wherever my laptop is. You, on the other hand, can't work from home. Am I right?"

She nodded.

Theo grasped her shoulder and gave it a firm squeeze. "I'll leave you two to it. Rachel, do you have any plywood in your garage?"

"Actually, yes. There are some small pieces on top of the workbench. Gideon left them after he built a platform for the back camera. The light and garage opener switch are to the right of the entry." She heard the heavy door open.

"I'm going to check on Iris for a sec." James spoke. "But when I get back, let's sit down and go over your case docket. I want to know as much as possible about each one, including the names of the defendants." He turned and she watched him retreat down the hallway.

Comfort conflicted with resistance as she processed the fact it'd be a sight she'd better get used to. James was moving in—and not just into her house.

Chapter 16

"I think you'd be fine sleeping in the guest room at this point. It's been well over a week since the brick." And the dead-flower delivery, which he noted Rachel didn't mention.

They sat at the dining room table, a pot of tea between them. Iris was in bed, and the routine they'd established had begun to feel normal to James.

Each night after Iris was down, they'd spend two to three hours scouring Rachel's case files, both as assistant DA and DA. And every night Rachel went to her bedroom alone and James camped out on the sofa.

"Your sofa's just as comfortable as the guest bed. Besides, I'd get zero sleep back there. I need to be up front." He knew he'd never get any rest if he wasn't near the house's main entry.

"You're a lawyer, not a police officer or security specialist."

"I'm in this with you. I've already missed out on too much time with both of you. I'm Iris's father. Nothing is coming between me and her." *And you.* He couldn't say the last but the urge to protect Rachel was as much a part of him as needing to breathe. He'd convinced himself that it was only because she was Iris's mother. That, in his effort to make up for lost time, he'd gone a little overboard, especially when they made love last week. He'd thought they'd gone to bed together again because they had a shared attraction. At least that's what he'd tried to convince himself. Because if that wasn't the primary reason, if he was developing feelings at a deeper level than ever before, James needed to move carefully. The last thing he wanted to do was push Rachel away by being too impatient and rushing whatever this connection between them might grow into.

"You're in that overthinking place again. Here. Have some tea." She'd mistaken his sudden quiet for something completely different, a good thing. It seemed a mutual decision to avoid physical contact, and he knew it was for the best. Yet her presence, her scent, her quick smile made it difficult to convince his body to take a step back.

"Thanks. I still don't know how you think this helps with clear thinking." He'd come to enjoy the spicy aroma and taste.

Laughter made her eyes sparkle, offered a relief from the heaviness of what they were fighting together. "Did I say that? It was just to get you to drink it. Ginger tea is my go-to since having Iris. I like peppermint, too, but it's best to keep it an occasional treat while I'm still breastfeeding."

"It never occurred to me that you have to be careful with something like herbal tea."

"Yeah, keeping it decaf isn't enough of a safety precaution."

"How long will you breastfeed?" He'd been mesmerized by how reverent the ritual was between mother and daughter, honored that Rachel didn't hide it all from him.

"I'd like to nurse her the entire year. Iris is ravenous and, as you know, needs more solid food each day. I'm not sure if she's going to want to nurse the entire twelve months. My mother says I quit around eleven months, only latching on for a bit at a time toward the end. Not that I totally rely on her anecdotal evidence. She had twelve kids, after all." She laughed and he joined in.

"You're such a great mother, Rachel. I don't know how you do it—nurse her morning and night, pump and freeze milk at work, oh, and be a full-time DA." His words came out without any forethought, unusual for him. But he'd been changing, becoming more comfortable around her. He knew his mental filters existed for good reason; he'd been burned by women before.

Rachel's different.

She shrugged, a blush on her smooth skin. "I never comprehended the work, the hours that a baby takes. But it's as though she's always been here, you know? Before Iris, I couldn't imagine having a child, not this soon. Although at thirty-four, I suppose I should have started thinking about it. Now that she's here, I can't for one instant imagine my life without her."

"Same. I don't have to do all the physical lifting you do. My gosh, you carried her for over nine months, labored with her, had her. But I feel the same as far as feeling she's always been a part of me."

"Yeah." Rachel nodded, tapped her hand on the stack of files that sat between their laptops. "We still haven't narrowed down any suspects."

"There are two I'd place as most likely to have thrown the brick. Your most recent case and Bethany."

"My money's on the Parson case. You're convinced it's Bethany. I can tell. And I appreciate that, James, because let's face it, you've been traumatized by her. I understand trauma. Why do you think my dad's crimes still haunt me?" Her hand reached across the table and covered his. A brief touch, but it burned. He fought to keep his palm flat down instead of turning it right side up, grasping her hand, pulling her toward him.

"Your father was a complicated man. But he was *your dad*, Rachel. Bethany was barely a friend. At this point I feel I owe her nothing, except to see that she gets the help she needs."

"If it turns out it's Bethany, we'll both make sure that happens."

"If it's a criminal you've prosecuted?"

"Then we turn to Theo and BLPD to weed out all the other jerks who helped this person harass me." Her beauty was stark against the exhaustion he'd noticed creeping in since they'd met in the restaurant. Sure, Rachel had new-mother exhaustion. But she'd had a verve in her step that he hated to see hammered away by the incessant threats.

"I'm going to do everything to catch whoever it is, Rachel."

"I know you are." She looked at her smartwatch. "I've got three cases tomorrow. How about you?"

"I'll work here 'til noon, then I'm in court through the rest of the day, too."

"See you same time, same place?" She stood and took both of their mugs in one hand, the teapot in the other. He moved the files to the opposite end of the table, away from Iris's high chair and where they'd all have breakfast together tomorrow morning.

"I wouldn't miss it." As he prepared for another night on the sofa, the sense that he was exactly where he was meant to be hit him harder than the thrill of winning any of his biggest cases ever had.

But there was at least one, possibly two criminals who weren't afraid of harming Rachel or Iris. Until they were stopped, his heart would have to wait.

Rachel's bed seemed humongous as she tried to get to sleep. Knowing James was in the front of the house brought as much comfort as it did frustration. It wasn't sexual frustration, either. Sure, that was a part of it, but whatever was going on between her and James was getting deeper, stronger. If it was just her heart on the line, she'd deal with it. She was a prosecuting attorney, the daughter of a man who'd betrayed the community. Risking her heart was scary but doable.

But not her daughter's.

Her phone vibrated on silent mode, and she was grateful for the distraction.

"Mom! What are you doing up at this hour?"

"Please, it's not that late. I had a project I needed to put to bed and I'm having a cup of chamomile in the tub."

Rachel laughed. Isa had been a bath lover from long back. "Maybe I should take one."

"Oh, trouble sleeping?"

"No, yes. I mean, well, maybe."

"I'm sure you're worried after all the goings on at your place. Theo assures me that you'll be fine. Between the PD and both you and James, the crooks don't have a chance."

"Thanks, Mom. I'd like to think that, too."

"So let me guess. Is it James? Please tell me you're still not making him sleep on the sofa. Your sex life is none of my business—"

"No, Mom, it's not." Her cheeks heated before she heard her tone. "I'm not ready to give in to it, Mom. I have no way of knowing if James is really interested in me because I'm me, or because of Iris."

"They're one and the same, honey. You can't separate the two—you come as a whole package. And whatever you do, don't base your relationship with James on mine with your dad. Your father made a lot of mistakes, no question, but we had a lot of happy times together before he went to the dark side."

"You've certainly worked through your grief and blaming yourself for his actions. I'm proud of you, Mom." She was. Her mother was the strongest person she knew.

"After twenty years, it's about time, isn't it?"

"Yes."

"I know I've said it before, but please believe me when I say that life is short. Don't waste any more time than you have to when it comes to a man you care about."

"You may be right, Mom." She couldn't think about her future with James. Not while she was looking over her shoulder every minute of every day.

"You sound a little sleepy. Any chance you'll get some rest now?" Isa asked.

Rachel yawned. "Yeah, I think I just might. Thanks for calling, Mom."

"Night, night."

They disconnected and Rachel lay back on her pillows, glad for the call but suddenly wide-awake. Again. Were her feelings for James that obvious to everyone?

Chapter 17

"Please, Rachel. Trust me on this." James reversed out of her mother's driveway, deftly switched gears on the manual transmission and drove them out of the subdivision. The weekend after the brick crashed through Rachel's window, James had surprised her with what he said was a "relaxation day." They were in his BMW, which seemed incongruous to the way he'd told her to dress. Both were in outdoor gear, as if going on a hike. But she hadn't noticed trekking poles in the trunk or back seat when they'd loaded all of Iris's paraphernalia and strapped her into her car seat earlier.

"I'm still not over the fact that you planned this with my mother behind my back. Although my mom sure loves any chance she can get to spend a day with Iris." She gave him a playful punch to his upper arm to make certain he knew she was kidding. "Actually, it's kind of nice to have something other than work to worry about."

And being stalked, no matter by whom. They'd pored over her caseload, checked and rechecked the backgrounds of the criminals she prosecuted. But little progress for their hours of labor. Their research had underscored the cunning presence of the underbelly of the community she loved and never wanted to see suffer at such brutal hands.

James's hand on her thigh spun her thoughts from investigative mode to her confused heart. He kept his focus on the road as he spoke.

"You need a break. And we need time alone together. Co-parents should be on the same page, know one another well enough to be a team."

"Sure. But what does that have to do with this mystery…day." She'd almost said "date." And he'd not made a move to take her back to bed since last week, when her world had forever changed with his lovemaking. No matter whether they somehow became more than co-parents— a place she couldn't let her heart go, not when she was in mortal fear for her daughter's safety—she knew deep down that no one else would ever be able to elicit such a primal, passionate response from her.

But life was about more than sex, even more than romance. She was a mother with a daughter to provide for and the DA for a county that deserved all she was able to give. Wouldn't becoming emotionally dependent on James be a distraction she couldn't afford?

"Rach, please let go. Trust me. It's going to be fun." He squeezed her thigh.

"I don't know how you do it. You always know my mood. Okay, I'm letting go." But as she looked out the window, saw the direction he was taking them, her anxiety edged in. "Wait a minute—if we're not hiking, and

I know you wouldn't bike without your mountain bike, please tell me we're not rafting. Isn't it too early in the season, anyway?"

"Okay, I won't tell you. And no, there are a couple who open earlier." The flash of white on his tanned skin reflected how thrilled he was to have planned this. And his complete ignorance of her white-water revulsion.

"James, I don't like to white-water raft."

"Because of what happened when you were twelve?"

"Let me guess. One of my siblings told you about my bad, nearly traumatic, rafting event as a young girl? All of them think I don't raft because I'm being stubborn. But they weren't the one left scared to death."

"I can confirm or deny nothing." James's smile was small but it was enough to trigger her emotions from that fateful day decades ago.

Shame, embarrassment and a sense of betrayal fought for first billing as she twisted in her seat to make her point. "I don't know which of my brothers or sisters told you, and I know it was one of them because Mom wasn't on the trip and doesn't know how traumatic it was for me. But I'm going to kill them when I see them."

"Careful with such a strong word." He maneuvered a mountain turn as well as his voice soothed her. She hated to admit it, but simply being next to him, in any capacity, calmed her. Except when she thought of sitting in a rubber raft.

"James, we flipped that day. Gideon and I got out of the water only because of luck." The rest of her siblings there had been old enough to basically stand and walk out where the river calmed, which was right after where both rafts had collided and flipped. Caleb and Morgan were seventeen; Oliver, Ezra and Dominic were fourteen; she was twelve, and Gideon was ten. The younger kids had stayed home with Isa, who would have had a stroke on the spot if she'd seen what Ben Colton's idea of fun had turned into. Rachel had never set foot on a river raft again.

"You made it out safe due to luck, or good safety precautions taken by your father?"

The reminder that Ben had loved his children, his family, the best he could, did little to stop the fear that pushed up her throat, tightened every muscle in her body.

"He had trained us well. I give him that." A harsh laugh escaped her. "It's ironic that all of my siblings still enjoy a day on the river."

"Why do you think you're the one that took it the other direction, Rach?" He was pulling off the highway now, and she did her best to ignore the road signs that screamed where the white-water rafting exits were.

"I don't know. It was terrifying, James. One minute we're bouncing along, yelling our heads off. My dad was in the raft with us—me, Gideon and Ezra—and the others were with his friend. Our rafts weren't supposed to get that close to each other, but there's no controlling the river rapids during snowmelt. Of course, today they won't let you on that stretch unless you're sixteen or older."

"Were you having fun until your raft overturned?"

"I was, yes. Yes. But it didn't just flip. I don't know what everyone else told you, but I remember we smashed into one another so hard my head knocked back and hit my dad's helmet. Then we capsized. I was under the water for what felt like hours, but I know couldn't have been more than a few seconds." It had been so cold, compared to the warm spring day. Exactly like today, in fact. "I'm a good swimmer. We all are. Mom and Dad didn't skimp on Red Cross swimming lessons."

"But you think your father took a shortcut with the rafting trip that day?"

"Maybe. I don't know. You don't have to be with an official guide or anything. And it would have cost a lot for all of us to go if we'd paid. Dad's friend had the two rafts that we used."

"So this is why Isa wished me luck earlier."

"You told her where we were going? And she didn't tell you not to bother? She wasn't there but she knows I don't raft."

"Yes and no. She didn't say anything but 'best of luck.'" She watched his profile as he merged onto a busy road. His profile reminded her of Iris's. Already, she could tell that her daughter, their daughter, was going to have her daddy's nose. Long, straight, definitive. And she had the same shape to her eyebrows.

James shot her a quick glance as he stopped at a light. "What?"

"It's remarkable how much Iris resembles you, do you know that?"

He chuckled, which for James was a soft grumble low in his throat. As sensuous as his tongue on the most intimate parts of her body. Too hot for comfort, Rachel's finger felt for the window button and lowered hers. James's brow rose, but he didn't acknowledge the bright red that she knew had to be visible on her face.

"I've been sending my family so many photos of her that they're going to all block me. But my mother, she's over the moon about her and keeps saying that Iris is an exact mini-me. I'll have to get some of my baby pictures the next time I'm home."

"We're already halfway to Denver." The nearest white water to Blue Larkspur was a few hours away, on the way to Denver. She looked out her window as the light turned green and they inched forward in with the long row of cars. "We should have brought Iris with us." It hadn't been more than an hour, and she'd started missing her baby before they left. James didn't display any regret at leaving her for the day, from what she could tell.

"I miss her, too." Surprise zinged through her center, warmed the spot under her rib cage.

"You do?"

"Of course I do," he said. "Granted, I missed out on a lot, but it doesn't make my bonding experience any less intense. I used to listen to my siblings talk about how hard it was to leave their babies for that first day of work, both my brothers and sisters, by the way, and while I thought I empathized, I had no clue. None at all."

"It's impossible to know the joy, love and abject terror having your own child can bring into your life. Not until you're a parent. That's my experience, anyway."

"My family wants to have both you and Iris over for dinner sometime soon,. As soon as I told them about Iris, and you, they were over the moon."

James never avoided questions or confrontation, from what she knew of him. She'd give him a pass, for now. Maybe he needed the break from the long hours with Iris. No matter that Emily was with their daughter during the workday, it was often a two-person job when it came to the tiny girl's care and feeding. How many times had she wished she had a partner to share the weight of the load?

"Next month, maybe?" She mentally skimmed her schedule, wondering where it might fit in.

"If not sooner. I'm hoping we could get out of work a little earlier on a Friday and drive up there. My brother has a huge house we can stay in, and my mother lives less than five minutes from him."

"I'll, um, have to check my calendar once we're home. Some last-minute meetings were planned yesterday and I don't know which days they're on."

"Great." He pulled under a large blue-and-yellow sign that proclaimed Colorado River Rapids as the world's most challenging. Her stomach dipped.

"I don't know about that sign. Isn't it false advertising? The snowmelt hasn't been as much as they'd hoped this year. But it's early yet, barely begun." *Please, please don't let this be awful.*

"Which should make our ride more on the relaxing side, then." He followed the parking attendant's arm signals and aimed for a spot that seemed miles from the entrance, on a grassy stretch of land next to the paved lot. "There's a lot more visitors today than the last time I was here, last year."

"This time last year I was just getting over my morning sickness." Not wanting to drive home the fact he'd missed it, she scrambled for a new topic. "Maybe there are more people here because it's a smoother day, and a good time to bring families of all ages." But a heavy downpour was predicted later, too. Which meant a possibly rougher ride. She had to stay off her weather app.

"Hmm." He maneuvered to back into his appointed spot, and even though his car had a rear dash cam, he relied only on his visual reference. With his arm across the back of the seat and him turned toward her, looking over his right shoulder through the rear window, it was impossible to ignore the scent that she'd come to associate with him. Fresh, sometimes minty, always pure James.

Go in another direction. Her current train of thought would lead to where any thoughts of James invariably did. Would he still be around, interested in her as more than Iris's mother, over the next months, years? How did she feel about that? How would she take it if he found someone else to partner with, possibly marry? Would Iris get along with any possible stepsiblings?

"Tell me what's on your mind, Rach." He shifted from Reverse to Drive. Had he noticed the emotional upheaval on her face?

"Why don't you use your rear camera?" *Good one. That'll distract him—not.*

"My camera, eh? Okay, I'll play along. It isn't accurate. I trust my eyes better than a backup camera." He finished parking and cut the engine.

"It's kind of scary, when I think about it."

"What, that I used my vision instead of a screen?"

"No, that we're more alike than I want to admit. We need to see the proof ourselves. About everything. You know, obsessive." She couldn't stop her chattering if she wanted to. The throngs of people heading toward the rafting tour office triggered a sense of inadequacy. Why couldn't she get past the accident from so long ago? Her siblings had.

"I'd like to think that's what makes us good attorneys."

"What's that?"

"Our attention to detail." He spoke slowly, eyeing her as if she were a bat caught in a net.

"Oh yes, yes, it does help with legal work." And other things. It meant that they didn't settle for second-best, that neither would be here alone with one another unless they very much wanted to.

He faced her in the car, as physically close as they'd been in a week, save for when dressing, bathing or feeding Iris together. "Look, I don't want you to be absolutely miserable all day. This is my bad. I thought that once you got used to the idea, you'd be able to enjoy it. We can forget the rafting and take an easy all-day hike. I know several spots—"

"Are you kidding me? And have my family find out that I chickened out? No. Freakin'. Way." She reached for her door handle. "I'll be fine. Where do we line up?"

Anger seethed in Bethany's intestines. Twisting, cramping, taking away any illusion that she had much time left to prove herself to James. To get rid of Rachel Colton.

Except it couldn't happen today, because when she'd been following the three of them over to Rachel's mother's house, her car had begun to sputter. Bethany couldn't afford anyone noticing her or her beater, no matter that she was careful to always follow at a decent distance. If she'd been smarter, she'd have spent her money on a GPS tracking device and stuck it to James's or Rachel's cars, instead of blowing her cash on the spy cameras. But it would have been torturous to not know what they were doing in that house.

She couldn't see the bedrooms or nursery, but there was enough action in the front room to let her know that

James and Rachel were getting too close. There hadn't been any sign of touching this week, but she didn't like how their heads had bent over the same computer screen too many times. Probably working on some dumb legal case that Rachel made up just to get James's attention. Women did that all the time with the men Bethany fell for. Rachel wasn't the first woman to get in the way of Bethany's love life. But she'd be the last.

It still infuriated her that James was being used by Rachel as a babysitter, too. He was at that house all day with the nanny and kid. Bethany saw the cops pull up last week, late at night, while she sat in the tree, two houses over. It hid her perfectly. She parked her car at a supermarket two miles away and walked into the neighborhood after dark. Usually she climbed down and went back to her car to sleep through the hours she'd learned that Rachel slept.

Not that she'd gotten a lot of sleep, not since it had occurred to her that the brat might be James's. But the thought of Rachel having that kind of hold on James made Bethany so angry. And gave her more reason to take care of Rachel Colton.

The night the cops showed up, something odd had happened at the house. A bunch of police cars had shown up. The cop presence had prevented her from getting out of the tree until early the next morning. She'd gotten lucky. The noise and big trucks gave her something to hide behind. It had been a real pain, acting like a perky jogger as she circled and left the large neighborhood. And she'd been tired for the rest of the day. But she'd gotten away, as she always did. Except that one time with the explosion in James's Denver condo.

She still didn't know why the cops were called to Rachel's that night, though. Probably another thing Miss DA did to cause more trauma-drama and get James to take pity on her and her squalling brat. Oh yeah, she'd heard that kid screaming more than once. James was going to be so much happier without the kid and clingy DA.

Soon, James.

It was a major bummer that her car had kept her from following James and Rachel, but there was a silver lining to the lousy day. Her vehicle had died, but not until she spotted the run-down, mom-and-pop place outside town. If not for the gullible auto mechanic who'd been so eager to help, she'd be getting around on some bike she'd stolen. It had only taken one calculated act to convince the guy that it was worth making her car run smooth again for the little cash she had left in her pocket.

She hauled her stuff back into her trunk and tried to ignore the cramps in her lower back. It was getting old, her routine of hiding her clothing and personal items in an abandoned homesite each and every time she watched or followed James and Rachel. But it was a necessary precaution in case she was pulled over. There was no need to give any clues away that she was living out of her car, that she fit the description of the woman they were looking for.

Maybe she'd missed out on whatever James and Rachel were doing at Isa Colton's place. But it wouldn't stop her from checking out Rachel's house.

She smirked to herself. The local cops were stupid. Their patrols around the DA's home were so regular that Bethany was able to beat them at their game. Walk by the house in between the cruisers, peek in windows when she could. But she'd had to be more careful this past week, since the incident that made all those police show up a week ago.

If only her video feeds were enough. It was one thing to see James on her tablet screen but nothing like seeing him live, in person. He looked drawn, fatigued, if the grainy footage was accurate. She'd put the life back in him soon.

Very soon.

"You can change your mind, Rachel. Don't be stubborn on my account." He felt like such a jerk, as if he'd mentally wrestled Rachel into white-water rafting. In a sense he had, not realizing how awful her past experience had been. Now that he did, he wanted to do anything but stir up her anxiety. She'd had more than her share with Bethany stalking them. But despite her misgivings, she refused to back down.

"No way. You're right, James. I need a break. This will be fun." She spoke through a forced smile that would usually make him laugh, but he was too worried about her anxiety.

"Get your helmets on after you fasten your life vests, please." Their welcome guide was a petite woman whose commanding voice belied her stature.

Rachel expertly donned her vest, but he noticed her fingers were trembling and she kept biting her lower lip.

"I mean it. Let's do something else." Guilt wrenched at his gut. "This was stupid of me."

"Stop it, James." Her stubbornness soaked through each word. He paused after tightening his helmet and faced her. Under her helmet, blue eyes sparked determination. "I'm a grown woman. If I didn't want to do this, I wouldn't. Besides, I think it's about time I stop allowing every single thing about my past run my life." Her eyes widened at her last, and she blinked. "I can't believe I said that."

A warm sense of identification with Rachel punched out from under his ribs, spreading across his abdomen. "I can. It's admirable that you've been so active in righting your father's wrongs. You've done more than anyone I know to repair and protect your family legacy. Many would have walked away." Hadn't he been in that category before he'd gone through the hell of being stalked, the joy of becoming a father? Chasing the next court win, the next raise?

"Including help spring a criminal from jail?" Her mouth twisted.

"You mean Ronald Spence?" He needed her to know it wasn't her fault that the shady character was about to walk free. "The Truth Foundation, and your involvement before you became DA, isn't going to lose its purpose or integrity because of this. Spence is who he is, from everything I've read. He'll show his true colors soon enough. If it turns out he's the innocent man he claims, all the better."

"But if not, he's got the potential to harm many. His connections are…vast." Her gaze darkened. "Maybe, instead of accepting the invitation to run for DA, I should have focused on the Truth Foundation, taken a private job."

"No. You're right where you're supposed to be." Standing with little more than inches between them, he was dumbstruck by his own words, exactly the thought that nudged him day and night. Was this where he was meant to be? Next to Rachel? Because that was where he wanted to be more than anywhere else. Save for being with his baby girl. He opened his mouth to tell her, then shut it.

Not the time, bro. Not with Bethany still out there.

"Maybe you're right. I don't know, and good job on distracting me from my nerves, by the way." Her grin belied her shaking hands. He leaned in and gave her a hug. Her body stiffened for a split second before melting against his. "Thanks for your patience with my neuroses. I have a lot more than a fear of rafting!"

"You're perfect, just the way you are." He stopped short of calling her babe. But only with effort.

Even with two layers of flotation device between them it was easy to know why it always felt natural to be with her. Rachel not only shared his enthusiasm for the law and debating various sides of an issue, his love of the outdoors, and now his adoration of Iris; Rachel understood him at a gut level. He'd never dated or been with a woman long-term who seemed to be able to read his mind. Making her happy had somehow become his life's mission.

"Mmm, this feels so good." She gave him an extra-tight squeeze before stepping back. Her eyes had brightened, the worry lines that framed her mouth gone.

"Looks like we're up." He walked to the ticket desk and displayed the verification code on his phone. He'd paid online.

"Kiriakis, party of two? Both adults? Experienced rafters?" The clerk looked at each of them.

"No, we're both pretty inexperienced."

"Not true." She looked up at him, determination etched in every line of her expression. "We can handle up to Class III. Just nothing more, please."

"Okay, will do. I need your wrists, please." The cashier wrapped the bracelets snugly on their wrists before pointing at an area where several small groups of people stood, awaiting their individual raft guides. "Before you go join the group, go to the gear cage. Select a wet suit, booties and life jacket that fit. Your guide will give you your oars."

The next two hours were full of preparation for the half-day trip. A staff member ensured their equipment fit correctly and took them through a few drills so they'd know the strokes they'd need on the river.

James watched for any signs that Rachel had changed her mind and wanted to back out. He'd call it quits at the least indication of doubt from her. The regret churning in his gut over his callous decision melted away as it appeared Rachel not only was willing to go through with it but she also seemed to be enjoying herself. The tension released from his shoulders and he unclenched his jaw, wiggling it.

Finally, they were free of the dangers that stalked them in Blue Larkspur.

Chapter 18

"**O**kay, you're all about to have the ride of your lives. Water conditions today are good, with the runoff just beginning. It won't be the fastest ride ever but it'll be thrilling nonetheless." Their guide was paid to be enthusiastic, but Rachel thought he could ease back on the "fastest" and "thrilling."

With James's constant gaze on her, she couldn't let him see her trepidation. Which had dissipated loads since she'd first realized his surprise day trip was rafting. So far, the staff had been positive and supportive, and she didn't expect anything different once they were launched into the river. And it was April, for heaven's sake. Not the height of summer, when the river's fury would be at its strongest.

"You doing okay?" He spoke quietly as they were herded along with the other groups onto a bus.

"I'm good. Honest. I'm ready. If we had to do one

more white-water or man-overboard drill in the parking lot, I was going to jump in the river on my own."

"Yeah, it seems a little much, but it won't when we navigate the rapids."

"I've heard that this part of the river is a lot of fun, and pretty tame. Are you sure you won't be bored?"

"Getting to spend the whole day with you? Never." The flash of—attraction?—in his eyes piqued her awareness. Except, the light in his gaze when he looked at her wasn't passing desire. It was something she wasn't ready to identify, not until she got her heart screwed on straight.

The bus pulled up to a concrete boat launch, and the rafters were quickly assigned rafts and guides. Rachel's curiosity rose when she realized it was only going to be her and James in their raft, plus the guide.

She nudged James's ribs. "Why is everyone else going in groups of six or eight?"

"Not sure. That's what we were supposed to be in."

"Hey, folks. I'm Chet." A fortyish man with an athletic build approached them. His grin was a mile wide and he literally took bouncing steps. "You must be the Colton group."

Rachel shot a glance at James. She didn't remember the ticket taker saying her name, but James must have included it when he did online registration.

"We are, but I thought we were in a bigger group."

"We had several large groups that requested Class I or II max today. The staff said you wanted Class III, and the company aims to please. Come right over here and we'll get started." He led them to a place away from the main crowd, to a smaller four-person raft.

Rachel's insides began to quake, but she ignored the

overreaction. It was simple anticipatory butterflies, nothing more. The drills, combined with all the equipment she'd donned, gave her a sense of safety she didn't have as a kid on the river.

You can do this.

James tugged on her vest, kept her back as the guy bounced ahead several steps.

"This isn't what I booked. Let's reschedule."

"James, it's okay. Really. We'd be bored silly on a Class I or II ride all day. And honestly? Being with you is all I care about." *Whoa.* Had she just said that? Trying to cover up her gabbing, she gave him a wide grin. "Let's go with it."

"Okay. Yes, let's do it." White teeth flashed before he leaned in and kissed her. Quick, definite, warming.

They caught up to Chet and, within minutes, were in the raft and floating on the wide, flat river. Chet wasn't a talker but stayed on the front bench while leaving them to the back one. It was easy to imagine being alone with James, telling him all of her deepest secrets and dreams.

Focus on the ride, girlfriend.

Trees loomed from both banks, many sporting the bright green buds that heralded spring. The first half hour was the kind of ride that would have gotten Rachel back on a river sooner than in over two decades. But she knew that it could change with little warning.

Not unlike her life over the past several weeks.

"Get ready to rumble, folks. Follow my signals." Chet shouted over his shoulder at the same moment she saw the rocks jutting from the river. Because the water was still low, many more boulders were visible than would be in a couple of months. Chills ran over her, and it wasn't from the weather. The wet suit kept her warm and dry.

"You've got this." James spoke in her ear so that Chet wouldn't hear. She tried to give him a brave smile and he winked. Tears welled at the simple gesture.

The rapids came on fast and hard, and Rachel focused on Chet's oar, where and how he was placing it, and copied his moves. The raft twisted and bumped, making her stomach dip. They raced past rocks that knifed out of the water and she hissed in her breath, prayed they'd clear. They did, but then they were catapulted toward a large wall of granite, faster and faster, with no reprieve in sight. Just when she thought their paddling was in vain, the raft turned left, avoiding the hazard, and they were once again on calm water.

Joy erupted from deep inside, and she let it bubble over in fits of laughter with a few whoops thrown in. "That was a rush!" She looked at James for confirmation. His smile matched her elation. Before she could stop herself, she leaned over and gave him a kiss, full on his lips as he'd done earlier. Rachel would have lingered longer at the way his mouth tasted, but the boat jerked, throwing her on her bottom.

"Please stay seated at all times, folks." Chet barely looked back at them.

"What are we, cattle?" She muttered the words for her own benefit, but James's chuckle told her he'd heard and agreed with her assessment. Awareness infused her from her throat, across her breasts and between her legs. Only James's laugh could turn her on as quickly as his tongue.

His profile against the rugged river was something she'd never forget. He caught her staring and grinned.

"Enjoying yourself, are you?"

"I am. I can't thank you enough."

"No thanks necessary. I'm glad it's not a total bust."

She looked around at the changing scenery. They'd left the wide, deceptively serene river behind them and they were moving faster through a narrower passage. Mountains rose on all sides, and as she looked forward she saw what she'd heard someone call the cattle chute. As in, they were going to move a lot faster through a bottleneck.

"Okay, get ready to ride through the chute, folks."

Rachel would have thought she'd be alarmed as they picked up speed, helpless to stop the raft's forward momentum as jagged rocks emerged from the water on either side. One oar in the water at the wrong angle and they'd be capsized or worse. But as she sat next to James, thigh-to-thigh, shoulder-to-shoulder, she knew she'd never felt more secure. Plus she'd studied the topographical map on display at the rafting center and knew that there was a lot more wide, calm water than rough in this particular part of the river.

"Look, up ahead." James pointed, the sun sparking gray flecks in the depths of his green eyes. The same as Iris's. "See that thin line? It looks like a tree trunk?"

She followed his finger out to maybe a quarter-mile ahead of them and saw what looked like a straight tree, but as she lifted her gaze higher, higher, there were no branches, no treetop.

"What is it?"

"It's where the river forks. We're going to the left, to the quieter side. The line is the way the rock was carved out eons ago."

"That's wild." She breathed out her wonder as the

increasing waves jostled the raft, pushing her into James's side. His arm came around her shoulders and they looked at one another.

"Is this okay?" The pure concern and awareness in his gaze, from the way he seemed to soak in her image to his steadying grasp on her upper arm, further stoked the desire that she constantly carried for him alone.

"It's perfect." She closed her eyes and lifted her lips for his kiss. This time they lingered. Let Chet do his job.

Suddenly the raft made a hard right and they were both thrown to James's side of the inflatable craft. A scream escaped her as she clung to James with one hand and the side of the craft with her other. With her feet no longer under Chet's bench, she had nothing to anchor her to the inflatable. Terror squeezed tight on her fight to stay in the raft.

"Stop!" James's shout to Chet sounded her mental warning alarms. Still on her knees in the space between their bench and Chet's, she righted herself and got on the seat. She tried to shove her feet under the front bench. Chet's weight crushed the inflatable seat and made an L-shape, but Chet was leaning so far forward that her feet weren't getting the grip they needed. She bounced high in the air, then hit the raft hard as the current increased.

They were going to capsize.

"Chet!" James leaned over and grabbed the guide's shoulder, tried to yank him back. But Chet was on some kind of mission, his focused paddle strokes steering them exactly where they weren't supposed to go.

To the Class VI rapids only the most experienced white-water rafters dared attempt.

In an instant, the images of him and Rachel being separated from the bigger groups, the way Chet had seemed to appear out of nowhere, and the threat Rachel's current defendant, Brian Parson, made in court fit together. Fury mowed through him and he prepared to act. This wasn't going to end like Rachel's childhood rafting incident.

It could end worse.

"Use your oar!" James pointed left and Rachel complied, grasping her oar's handle and paddling to counteract Chet's deadly maneuvers. James mirrored her actions on his side of the raft.

Their movements fought with Chet's for what felt like hours. Water sprayed in his face and he strained to see if their efforts were turning the boat. His shoulders burned along with every muscle in his body. Rachel kept up, but even his pride in her efforts wasn't enough to sustain the energy they needed to fight Chet's frenzied strokes. The water's frigid temperature was evident as it repeatedly hit his face.

Keep going, keep going.

While they were able to slow Chet's forward momentum they weren't able to get the raft turned to the left.

"James!" Her scream tore through him.

"Rachel! Hang on!" He grabbed her arm and settled her in the raft's center. She put her oar between her legs and gripped the raft's bench in front of her.

Now or never.

James dropped his oar and dove for Chet, grabbed him around his neck and pulled him backward. Chet's arm swung back, oar in hand, and sideswiped James on the head, against his cheekbone. Bright spots danced in his sight, but he didn't loosen his hold on Chet, who kicked his legs out, one foot landing square in James's face. He tasted blood but didn't stop. He couldn't. Rachel's life depended on him.

The fight rocked the raft more than the river and his hands were wet, cold and bloodied as he struggled to stop Chet. The raft cleared the rapids right before they passed the fork in the water and their ride leveled out, flat again.

James pinned Chet down, the man gasping for air.

"Why did you do that?" James shouted, needing answers. "Who are you working for?"

Chet didn't answer, and the roar of the river prevented further discussion.

It was too late. The raft headed for the wrong side of the fork, to the right, to the stretch of Class VI rapids. James remembered the map's description, in bold red letters.

ONLY FOR ADVANCED MASTER RAFTERS

Chapter 19

Was this how her life would end? After a lifetime of striving to follow in her father's legal footsteps minus the criminal turn, she was going to die in a river-rafting accident?

Images of Iris flashed in her mind, of the day she was born. Of when she'd first met James, how everything had seemed fresh and all possibilities were on the table. And the sight of James with Iris, holding their daughter, his smile reaching out to Rachel and triggering the idea that they had an instant-family connection.

At least Iris would have many aunts and uncles to help raise her, keep Rachel's memory alive.

"No!" The shock in James's voice forced her back to the present, to the sight of Chet purposefully jumping out of the raft into the seething frigid waters. James immediately tossed in the safety line, but his attempt to rescue Chet was unwanted. Chet grabbed the line, tugged hard as if to bring James in the water with him, before raising both hands, showing they were empty and he was not interested in getting back. The fork and knife-edge stone outcropping neared, and she was certain they were about to witness Chet's body being smashed to bits against the granite.

A woman somewhere screamed and with a start she realized it was her. She was screaming, out of control as James put a hand on either of her shoulders, one still holding his oar.

"He's headed for that bank." He pointed. Incredulous, she watched as Chet appeared to float atop the water, using his vest and the current to get him where he wanted. Chet stood up in about a foot of water, the current near the shore remarkably calmer, no matter it was less than one hundred meters from the raft and teeming water. Facing them, he offered a smile she'd always remember as the look of pure evil. Along with a rude hand gesture.

Chet had wanted them to drown!

Brian Parson's threat rang through her mind. *"I'll see you in hell, Rachel Colton."*

"Listen to me, Rachel." James tapped on her helmet to get her attention as he enunciated slowly while he yelled, waiting for her to nod and acknowledge his words after each sentence. The raft stopped heaving, though it moved more quickly as the current shifted.

"We can do this. Follow my lead," he shouted.

"But Chet!" Chet needed to be apprehended. "I'll call Theo!"

"No time. There probably isn't any service, anyway. Look." He pointed toward the right side of the river, to a bank where a group of three men stood, throwing a line to a bright orange speck—Chet. "He planned this. This was one of your defendant's men. We'll call Theo when we're safe."

"Could it be Bethany, James? I can't tell if they're all men from here."

"It doesn't matter who it is. All we need to focus on is staying above water and safe."

Safe.

James's words confirmed her fear. The sheer rock cliff that careened toward them was going to kill them.

"James! I can't do this!"

"Do what I do, and we'll get through it, okay?" His eyes blazed with intent. It was impossible to argue with his determination. "This is fast but a good place to catch our breath. We'll get through the rapids."

She nodded.

Before they had to begin paddling through white water she took her phone, in its waterproof case, and snapped as many shots of Chet and the other men as possible. When James saw her, he grinned.

"I'm at least good for proof!" She yelled over the roar of the water, increasing in decibels with each second.

"We'll need it to call in for our pickup. Put it away, fast!"

Rachel complied, but her exultation that she'd captured decent shots of Chet and his fellow culprits deflated as quickly as the water turned from fast but smooth to dangerously choppy. She'd no sooner zipped her phone securely into the fanny pack she'd worn over her wet suit than James was touching her shoulder, indicating how she needed to hold her oar.

The next two hours were the scariest of Rachel's

life. Or at least, they should have been. Except she had the steadiest guy next to her, no matter how rough the ride got. As they progressed downriver, she knew that if she let her concentration slip the least bit, she risked upending the trip for both of them—literally. While they were in wet suits and wore vests, there was no one around to throw them a line, no other rafts in sight. She vowed that as soon as there was a chance she'd try for a signal and call Theo.

Finally they turned a long, slow bend and she allowed herself to look around at Colorado's spring beauty in full display. The midday sun reflected off the water, its clear depths belying the miles of rapids they'd traversed.

"How did Lewis and Clark do it?" She marveled at the rawness, centuries later, of their surroundings.

"They hiked a lot of it, carrying a canoe." His dry response made her smile.

"If you'd told me we'd be joking after that…"

"Now would be a good time to see if we have reception, call in to the tour company. I can do it." He had his phone out and Rachel couldn't stop tears of relief from welling when she saw he'd made a connection. She listened as he gave a rundown of what had happened and requested a pickup somewhere near a place called Miner's Exit within an hour or so.

When he disconnected, his eyes were full of concern. "I need you to call Theo, tell him what's happened. Send him the photos. Hurry."

"Of course. Good thinking." She'd been so relieved to have cleared the rapids that she'd momentarily forgotten what got them in this exact location to begin with. As soon as she'd left Theo a voice mail and sent the photos, the familiar crawl of discomfort up her neck, across her chest returned.

"Why did you tell me to hurry? And what's Miner's Exit?"

"Miner's Exit is our last challenge today."

Her heart threw itself against her rib cage. "What are you saying? You mean there are more rapids?" Her throat was raw and she fought against the disappointment that squeezed at her tear ducts and hoped James thought any wetness on her cheeks was from river water.

"Babe, you're doing great, and I know you can handle the next stretch."

"Can the empowerment coaching and give it to me straight, Kiriakis."

"There's a reason Chet, and whoever employs him, sent us to this part of the river. It's notoriously unpredictable, no matter the time of year. Since snowmelt hasn't started in earnest yet, the rocks are an issue."

"So we paddle around them." Like the other rocks they'd avoided, some just inches below the surface.

"Some of the rapids have crevices that few have survived, if they go under. Our entire focus is to stay in the raft."

"Isn't it always?"

"More so this time, Rachel."

Regret and sorrow flooded her thoughts. "I'm so sorry, James. I got you into this. This is the work of Parson, I know it."

"You're kidding me. It could be Bethany. Who knows? Either way, I'm the one who planned a rafting trip and didn't cancel after I found out your repulsion to white water."

"How would Parson or Bethany even know we were coming here?"

"I used my cell phone and laptop from your house. You know better than I do how resourceful the local crime rings are. It's easy to intercept a call, and if someone was monitoring your home, they could have hacked my computer."

"But everything's encrypted."

"I had to phone to verify my credit card. Their site was down that day for maintenance. That has to be it. It wasn't Bethany—I can't imagine she's that computer savvy. Her expertise seems to be more with shock actions, like the explosive. But a crime syndicate has many resources. They intercepted my call, I'm almost positive. It's the only way this makes sense." He shook his head. "I regret every bit of this, Rachel."

"Please don't. It seems we have an issue."

His eyes filled with surprise. "Issue? You mean besides being stalked by my ex, and now one of the criminals you're going to put away?"

"Nope. The problem with us, as I see it, James, is that we get one another in trouble every time we're together."

"Iris is anything but trouble."

"But she wasn't planned. We can't ignore that, no matter how much we love her now. We didn't plan to be the victims of bad guys, but we are. Folks like that are going to do what they're going to do. It doesn't matter at this point. All I care about is getting home safe. You're going to get us there."

"You trust me?" He spoke with a tentativeness she'd never heard in his voice.

"Implicitly." She looked downriver, to where the wide calm appeared to drop from sight. To where they'd face life-threatening rapids. "I suggest we use our special mojo, whatever it is, and finish up this ride in style. I completely trust your judgment. Wherever you tell me to paddle, I'm on it."

James had told Rachel the truth; he'd ridden through a similar stretch of the river more than once. Maybe as many as four times. But it hadn't been on Class VI, he was certain. And he'd been a heck of a lot younger, and there had always been a guide with his group.

He quietly planned his strategy, humbled by Rachel's complete reliance on him. His insides were tight as wet knots and he made himself take a few deep breaths, consciously relaxed his shoulders.

Not for the first time he wished the rapids, or the threat of facing the criminals, were the worst of his concerns. Rachel was his biggest worry. One look at her pinched expression, the way her eyes flashed stubborn sparks while her body quaked with fear, sent a shock of terror through him. It was his fault that Rachel was being pushed to her mental limits. Today, the past few weeks, the time she'd been pregnant and then a single mom without his help, it all added up. He vowed to get them to safety and protect her and Iris no matter the cost to his life. If he had to quit his new job to guard them 24/7, he would.

"Less staring at me and more looking at the river, Kiriakis." Her voice trembled but without her customary spunk. Surprise sent a warm shock through his chest.

"On it, Colton."

The change in tempo was deceptive as they slowed to a comparative crawl after being rushed through the gorge.

"Maybe the rapids won't be so bad today." But Rachel's white knuckles betrayed her attempt to remain positive.

"Hey." He covered her hands with his. "You've got this. The Arkansas River has nothing on us."

She smiled with trembling lips and wide eyes, and he wondered if her confidence in him was warranted.

"James!" The craft swayed, and they were in the rapids.

The next forty minutes were the most challenging James had ever experienced. As before, Rachel stayed with him, not once complaining or setting her oar on her lap in exhaustion.

His shoulders and triceps started to complain when they had about three minutes left, from what he'd calculated it should take for the trip. But instead of the usual aches and pains of a grueling workout, a searing pain in his right shoulder was his only warning before he lost his grip on the oar. His left hand held on, but he couldn't direct the raft the way he'd been.

"What's wrong?" Rachel screamed more than yelled, her voice barely perceptible above the din of the current.

"My shoulder!"

"Tell me what to do!"

"You're doing it!" He had to focus, ignore the pain, keep Rachel safe. It was all that mattered.

Rachel tried to ignore the fear and panic that fought to take over her thoughts, tripping them into existential dread. The river was unforgiving, and her body was at its limit.

"Left, left!" James directed her like a coxswain, his direction always spot-on, but the inflatable raft wasn't a crew shell and her efforts were all the more difficult thanks to the personal flotation device the river trip guide had buckled her into.

You can do it. Almost there.

The mantra was harder to hang on to and on the verge of becoming laughable. The possibility that she and James wouldn't make it through these rapids pricked and stabbed at her hard-won positivity.

"No!" She paddled furiously, using the adrenaline that seemed to come from nowhere.

"Slower, easy." Sternness laced his shout and she knew she'd overcompensated. "That's it."

"How much long—" Her request was denied more quickly than any court proceeding as the raft lurched into another stretch of churning water. The harsh motion sent James, unable to balance with an injured arm, into the space between the two benches. The momentum of his weight tipped the craft precariously on its back edge and James slid into the frothy water as she was tossed backward, hitting the waves bottom-first.

V-shape, legs up, let the current take you. Her body had somehow absorbed the safety video and she stared at her feet, up in front of her, her arms at her sides. The PFD kept her buoyant and she lifted her arms up, out of the way of submerged rocks.

James.

"James!" She tried to yell, but the spray and exertion of the last hours captured her breath, making her voice tiny. The current spun her, lifted her, dropped her like a rock.

And then, quiet calm. She'd made it through the rapids! Sunlight dappled the water lapping the beach almost directly in front of her. Several people stood there, waving and shouting. Fear smothered her exultation. Were they Chet's buddies?

Something large bumped her and she turned her head, afraid to look. But when she saw James floating next to her, his grin wide, it immediately dispelled her trepidation.

"You did it, Rachel!" He whooped and pumped his fist, then grimaced.

"*We* did it. We made it."

"Here!" Shouts reached them, and she saw the familiar rafting-company logo emblazoned on a truck, the safety lines being tossed toward them.

"Grab one of the ropes, Rachel." James grabbed her hand and they half swam, half floated together until she was able to grab one of the lifelines. "Let me hang on to you, while you hold on to the rope. We're there, babe!"

Chapter 20

"We're not going to agree on this." Rachel wiped Iris's mouth of the butternut-squash-and-cereal blend she'd chowed down on for dinner. "You're convinced Bethany is behind everything bad that's happened to me, to us, and I think it's more likely the work of Brian Parson and his fellow thugs. My siblings regularly post what they think are funny memes about white-water rafting to my social media page. I set my privacy settings tight but nothing's impenetrable, not at all. I'm certain he pulled strings to sabotage our raft."

It'd been two weeks since the white-water-raft event, and since then, Brian Parson admitted he'd "turned on" his network to "send the DA a solid message." He'd said "Get me convicted at your own risk." She'd gone on to rest her case against him, and he'd been found guilty of all counts of racketeering and assault and now faced additional charges of kidnapping, attempted assault and possible attempted homicide for the rafting event. Chet, the pseudo raft guide, and his jerk associates, like the rats they were, had scattered and disappeared, still at large. Theo expected they'd show up again before long. It was a matter of time for such lowlifes.

James methodically rinsed and loaded dishes into the dishwasher as they talked across the island. Rachel had rolled the high chair to the counter so that she could more easily hand the removable tray to James for cleaning. "Here you go."

His hands were sexier while soapy, and for some reason, that inexplicably annoyed her. "You really should have let me do the dishes. How's your shoulder?"

"Good as new, almost." He grinned. The orthopedic doc who examined his shoulder after their boating adventure had instructed James to rest it, take ibuprofen and ice as necessary. He'd been in daily physical therapy, which he swore up and down had worked miracles.

"You and I are alike. We don't want to ever take a break from work. We're lucky we enjoy what we do so much. But that means it's never a good time to get things done for ourselves."

"You mean like your intention to get back to a regular workout routine? Which, by the way, other than for your stress levels, you absolutely don't need." His words stroked her awareness, raised the tiniest hairs on her forearm, her nape. And got the fire in her center burning for him.

"No, I mean like rotator cuff surgery for reinjuring that same shoulder. I get that you don't want to even think about being laid up for a few days. But they said it won't be as bad as when you were in college. Surgical techniques have improved." That's what he'd told her right after. But once they got back into their regular routines, James had pooh-poohed any reference to his injury, saying it had pained him most in the moment, after all the paddling they'd done.

"I'm not committing to such major surgery right now. No way." He placed the items they didn't put in the washer in the rack atop the counter and dried his hands. "We've both got too much going on."

"Since Parson is locked up, you mean you're not considering it until Bethany is out of our lives, don't you? Have you considered that maybe Parson has been responsible for all of our troubles this last month or so?"

"No. I wish we had concrete evidence on Bethany, and I know you do, too. You're going to have to trust me on this one, Rachel. I know her ways. She's behind your fuel-tank contamination and the restaurant explosion, I'm positive."

"But we haven't had any incidents for two weeks." Not since Brian Parson claimed responsibility for the brick through her window and sending Chet to sabotage the rafting excursion.

"I'm not considering moving out until we know for certain Bethany's been shut down. She hasn't shown up back in Denver since I left, so it tracks with her being here."

"Her mother doesn't seem worried, according to Theo." Theo had investigated Bethany's history personally. "She told him that Bethany has had periods of disappearing like this throughout her life."

"And I've no doubt they line up with the other men she's harassed. Her behavior has escalated over the last five years, remember. She'd been known for doing a nasty thing or two, like showing up unexpectedly at a place of employment, before moving on to her next victim, that is, another man to date. The man before me had a dead rat left on his doorstep. The only reason the police think she stopped is because she met me. She won't stop until she's forced to."

Rachel watched him finish up in the kitchen, with Iris settling against her, sleepy and ready for a quick bath before bed. She'd miss talking to him like this, after dinner, as the day wound down. Doubt seeped into her heart. James wasn't her father. Maybe she should think about the "more" he'd mentioned more than once.

"Here, I'll take her while you run her bath." He held out his arms, but she noticed that his injured one wasn't outstretched as far.

"Why don't you relax tonight? You did the dishes. I'll call for you when she's ready to go down."

"Fair enough." The fact that he didn't argue confirmed that he was still hurting. Rachel bit back a grin but not before his gaze landed on her mouth.

"Tell me."

"I never thought it was possible, but I've met someone as stubborn as me."

"Iris?" His feigned innocence tugged on her funny bone and she laughed.

"Oh, she's got both of our genes, I'm certain." She stood only a foot from James and he leaned in and planted a kiss on the baby's head, as he often did. But tonight she couldn't take her gaze off his profile, his mouth, his scent.

As if he read her mind, he didn't pull back all the way but instead kissed her full on the mouth. His lips were firm, the kiss validation that he felt the attraction between them, too.

His eyes were heavy lidded, his pupils dilated when he pulled back. Iris reached out and grabbed a hunk of Rachel's hair.

"Ow, baby!" She looked away, needing the break between them, from his intensity.

"Rach." Imploring, his request reverberated with need.

"Yes?"

"I've never stopped wanting to be with you. I know we've had this silent agreement to keep our distance, but—"

She held up her free hand. "Wait. We'll finish this conversation after Iris is asleep."

"I want more than talking, babe." His laughing reply followed her down the hallway to Iris's room.

Bethany could barely make out their figures on the screen when she was this mad. It had taken her days to work out a way to get more cash without being traced, which meant she'd had to go back to Denver and ask her mother for a money order. Her mom was useless most days but had agreed to keep this visit a secret when Bethany had promised she'd buy her mother a new car with her next job. She'd been fired from her most recent place of employment but the lack of a paycheck didn't bother her. She'd have James in hand soon enough.

All she had to do was get James away from the brat and its mother, Rachel Colton. When she and James returned to Denver, everything would be wonderful and she'd be able to find an even better job, making more money. And James was generous. He'd contribute to her mother's car fund.

Mom had said that some detective type had been sniffing around, but she promised she hadn't ratted Bethany out. Her mother knew what was best for herself. Not only would Bethany's promise of new wheels disappear, but Mom might need an attitude readjustment in the form of a crack to her head. Bethany had given her mother some lessons over the years, mostly in the form of cutting her off financially. She'd only had to drive one lesson home by hurting her mother a few years back, when she told the cops where her daughter was hiding out.

Yeah, she'd fixed her mother but good that time. But it was nothing like what she planned to do to Rachel Colton and her kid.

Not even close.

James couldn't stop thinking about Rachel's lips, her soft skin, the way her inviting smile told him that she wanted him, too. He walked around the living room, knowing he should have gone for a run earlier today when he'd had the chance. But he hadn't been able to shake the sense of danger that clung to him, even after that loser Brian Parson admitted he'd orchestrated Chet's life-threatening ruse. A week out and the terror still woke him at night, bathed him in cold sweat, his heart racing to beat the nightmare of continuous white water and being unable to find Rachel.

His gaze caught on the fireplace mantel, where Rachel kept several knickknacks including a beautiful photo of her and Iris. He fingered the glazed pottery she'd mentioned she liked to collect from local Colorado artists. One vase in particular had the same shade as her eyes. He lifted it absentmindedly, killing time until she put their baby to bed.

A *plunk* caught his attention and he made sure he hadn't tipped the vase, spilling any contents out. No. It remained upright in his hand. Investigating further, he saw a small black button on the oak shelf and picked it up. And realized it wasn't a button, but a tiny glass lens about the size of a dime with a short wire coming out the back. His mind tried to convince himself it wasn't what it obviously was.

"James!" Rachel called to him from the nursery. Iris was ready for bed.

"Coming." He pocketed the camera, and quickly scanned the rest of the room for more. Sure enough, he found two more, one on the top edge of the television, and one in the corner of a bookshelf. Maybe Rachel had placed them there, the usual nanny cam. He hoped she had.

Rachel stared at the three small disc-shaped cameras in James's palm. They stood in the hallway, outside the nursery, where Iris had fallen asleep to her father's voice reading *Goodnight Moon*.

"Those aren't mine. My brother installed outside cameras for me at about the same time you arrived in town. The security specialists I hired upgraded that system. This isn't their work." She ran her hands over her head. "Oh my goodness, James. I've been so busy between getting you acquainted with Iris and my caseloads that I never noticed these. We've got to check the kitchen, the rest of the house. What if there are some in the baby's room?" Her pitch rose of its own volition, and

Rachel fought tears as her body began to shake. Neither reaction was from fear, but from deep-seated anger. How dare anyone get this close to her, to her child?

"Let's go into the living room and call Theo."

They sat next to one another on the sofa and she put her cell on speaker. She had Theo on speed dial as "Police Chief." She'd entered him into her phone years ago, as he was such a close family friend. Never would she have guessed she'd come to rely on him as much as she had these past weeks.

From how her mother behaved around the chief, she had to wonder if Isa was relying on Theo for far more than friendship these days. But there was no time to ponder family concerns tonight. She had to keep her focus narrowed on the safety of her immediate family. If anything happened to Iris, she'd never forgive herself.

Don't go there.

It took Theo a bit to answer, and when he did, she heard laughter—and it sounded suspiciously similar to Isa's. Rachel wouldn't begrudge anyone some fun, but with her family's safety on the line, indignation rumbled under her breastbone.

"What can I do you for, Rachel?" Theo's voice vibrated with humor, too, as if he and whomever he was with had shared a great joke. Her initial annoyance melted into sweet relief. Theo was the one man she'd been able to rely upon since her father's death, besides her brothers.

You can rely on James. She paused, her words stuck in her throat.

"Rachel? You there?" No hint of laughter this time.

"Theo. Yes, yes, I'm here. I'm sorry to bother you at this time of night, but I'm afraid there's a new development—an answer, really—to the question of how whoever's stalking me, or James, or both of us has figured out our movement patterns." She summarized what James had found.

"Do any of your windows or doors show signs of a break-in?" Theo was in full-on cop mode again.

"No, I checked." James spoke. Their gazes caught, and she realized he'd been busy while she was giving Iris her bath. "Every single window and door is secure. And judging by the dust that was on them when I found these camera devices, they've been here awhile."

"At least since the brick necessitated the woodwork repair on the transom." She relied on Emily to pick up around the house, but emphasized that the nanny's focus should always be on Iris, not cleaning. "I've been meaning to get a housekeeper, but it's not the right time."

"Good thing you haven't yet, Rachel. As James said, the dust lets us know the cameras have been there for at least a couple weeks. Plus your house is a newer build and they don't get as dusty as the older places." The way Theo broke it down into its simplest facts reassured her, almost as much as knowing James was still staying in her house.

"I agree. The air filters on my HVAC are top-of-the-line and keep the dust to a minimum. My guess is that these cameras have been here for several weeks." Fear worked its paralyzing grip up her spine as the ramifications of being watched for so long pressed in on her. Warm hands clasped her shoulders and began to knead. *James*. She mouthed "thank you" to him and then relaxed under his deft touch.

They continued to talk to Theo for the next several minutes, telling him the various cases they'd reviewed, listing possible suspects. But it all came back to Bethany.

"Listen, Theo, I understand that I'm looking at it through my unique perspective, having been stalked by Bethany Austin for so long. But I'm thinking that she placed these cameras." James's fingers stopped their magic on her shoulders as he gave all his attention to Theo. She immediately missed the connection of his skin on hers.

"It's possible James is right, Theo, but my money's still on Parson's criminal connections. It would explain how they knew our movements, and if there are mics embedded in the cameras, it all but confirms it. They would have heard James make the reservations, no need for a cell phone intercept."

James stood up and went to where he'd left the cameras, on the kitchen counter.

He frowned as he peered at the discs, sealed in a plastic bag. "I can't tell if there's a mic in these or not."

"Leave them be, and I'll have an officer stop by to collect them as evidence. Our tech expert will take a look at them. In the meantime, continue with your security measures—make sure all blinds are closed, leave all outdoor lights on 24/7 and expect an officer to stop by periodically to visibly check on you."

"Got it. Thank you, Theo." She almost added "Hi, Mom" but thought better of it. If it was Isa's voice she'd heard at the start of the call, her mother didn't want her to know she was there or she would have spoken up. And if it was another woman, Rachel didn't want to know. As the call ended, she recognized the sensation squeezing her heart. Regret at the thought of Theo caring for another person instead of her mother. She shook her head, silently told herself it was the stress of worrying about Iris's safety that had her thinking the errant thoughts.

"What's wrong?" James stared at her, his eyes bright with compassion.

"You mean minus being targeted by a bad person? I'm wondering if I should take Iris to my mother's, but the last thing I want is for whoever's doing this to go after her, too."

"If it's Bethany, she wants me, not you. Her pattern has always been to frighten, not actually harm anyone."

"I'm sorry I didn't back you up in front of Theo, but I don't think it's Bethany any longer, if ever. James, Theo's right. The reach of these thugs in a small town like Blue Larkspur is vast. Strings are pulled with the blink of an eye. For all we know, Parson knows you've been stalked and has made all these incidents appear to be related to Bethany. It makes sense, as I was working to put him away for a solid few months before you arrived in town. If it is him, then there's nothing to be concerned about as he's been found guilty on all charges, and after his harsh sentence yesterday, it should send a message to all the crooks to back off. That threats aren't going to keep justice from being served. You found the mics, so there's that, too. For all we know, they're not operational any longer."

"You could be right." James used the classic I-don't-agree-but-whatever line with a shrug.

Heat pierced her heart, but unlike moments earlier, it wasn't passion. "Excuse me?"

"You've blown off every suggestion I make that Bethany is behind all of this."

"That's not true. But why does it matter who's behind these acts when the bottom line is that harm could come to our baby?"

"No harm is coming to either of you as long as I'm here."

"Really? Because last time I checked, your presence didn't keep that loser Chet from almost getting us killed on the river. And what about the brick? And the explosion the first night we had dinner?" It didn't matter that she heard how strident her accusations sounded; the dam holding back her fear had burst open. Cold knowing washed through her veins, making her shiver.

She was a DA. It didn't matter that it was a new-to-her position. She'd worked in the prosecuting office long enough to know that a determined criminal could get what they wanted more often than not. Especially one connected to an established criminal ring, like her most recent defendant. Hadn't she seen it first with her own family, when her father had succumbed to the pressure to break the law?

"Hey, I hear you. It's been a scary, chaotic time. But let's keep the risk in perspective. Your defendant has been sentenced, so any pressure from him should be over."

"For now. The crime syndicates never completely go away, or if they do, another one pops up. Criminal law is a lot different from corporate." She put her hands on her hips. "Let's say you're right, and we don't have to worry about the likes of Chet again. What about Bethany? If she's behind even a fraction of these incidents, as you're so convinced, how are we going to stop her? Short of catching her in the act? What if Bethany's next stunt puts Iris in danger? I'd never forgive myself."

The air between them was heavy, spiked with the silent part of her declaration.

I'll never forgive you.

James's eyes narrowed and he leaned forward but remained standing at the counter. "Don't you think I'd do anything to have prevented those things from happening? I haven't risked losing a new job by working here, from your house, for kicks. I would never live with myself if anything happened to you or Iris. Our daughter is my top priority."

The heat in her gut turned sour as she recognized how harsh she'd been. James was feeling the pressure of the past weeks, just like her. She forced herself to take a few breaths before she replied.

"I know you haven't caused any of this. I don't blame you for Bethany, although—"

"If it is her, I brought her into your and Iris's life." His eyes blazed with anger and frustration, matching hers. But what she wasn't feeling yet saw in his gaze was the one thing she'd feared since she'd let him into her life again, let him become such a loving father to Iris.

Regret. James definitely regretted all that had befallen them since he'd arrived in Blue Larkspur. Her logical mind tried to reason and tell her that his regret had nothing to do with her, personally. With their relationship. Relationships were something she'd avoided, never wanted. Nothing serious, anyway. The wounds of her father's betrayal to her family ran deep. As she looked at James her heart wept with how much he'd come to mean to her, because anything besides coming together to raise Iris was too scary, too risky for her. She wasn't willing to do what committing to James would require. Trusting him with her heart, no holds barred.

You're co-parents, bottom line.

"It's been a long few weeks, James. Today was killer. I think we both need to sleep on this and regroup in the morning."

"And what then, Rachel? Spit it out." His expression was thunderous, and she got it—she wanted to scream her frustration out and would have, if it wouldn't wake their precious child.

"There's nothing for me to say. Nothing at all."

Chapter 21

When James woke, there was no brew strong enough to shake off the uneasy night he'd spent on the sofa. The cameras and what they represented had upset everything he'd been so certain about only a day earlier. That his presence alone kept Iris and Rachel safe. The white-water fiasco should have alerted him that there was more than one bad guy in Blue Larkspur, more than a single entity that wanted either Rachel, as DA, or him, as her partner, under their thumb. The police chief informed them that it appeared as though Bethany was behind what could have been a lethal rafting trip. James experienced no satisfaction at having been right about Bethany and her capabilities. It didn't erase all the other threats aimed at Rachel, from multiple sources.

He tossed a bagel into the toaster, *Rachel's* toaster, scrambled up the eggs he'd been making for them both each morning of his stay. He'd thought about not doing it this morning, to make the break cleaner, but Rachel was Iris's mom. He owed her this much.

She's more than your baby's mother.

His stomach twisted, and that unfamiliar ache deep in his chest cranked back up. It wasn't his heart; he knew he was in decent cardio shape, or had been before coming to Blue Larkspur and all it had dumped on him. Images of crashing into Rachel on the courthouse steps, running from the restaurant that first night out together, meeting Iris. Seeing his child for the first time, those eyes looking at him, the immediate connection. He hadn't needed the DNA test but did it for his daughter's benefit. He wanted her to always know that she was part of him.

And still would be—just on a different basis than living with her and her mother afforded him. He did a quick mental calculation. He could sell his swanky condo downtown and find a house closer to this neighborhood. Iris could spend time between his and Rachel's place; many children did so. His stomach twisted again. It wasn't ideal. He'd missed out on having a father since his dad had died when he was still only six years old. The last thing he wanted was for Iris to not have her dad with her 24/7.

"Morning." Rachel's voice was a hollow version of itself, and no amount of makeup could erase the dark circles under her beautiful eyes. His resolve to leave wavered. His mind screamed at him to beg her to let him stay.

No. She'd made it clear it was time to move on.

"Hey. Your eggs and half a bagel are ready."

"Thanks, but you don't have to do this. Make me food." She moved robotically, filling her coffee mug.

"You mean you don't want me to."

"That's probably best, isn't it?" She sighed, ran her fingers through her messy hair. "James. This isn't about you. I don't want you to leave here thinking that. We're good together, as Iris's parents. I'm not willing to risk that all because we're good in bed together."

"Good in bed...we're on different pages here, Rachel. Yes, we're very compatible in many ways, but there's more. I know you know there is." That's what angered him the most. Rachel was willfully turning her back on the possibility of not only a future together, but an incredible one at that.

"You've known about my father, what his misdeeds did to our family, from the beginning. I've been conditioned from a young age to have a healthy mistrust of men. Not what you want to hear, but I can't change who I am. It's unfair of you to expect me to be able to take a chance on lo—" She stopped herself, shook her head. "A chance on anything permanent. Other than being here for Iris."

"I never saw you as a coward, Rachel." He held back his temper, but only from years of courtroom experience. Some things cut too deep to express in words, anyway.

"So you agree we need to keep our lives separate." Her expression was as flat as her statement. Her gaze caught on the table, the neat stack of computer equipment, his suitcase. Packed.

"We need space, I'll grant you that. I'll get back to you within a few days. I'm looking for a place near here, so that we can share custody as easily as possible."

"That sounds good." She sipped her coffee, didn't so much as glance up from her phone. When he heard the front door unlock a full hour before the usual time, Rachel finally spoke. "I have to be in court earlier than usual today. I asked Emily to show up now. Theo's put all of his assets on me and my family. Bethany will be caught the moment she makes her next move. You're free to go, James."

Their gazes met, and he fought against the powerful urge to walk around the counter, pull her into his arms and break down her solid ice wall of defensiveness with his kiss.

She's Iris's mother. Period. He'd done nothing to help them in the end. He'd only brought more danger with him. If Bethany was around, and his gut told him she was, it was best for him to draw her away from all things Rachel and Iris.

"Okay, then. I'll text you when I have a place near here to move into."

"Sounds good." Iris's cry pierced the room, via the baby monitor. He put his bags down, ready to go to his baby. But Emily walked into the kitchen and smiled.

"I'll go get her. You two get ready."

"Right." James grabbed his things and headed for the front door. Only after he'd thrown his stuff into his car and backed out of the driveway did he rub on his chest, trying to unfurl the tight ball under his rib cage.

If his cardiac health was good, what was this pain in his heart?

Can it be love?

The next week, Rachel fell back into the routine she'd had before James, before being attacked and stalked.

Well, almost. Emily's constant presence combined with her mother's frequent visits gave her the reassurance that everything really was okay. Back to normal. Parson had been sent to jail, no further "Bethany" incidents had happened, and Rachel had her evenings to herself again once Iris was asleep.

There were no more long nights in front of her laptop, searching for clues as to who'd want to harm her. No late-night coffee talk...or any other activity.

Her cheeks heated as she pulled into her driveway, grateful the grueling workweek was behind her. It had been the longest she'd had yet as DA. Not that she could put her finger on what exactly had been so rough. Her caseload had never changed, so it wasn't that. She'd been able to be home for dinner each night, giving her maximum time with her baby girl.

You miss James.

Yes, so what? She missed having someone, another adult, to talk to after Emily and Isa left. It wasn't as if James was gone...forever. He was Iris's dad, and no matter how she'd begun to doubt their ability to maintain anything but the most professional of relationships, she believed he'd be back for Iris.

Her heart pounded in her ears and she gulped, fighting back the onslaught of an emotion she'd thought long buried. The driving force behind her frantic adolescence, always needing to be the best at the law, to right her father's wrongs.

Sorrow. The old frenemy snaked around her heart and began to peel back the layers of her defenses, which weren't many. Not since she'd allowed James and how he'd cared for her, for Iris to invade her fortifications. Sinking to the cold kitchen floor, she rested her head on her knees and let the tears flow. A good, solid boo-hoo was just what she needed.

If she acknowledged her grief at the breakdown of their non-relationship, it would have to stop hurting, wouldn't it?

Chapter 22

"I told you, Jake, she's not going to be that kind of co-parent. She's already let me bond with Iris, and I don't anticipate any problems going forward." James spoke to his brother as he sipped his first coffee of the weekend. Clad in a black T-shirt and sweatpants, he was glad it was Saturday, his day to regroup. And grateful that his entire family knew all about Iris. They couldn't wait to meet her, either, but James wanted to do this on Rachel's timeline.

"Right. So tell me, why aren't you still living there, again?"

"We've figured out that the harassment and threats were most likely related to a recent case she's prosecuted. Not to Bethany."

"You don't sound so certain, bro."

"I'm not, frankly. I do think Bethany's behind at least

several of the incidents, and I've no doubt she somehow followed me here. There's only been one sighting of her in Denver since I moved to Blue Larkspur, and that was to visit her mother. Probably to get more cash for living expenses so that she can stay off the grid." Theo had texted him the information in the middle of the night.

"At least with me out of Rachel's place, I feel I've directed her future actions toward me, not at Rachel and Iris."

"Do you think there's any way she knows there's more between you and Rachel or that Iris is your daughter?" Jake's voice strummed with the same frustration that churned in James's gut. He'd do anything at this point to know Bethany wasn't around, wasn't about to strike again.

"Who said there's anything between me and Rachel besides being Iris's parents?" Playing coy wasn't his favorite thing.

"Bro, I know you. You're a good man, and you'd stay with anyone who needed guarding. It's what made you such a great Boy Scout. You have integrity, which I'd like to think I imparted to you."

"Still modest, aren't you?" He had to tease his older brother even in the midst of his own misery. Jake was the one who'd taken his senior-sibling responsibilities seriously after their father died. James had zero doubt that his work ethic and sense of honor were direct results of Jake's efforts.

"You know it."

They jokingly sparred for the next several minutes, catching each other up on life, until a doorbell sounded.

"Sorry, Jake, I've got to go. Someone's at the door."

"Hopefully it's Rachel. She's come to tell you she can't live without you."

"Ah…" Words lodged in his throat. Dang it, but Jake knew him too well. Yes, he *did* hope it was Rachel ringing his bell. "I'll keep you posted."

"Sure you will." Jake's chuckle was the last he heard as he disconnected and tapped into his doorbell app. The new condo had the same kind of security that Gideon had installed for Rachel. But like any security, it was limited by its hardware, and his camera didn't show anyone standing either in the front lobby or his condo door. He quickly dialed reception, which operated 24/7.

"This is James Kiriakis, condo 473. My doorbell just rang, but I don't see anyone at either door. Did one of you happen to go ring the bell?"

"No, sir, but we'll get on it and call you back if we come up with anything."

He disconnected and walked to his door, needing to see for himself if someone stood out of camera range. After validating the corridor was clear via the peephole, he slowly opened the door and peered up and down the hallway.

And saw the huge vase filled with dead flowers, a dozen withered roses, on the accent table diagonal to his entrance, just out of view of his security camera. Bile fueled his souring stomach, and he fought nausea as he forced himself to walk the few steps to the desperate object.

A single sealed envelope rested against the vase, which he noted held no water. Why would it? Dead plants didn't need hydration. He snatched the creamy white enclosure and ripped it open, pulled out a folded-up sheet of computer paper.

No more games. This isn't a warning or for attention. You know it's me. I hope you said a proper
good-bye to the two nuisances in your life.
See you soon, lover.
Bethany

He crushed the paper in his hand, the sharp bite
of its edge slicing into his dry palm. He knew he'd
been right all along, but the validation did nothing to
soothe him.

No, nothing would make him able to rest and breathe
and live again. Not until he stopped Bethany.

He ran back the few feet to his foyer, grabbed his car
keys and bolted back out the door, dialing Rachel as he
fled. He had to make it back to Rachel's ASAP, before
Bethany did. Before…

Before she wasn't here anymore.

No!

Rachel didn't pick up and he didn't want to waste
time leaving a message. He placed a call to 9-1-1, alerted
them that the DA was in peril, then called Theo. The
last call also went to voice mail, but this time he left
a message.

"Theo, it's James. Bethany's going after Rachel and
I need you to send police now. Please." He threw his
phone on the seat and shifted into gear, roared out of
the condo's parking garage. As he sped through town
toward Rachel and Iris, the sickening swirl of bile in
his stomach warred with a newfound reality that he
should have seen weeks ago. Over a year ago, when he
met Rachel.

He was racing toward his home—his family. The only
woman for him.

But was love enough to keep Bethany's unstable actions away from Rachel and Iris?

It was too easy, in the end. All the weeks living in her car, going hungry because she needed the gas money more, paid off. Because now she knew Rachel's schedule better than the stupid woman knew herself. She knew the exact times the babysitter showed up and when she left. The times the kid needed to eat and nap.

She knew that Rachel hadn't been sleeping this past week. Right after she realized the cameras had been found, Bethany wanted to run inside Rachel's house without a plan, just make the biggest, scariest mess she knew how to. But James had held her back, because he'd given her hope. He hadn't been completely charmed by Rachel and her evil ways. If he had, he wouldn't have left. By Bethany's count, James had been away from Rachel and the kid for eight nights. Which made her think maybe the kid wasn't his, after all. Rachel probably tried to convince James that it was his kid.

Bethany had seen him leave his Blue Larkspur condo only once, after visiting the kid before Rachel got home. Yesterday, James walked up the driveway pushing a baby stroller and took the kid back into the house, right before Bethany could get down from the tree she'd climbed up to sit in, in the wooded grove across the street.

Bethany was mad at herself for missing the chance to talk to him one-on-one. It would have been perfect to "run" into him on the sidewalk, in a different part of the neighborhood. He wouldn't have been able to move or alert the cops, not with her standing right next to that witch's squalling brat. But she'd arrived late, as she'd had to go buy some supplies for her ultimate plan. The endgame for Rachel Colton. Maybe the kid, too. Bethany wasn't one to want to deliberately hurt a kid. It wasn't the brat's fault that her mother was such a jerk. Bethany understood this more than anyone else. Hadn't her own mother betrayed her, hurt her, made fun of her time and time again? Bethany had struggled in school. Her guidance counselor told her it was okay, it was because she was dyslexic. And something about her brain just being different. But her mother had another term for it. "You're stupid, Bethany. Stupid and ugly. Learn to not expect much out of life."

No, no, no. No going back to the hateful memories. She'd gotten free of that, only used her mother as she needed to these days. Bethany was her own woman.

Laughter welled in her throat and she made sure she was wedged in the V of the tree branches, balanced with her two legs astride a thick bough as she slapped both hands over her mouth. This was happening more and more. The giggles. It was because she was anticipating the joy James would feel when he realized she'd taken care of everything for them.

James was too naive to realize how he'd been manipulated by Rachel and the kid. It made her angry to think about it. It would have been a lot easier for them both if James had stopped fighting his attraction for her and just admitted she was the only one for him sooner.

"Oh, James. You silly boy. You'll have it all figured out soon enough." And if he didn't, she'd fill him in.

But first, it was adios to Blue Larkspur's district attorney.

* * *

Rachel's phone woke her early Saturday morning, before Iris's wake-up babble. She grappled for the device, but her fingers shoved it off the nightstand, and the sound of it hitting the floor was immediately followed by Iris's cry for her mama. She rubbed her eyes, peered at the clock. A full hour before they usually rose on a Saturday, but her little girl had heard movement and wanted up and at 'em.

She scrambled into her pajama bottoms, having slept in an old 5K race T-shirt, and made a quick pit stop in the bathroom to splash water on her face and brush her teeth before going into the nursery.

Iris's eyes were wide and full of the wonder of a new day as she looked up from all fours on her crib mattress.

"Good thing we lowered your mattress last week, huh?" Rachel had done it out of precaution when Iris began trying to pull herself up on the crib bars. It wouldn't be much longer before the baby would pull to standing.

"Come here, precious." She cuddled the wide-awake infant to her chest, breathed in her unique scent. Already the baby-fresh fragrance had faded from Iris's scalp. Rachel's heart twinged. Everyone from Isa to Emily to her siblings told her that the time raising a child would go fast, but she'd not believed it when she and Iris had yet another sleepless night due to colic or teething. Yet Iris was almost eight months old. Where had the time gone?

James.

"Yeah, your daddy has certainly taken up our time, hasn't he?" She giggled and cooed with Iris as she changed her diaper and put the girl into a pale green romper. James. She missed him, and not just because he was such a great parenting partner. Their long talks, the fact that they both enjoyed geeking out over the most minute legal details, had all come to light as they'd pored over her cases, past and present. James had been the first to conclude that if she was being pursued by one of the bad guys she'd prosecuted, it was Parson. And he'd been right.

But he'd never let go of his belief that Bethany was behind some of the mishaps that had befallen her. And Parson had confessed to several things, from the brick to the white-water rafting incident, but not to any kind of surveillance or threatening packages. He'd remarked that his higher-ups were more direct than sending a box in the mail. The brick through her window was a perfect example.

Yet there hadn't been anything suspicious, other than the spy cameras James discovered, since they'd returned from their rafting trip.

James. She missed him so much. What a fool she'd been. These past days had given her time to think, contemplate, measure what mattered most to her. It wasn't her career, or even her family, as much as she loved both. It was the child in her arms and the man who'd fathered her. The man who'd accepted Rachel for who she was and didn't try to mold her to fit his idea of who she should be.

Did she still have trust issues? Of course. She accepted that she might always wrestle with the demons of her past at different times in her life. Who didn't? But none of it was worth missing out on a life with the one man who understood her without judgment and cared for her the most.

Another tug at her heart, this one soaked with regret. James said he'd reach out to her when he was ready, but did she have to wait for his call?

It was time to tell James her truth. How he'd captured her heart.

"What do you say we surprise your daddy with a visit?" She tucked Iris onto her hip and went back into her room to grab her phone. She'd go slowly, not scare James off with an outright proclamation of love. But she'd tell him, nonetheless. He deserved to—

A strange woman stood in her room, in front of the open sliding doors.

Rachel stopped midstride and stared at the woman standing in her bedroom, holding the meat cleaver from the kitchen block in her raised hand. Her features matched the photos James had shown her of Bethany, but this woman's face was drawn, her normally bright brown eyes dull, sunken. A stained, faded navy hoodie covered her dingy white T-shirt and battered jeans. When her glance reached Bethany's feet, her stomach flipped. The woman wore sturdy hiking boots, meant for adventure. Judging by the bag at her feet, spilling over with heavy rope and—was that a pair of bolt cutters?—other paraphernalia, it wasn't going to be a fun kind of trip.

"Ma ma!" Iris wriggled and Rachel tightened her arms around her baby. Her heart. Her life.

"Hello, Rachel." Bethany's monotone was creepier than her appearance. "I'm Bethany. The woman James loves."

"Why don't you put the knife down, Bethany?"

"Rule number one, Rachel Colton? Don't even think you can tell me what to do, or it's the end for both you and your kid." She made a stabbing motion with the cleaver. Her eyes were vacant, and while Bethany's gaze targeted Rachel and Iris, Rachel sensed the woman didn't really see them. All she saw was what she thought stood between her and a life with James.

James had been right. Bethany was not only still stalking him, and Rachel, but was in Blue Larkspur. In her home.

Threatening her baby.

Chapter 23

Fear grabbed Rachel by the throat and dug in, triggering a whole-body reaction that included shaking, dizziness and panic. It was as if she was in a long, dark tunnel with Bethany blocking any possible light at the end. As if there was no way she could save Iris.

"Move. Now." Bethany waved the weapon at her, and Rachel instinctively clutched Iris to her as tightly as possible while her mind screamed *Run! Run! Run!*

"Where do you want us to go?"

"Shut up and listen to me or you're both dead. D-E-A-D, get it, Little Miss District Attorney?"

If she thought Parson's sneering threat at the end of his case had been scary, it was child's play compared to the sheer hatred that dripped off this woman's every word. Rachel was the focus of Bethany's rage, 100 percent. And by proxy, Iris was in the lost soul's crosshairs, too.

"I know you want James. He's yours, Bethany. He doesn't live here anymore." Rachel knew enough to realize she had to appease Bethany no matter what, even with lies. Whatever the woman would believe, whatever it took to disarm her.

"James is already mine, Rachel. He's always been mine. That's not a question." She cocked her head. The movement reminded Rachel of a marionette. "Don't make me tell you to move again."

"Fine, but I'm not walking my child anywhere near you. If you want me in the kitchen, you go there first. You seem to know the layout of my house."

Keep them talking. Theo's voice came back to her, from when he'd gone over what Rachel needed to do if she ever found herself in a hostage situation. It was part of her DA indoctrination and security training.

"I told you to be quiet. That goes double for the brat." But Bethany was backing up, through the door, and motioned for her to follow, to keep moving forward.

Rachel assessed her options as she walked toward the kitchen, Iris in her arms. She had no weapon with which to fight Bethany or that gleaming meat cleaver. Panic choked at her throat and she fought back against the sensation that she was walking to her own execution.

No. Not with her daughter pressed against her heart.

"Let me put the baby in her crib, Bethany. She doesn't need to see any of this."

"She'll see whatever I want her to." Bethany walked backward, and Rachel realized the woman did, in fact, know her home as well as anyone who'd spent time here. Shivers of revulsion wracked her, made her teeth chatter.

"D-d-did you put those cameras in my house, Bethany?"

"Yeah, I sure did." For as frightened as Rachel felt, all that emanated from Bethany was a sarcastic cockiness. Bethany thought she'd figured things out, finally had her quarry in her sights. "And guess what, Rachel? You didn't find them all, you stupid—" She ran into the corner of the heavy granite countertop with her hip and winced. "Damn this granite, this overblown house."

"Please, Bethany. Let's go outside and talk about this. We can leave Iris in the house. You and I will talk in the backyard. No witnesses, just us." If she could get Bethany outside, there was a good chance one of the officers was already outside and would have a clearer shot of Bethany than through one of her windows. Which, she realized, with a sick sink of her stomach, were all closed up, blinds and curtains drawn to keep Bethany from seeing inside.

The four walls of the great room seemed to move, and it wasn't fun like at an amusement park's haunted house. More like her worst nightmare turned into a true-life horror scene.

Save Iris.

The single thought pinged about her mind, echoed by heartbeats so fierce she was certain Bethany heard them. She struggled to keep her breathing even, to not betray her terror. Bethany's expression changed so rapidly over the course of a few seconds—from rage to anger to humor—that it was a struggle to keep up.

Breathe.

Rachel wasn't certain where it was coming from, but instinct told her to project as calm of a demeanor as possible. To show zero fear, no amount of concern over

Bethany's potentially life-threatening demands. But as she watched the kitchen's overhead lighting glint off the cleaver that Bethany held in an almost loving manner, there was no denying that her time on this earth was limited. Perhaps extremely, as in whenever Bethany decided to lunge at her.

No. She shoved the image from her stressed mind and focused instead on doing what she did best. Drawing out the witness's true nature.

Make her talk.

"Stay back from the house, James." Theo's voice thundered over the hands-free system in James's car. He'd returned James's call when there was still five minutes left in his drive to Rachel's.

"Only if your units are already there." But he knew that didn't matter, either. No way was he going to leave Rachel to face Bethany on her own. "I'm hoping Bethany didn't get there yet."

"Chances of that are nil, James. I have to deal with reality. If it is Bethany, if she left those flowers for you with the message, she had at least a—what?—five-minute lead?"

"Yes." He cursed himself. "I should have never moved out last week."

"Nothing you could have done would stop someone during a psychotic break from acting on their troubled thoughts."

"We both know that's BS."

"Listen to me, son. My cruisers are seven minutes out, and I'm three. Do not, I repeat, do not go in that house on your own."

James glanced at the clock on his dashboard and saw

that his ETA was, at most, only thirty seconds ahead of Theo. "Hopefully by then she'll have called me back."

But his phone remained silent after Theo disconnected, the only sound in the car besides the engine his ragged gasps for air.

"Don't move! I'm not telling you again." Bethany sidled over to the counter where the knife block sat and reached with her empty hand for another knife. Rachel wanted to look around for a make-shift weapon but couldn't afford for Bethany to think she was anything but helpless, and Bethany's gaze never left hers. If the woman didn't expect her to try to make a run for it, all the better.

It was becoming more clear with each passing second and the lack of anyone showing up—how could they, when no one knew Bethany was here?—that Rachel was going to have to do the unthinkable.

Fight back against a woman who held two lethal weapons aimed at her. All while keeping Iris safe.

"Can we talk this out?"

"Shut up!" Bethany screamed at the same moment the front door, visible to Rachel over Bethany's shoulder, opened. James walked in and headed straight for Rachel and Iris, but stopped short when he saw the knives.

"No, don't!" She tried to warn him about Bethany, but it was too late. He was already too far into the house. James stood behind Bethany by no more than six feet. Bethany could turn and shove those knives into him.

No. Stay focused. Save Iris.

"What are you doing here? Or have you come to help me get rid of the only thing between us?" Bethany switched to a cloyingly sweet tone that was scarier than her angry persona, looking at him over her shoulder while keeping both knives pointed at Rachel and Iris. In the close confines of the kitchen, there was no more than six inches from the end of the blades to her arms that held Iris.

"I've come to talk to you." James acted as if he came upon a murderous scene on a regular basis. There was no sign of the concern he'd expressed to Rachel about his sense that Bethany still stalked him. *This must be how he appears in court.*

She hoped that like his case record, James would win over Bethany and put an end to this terror.

"So you got my message." She smiled at James as if he were a pet.

"The flowers you left me? Yes. Bethany, please." He held his hands up in the universal gesture of appeasement. "Put the knives down. It isn't worth it."

"Not until I finish what I started. It has to be perfect, James. Just you and me. Only us. Stand over there or I'll cut them both."

"No!" The sob wrenched from Rachel, from a place deep inside, where her mother's soul lay.

"Rachel." James's eyes were intent and in the split second before Bethany looked at him again, he gave a quick nod toward the living room, mouthing the word "sofa." She nodded back when Bethany turned to him.

"Stop talking to her!"

"Leave them alone, Bethany. This is between you and me. Let Rachel and Iris go."

"Why do you care so much about her and her brat? Don't you see she's just using you to help with the kid? No one loves you like I do, James."

"I know that now, Bethany. Let's talk about it like adults." He took a step closer. Rachel sucked in her breath, afraid that Bethany would lunge forward at any moment. She had to get Iris to safety. But the knives—she or James might survive an injury from either weapon, but her child's tender flesh wouldn't.

"Stop it right now!" Bethany turned toward James, and Rachel took the first opening she'd had to secure Iris's safety. She darted from the kitchen into the living room, the sofa her target. If she could just get Iris away from—

"Don't move another inch or you're both dead!" Bethany's voice boomed through the air. "James, stay right where you are or I'll throw these knives. Remember how good I was when we threw axes in Bear's Tavern in Denver, James?"

"Wait, Rachel." James's tone stilled her, anchored her, drove the deepest fear into her heart. She placed Iris on the deep seat, far from the edge, giving the baby the protection of the sofa's back.

"Raise your arms!" Bethany shrieked the order, spittle flying from her mouth. Even Bethany's expression and posture were completely different than the photos James had shown her. The once-beautiful woman was a seething ball of anger and frustration. Two emotions that drove the worst of crimes.

"I'll do whatever you say. Please leave our baby be. She's innocent."

Bethany's head tilted so roughly she appeared like a doll ready to break apart. "What do you mean, 'our baby'?"

Rachel's mistake turned her stomach into a twisted ball of concertina wire as her raised arms shook.

"It's not important right now, Bethany. What matters is that you and I have the conversation we need to have. Quietly. Here, at the table." James motioned to the large dining table where they'd spent so many hours.

Would she ever have that kind of time with him again? Staring down two deadly blades held by a most unreliable criminal, the answer was clear.

These were her last moments alive. But she wasn't going to let Bethany hurt Iris.

"Stop talking! I'm not listening to you anymore. You've been seduced by the demoness! You believe her bastard child is yours!"

"Bethany, calm—"

"Noooo!" As she screamed, she threw one, then both knives at Rachel.

Rachel acted the second she saw Bethany's wrists twist, her fingers releasing their grip on the weapons. She did what any mother in the same situation would do.

Rachel covered her baby with her body, prepared to take the blades.

Chapter 24

"No!" James dove toward Bethany, aiming to tackle her at her knees. But before he made contact, a single gunshot sounded and Bethany collapsed on the floor. Landing on all fours, he immediately scrambled and ran to the sofa. To all that mattered. Footsteps sounded all around him, and he was dimly aware of several uniformed officers charging the scene, but all he needed was right in front of him.

"Da!" Iris reached pudgy arms and he grasped her to him, inhaled her baby scent. He was a split second ahead of Rachel, who was on her knees next to the sofa where she'd pushed herself up from covering the baby. Blood dripped down the side of Rachel's face.

"Rachel, it's okay. I've got her." He used his free hand to urge her to sit all the way back on her bottom as he peered at the injury. "You're hurt."

Her eyes, wide with the adrenaline he knew matched his own, fixed on him and they shared a moment of soul communication, as intimate as when he'd moved inside her. When they'd made Iris.

"I am?" She must have seen where he stared and reached up her hands to her face, then traced the wetness. "Oh my goodness! It has to be a surface scratch. It doesn't hurt."

James wasn't so sure. "EMT!" He bellowed the request as he cupped Iris's tiny ears. "Front room!"

"Clear!" An officer shouted from the back of the house.

"Clear!" Another holstered a weapon near the front door.

"Are you both okay?" Theo stood beside them, his weapon facing the floor. EMTs burst into the house, and Theo pointed the first two toward the kitchen, to where Bethany lay moaning. She'd taken a bullet to her leg from what James could tell, and appeared fully conscious.

"I'm…fine?" Rachel looked at the blood on her hands, still dazed.

"Over here." Theo directed the next available EMT over to Rachel and stepped aside to allow the first responder room.

"We're good." James knew he'd never let Iris go again. Ever.

"Come over here." Theo holstered his gun and motioned for two other men to come forward. James recognized Caleb, Rachel's oldest sibling, but not the other man. He wore his dark blond hair in a longish, shaggy style. His hair and blue eyes were darker shades than Rachel's, but the Colton resemblance was unmistakable. It had to be one of her other brothers.

"Caleb. James Kiriakis." He nodded to Caleb, and held out his hand to the other man, who stared at it for a full heartbeat before meeting it with a firm grip.

"Dominic Colton." James's gut felt the invisible yet tangible punch Rachel's FBI agent brother threw him. He'd heard all about Dominic when Rachel told him she'd been afraid her brothers would want to beat him up when they found out he was Iris's father. Dominic's eyes blazed with fierce protection.

"Dom!" Rachel tried to stand, but the EMT attending her kept her seated. "What are you doing here? Caleb, how did you two know to come now?"

"There's a thing called a cell phone, sister." Dominic walked over and placed a quick kiss on Rachel's cheek.

Caleb nodded. "We heard the request for backup go out, and Mom texted us at the same time, saying Theo was headed here."

All eyes turned to the Blue Larkspur Chief of Police.

Theo shrugged. "Isa and I were playing cards at her place. I made her stay put and promised I'd give her any update ASAP. So if you'll all excuse me…" He nodded, held up his phone, walked out of the living room.

"Wait, what was he doing at Mom's again?" Dominic had lines between his eyebrows that James recognized. He and his siblings had been very protective of his mother after their dad passed. Unlike Isa, though, Helen hadn't waited twenty years to find a new love.

"Stop it. Mom's entitled to her own life. And what are you doing in Blue Larkspur anyway, Dom? I thought your work kept your head low to the ground." Rachel spoke as the EMT applied butterfly bandages to a long but superficial cut that ran the length of her hairline from her forehead to her temple. James recalled that she'd mentioned Dom worked undercover in Denver. But her brother wasn't his concern right now. His gaze followed the EMTs working on Rachel's injury. Fear sliced through him as he processed the reality that she'd been spared more serious injury, even her life, by ducking in time. She'd saved Iris.

"I don't have much time. Caleb picked me up at the airport. I'm due to go back undercover but I don't have to, Rachel. I can stay here if you need me."

"Don't be ridiculous. Other than this stupid cut, I'm fine. And listen, all of you. James didn't know about Iris, that he had a daughter, until I told him which was very recently. So no ganging up on him. Got it?" Rachel's irritation normally would make James smile, but he hadn't gotten over how close he'd come to losing her. Losing Iris. All that mattered to him.

"I hear you, sis. So tell me, James, how is it that my sister and niece's lives have been threatened by your stalker?" Dominic's unforgiving gaze was back on him, and James shifted Iris to his other arm. The baby's face brightened at the sight of her uncles and Caleb held up his arms. James handed his daughter over, needing his full attention available for the justifiable inquisition.

"I messed up."

"No, you didn't. I did, so did Theo, frankly." Rachel had heard enough. She batted away the EMT's hands and walked to James's side. Wrapping her arms around his waist, she rested the uninjured side of her head on his shoulder. As they stood together, Bethany was wheeled out on a stretcher. The EMTs weren't in the same hurry they'd been when they arrived, and Rachel overheard Theo tell Isa that Bethany had a super-ficial injury.

"No offense, sis, but you need to rest." Caleb's brow lifted in that comical way that made her giggle. His humorous expression belied the concern in his eyes.

"I'm fine. You've hurt me worse when we were kids and beating up on each other. Listen, none of us believed James, that Bethany was behind all the awful things that kept happening." She ran down the litany of offenses, ending with being held hostage by knifepoint as she embraced their baby daughter. "One incident, a brick through my window, followed by a sabotaged raft ride, is attributable to my most recent case. That criminal is behind bars and the syndicate who carried out his order has been given fair warning about messing with this DA."

"So everything else was due to his former girlfriend?" A stab of annoyance pierced through Rachel's relief, but James answered first.

"Yes. This was all on me."

Dominic's lips formed a tight line and he turned away to speak to Caleb in quiet tones.

"Hey." Rachel tugged on James's collar, and he was powerless to resist her. A surge of relief layered in recognition and another stronger emotion compelled him to wrap her as tightly as possible to him, burying his face in her hair. "You handled my brothers well. I give you credit."

"My God, Rachel. Your brothers love you. They have a right to know it's my fault. I thought you, that you and Iris—" His throat constricted and his eyes burned with the terror that he'd fought since seeing the roses from Bethany.

"We're okay. Theo saved us all."

"No, *you* saved you and Iris. That was brilliant, putting her on the sofa."

She pushed back enough to look at him straight-on. "No, we were brilliant, James. We did it together. You gave the perfect distraction and had already communicated to me, without one word, may I add, to run into the living room. *We* saved our baby, James."

He wasn't about to argue with the most beautiful woman in his world, today or ever. Knowing her brothers looked on with disapproval mattered little to nothing, not when the love of his life looked at him with the same amount of love that pumped through his veins for her.

"I love you, Rachel. I love you as my partner, my soulmate, as Iris's mother. Forever."

Tears filled her eyes, changing the cornflower blue to bright aquamarine. She blinked. "I love you, too. Do you think we have a chance to be a real family?"

"Yes." He couldn't hold back any longer. He kissed her with abandon, stamping what he'd been unable to articulate until now on her very responsive lips. It didn't matter that they had an audience comprised of some very hard-to-please brothers, or that the Colton family protector and police chief looked on. All that mattered was that his family was safe, and Rachel was in his arms.

Chapter 25

"It's nice to have you all here together." Isa spoke to Rachel as they set out the food for the next Sunday Colton dinner, just days after Bethany's arrest. A combination of catered and potluck covered the expansive quartz-topped island in Isa's updated kitchen.

"Well, not all of us." Half of her siblings weren't there, but like her mother, Rachel was thrilled to be enjoying a Sunday that didn't have the ever-present threat of Parson or Bethany hanging over it. Warm gratitude spread under her breastbone each time she glanced up to see James and know that this wasn't temporary—they were going to go for it.

"Why don't you go over to him? I can finish up here." Isa nodded toward where James stood, Iris in his arms, conversing with Caleb, Gideon and Theo. Dominic was out on the patio with Aubrey and Jasper, the ranch co-owners taking a rare afternoon off together. Ezra, even though he lived with Isa, wasn't home as the Army had sent him TDY, away on temporary duty, for the weekend.

"No, Mom. Not yet. You can't do this all by yourself."

"Actually, I can." Isa grinned. "So you and James have decided to be a couple, for real?"

Her floral-printed blouse, one she thought perfect for the spring afternoon, suddenly felt like her heaviest down jacket. She blew out a quick breath, shrugged. "We've decided to commit to one another and to our family, yes."

"Relax." Isa touched her cheek with her finger. "Stop blushing, for heaven's sake. I'm not asking about your bedroom activity."

"Mom!"

Isa laughed. "I'm just teasing and you know it."

"You seem a lot happier these days, Mom." She suspected it was about more than Rachel's trauma-drama being resolved.

"I am. You've made me open my mind, Rachel. Remember our talk about letting love in again? You were right."

"You're the one who told me to open my heart."

"Was I?" Isa laughed. "Then, I guess I'm taking my own advice." Her gaze searched the room, looked through the windows to where Theo stood on the patio.

"I'm happy for you, Mom." She didn't want to push it, to go so far as to say she knew her Mom had a boyfriend—Theo. Besides, *boyfriend* seemed too casual. Isa and Theo both did not do anything in their lives casually.

"You can't blame me for feeling protective toward you and my sole grandchild." Isa fell back on one of her master skills—hanging the subject. "At first I was concerned that you both were reacting to the traumatic events of the last month, especially last week. I'm relieved beyond measure that nothing lasting happened to you or Iris. To any of you."

"Me, too." She'd not spoken to her mother about the specifics of having two knives thrown at her by Bethany, of seeing the woman taken out by Theo in her home. "Theo saved the day. That's for sure." Rachel was so grateful for Theo, for what he'd done for their family. He'd saved Iris's, and James's, and her own life.

"Well, as much as it's true he fired the deciding shot, it's been explained to me that you and James worked together as the perfect team to save your daughter. I can't ask for more."

"Thanks, Mom."

"And that woman—Bethany—let's keep her in our prayers that she gets the help she needs." Isa shook her head. "She's got a long road ahead of her."

"She does." Rachel didn't want to go into details with her mother, not today. But she, too, was at peace with what happened to Bethany. The woman was in a psychiatric facility for evaluation. If she was deemed mentally competent, she'd stand trial.

"No way would I ever allow Isa's daughter or granddaughter to get hurt." A deep baritone sounded to her right. "Isa would never forgive me. None of the Colton women would, I'm certain." Theo had walked up behind her but kept going until he stood next to Isa. He gave her mother a smile not unlike the special glances she and James shared. Rachel wondered if Theo was the man Isa had been talking about before.

"She's still going to have to pay for her crimes, Rachel. And for the record, I had to fire my weapon. No way was anyone going to harm a Colton woman, or girl, on my watch. I'm as happy as all of you to have the Bethany Austin case closed. I only wish Ronald Spence wasn't still free, but justice will be served."

"I agree with Theo." Isa's eyes twinkled only for Theo. *Of course you agree with him.* Rachel allowed a small giggle to escape her before she turned away from the buffet before the couple asked any questions. She wanted to be next to *her* family—her immediate family.

James and Iris greeted her with smiles and the resemblance between them took her breath away.

"What?" Lines appeared on the bridge of his nose, the same place Iris got them when she didn't like the taste of mashed carrots. "You look upset."

She quickly wound her arms around his waist and kissed him fully on the lips. Iris chortled and grabbed a hank of Rachel's hair.

"I'm not upset at all. More like awed—I am the luckiest woman on the planet!"

His green irises deepened to jade as their gazes locked. She leaned in for another kiss, but he held up his free hand. "Hang on a sec."

He strode over to Isa and gave her the baby. Turning to face everyone, who had gathered around the food, he held up his hands.

"Hey, Colton family." She noticed that Dominic and Caleb didn't lunge for James at his pronouncement. They were coming around to what she already knew. James was solid—a man of integrity. The best soulmate for her and father for Iris. "I was going to wait until more of you were here, but I'm learning that with twelve of you, that's not a common thing and I can't wait any longer." Without preamble he walked back to Rachel and bent down on one knee, pulled a small velvet box from his jean pocket.

"Rachel Colton, will you eternally bless me by becoming my wife?"

She couldn't see clearly through the tears, but it didn't matter what the ring looked like, or the expression on James's face. The certainty of their love was already stamped on her heart, in the depths of her soul.

"Yes. Yes, yes, yes!"

They embraced as a chorus of Colton agreement exploded around them. Rachel reiterated her confirmation with her lips, meeting his without reservation.

* * * * *

Don't miss the previous installments in the Coltons of Colorado miniseries:

Colton's Pursuit of Justice
by Marie Ferrarella
Snowed In With a Colton
by Lisa Childs
Colton's Dangerous Reunion
by Justine Davis

*Available now from
Harlequin Romantic Suspense!*

And keep an eye out for Book Five,
Undercover Colton
*by Addison Fox,
available next month.*

He winced. "Yeah, I remember…"

A smile tugged at the corners of her mouth, pulling up her lips. "Don't go looking for any flowers from me as an apology."

"There's something else I'd rather have from you," he said, and the intensity of his blue-eyed stare had her pulse racing. Then he leaned forward and brushed his mouth across hers.

And shock gripped her so hard, her heart seemed to stop beating for a moment before resuming at a frantic pace. He'd kissed her before, but it still caught her by surprise. Not the kiss so much as the passion that coursed through her. She'd never felt so much desire from just a kiss. And why this man out of all the men she'd dated over the years?

Why Owen James, who'd hurt her in high school with his cruelty? Who hadn't saved her mother?

Why would she be so attracted to him?

It wasn't just because of his flowers and his apology. She'd felt this passion last night before he'd come bearing the roses and his mea culpa.

She'd worried about him yesterday, but just like in high school, she didn't believe it was possible that he really cared about her, that he wanted her. Was he up to something? What did he want from her?

His mouth brushed across hers again. Then his lips nipped at hers, and a gasp escaped her. He deepened the kiss, and she tasted his passion.

He wanted her as badly as she wanted him.

And that was bad…

Very bad.

Because she had a feeling that if she let herself give in to her desire, she would be the one who wound up hurt next…

Don't miss
Hotshot Hero Under Fire *by Lisa Childs,*
available June 2022 wherever
Harlequin Romantic Suspense books and ebooks are sold.

Harlequin.com